CRITICS RAVE FOR C. J. BARRY!

UNLEASHED

"Action, adventure, and a love that transcends galaxies abound in this thrilling novel by up-and-coming author C. J. Barry. Full of witty dialogue and one hysterically funny heroine, *Unleashed* is a rollicking tale that hits on many levels...there is never a dull moment!" —*Romance Reviews Today*

"Humor adds zip to this grand adventure tale...exciting and spellbinding." —*Romantic Times*

"C. J. Barry provides readers with a wild, fun science fiction romance that will make true believers out of those who naysay *E.T....* exhilarating."
—*Midwest Book Review*

"I bow at C. J. Barry's feet. She is able to revisit the same world, give it a twist and make it entirely new...she creates full, multi-dimensional characters who make the book a blast."
—*ScribesWorld Reviews*

UNRAVELED

"Ms. Barry's storytelling immediately draws readers into this futuristic world, with deftly woven plots, and twists in each chapter.... Another winner from up-and-coming author C. J. Barry, *Unraveled* is sure ~~~~~~~~~~~~~~~~~~~~~~ ay

"Delightful...loade~~~~~~~~~~~~~~~~~~~~~~~ng romance...C. J. Ba~~~~~~~~~~~~~~~~~~r." ew

MORE PRAISE FOR AWARD-WINNING AUTHOR C. J. BARRY!

UNEARTHED
*P.E.A.R.L. Award-winner (Best Science Fiction)
*Holt Medallion finalist
(Paranormal/Time Travel/Futuristic)
*PRISM Award-winner (Best Futuristic)
*Romantic Times pick for
Best Futuristic Romance of the Year (2003)

CAUGHT!

He spun her around and pushed her toward the bed. She fell face-first and rolled onto her back a split second before his entire weight landed on top of her, pinning her arms beneath him.

"Bastard!" she yelled, trying to throw him off her by arching her body.

"Are you almost done?" The aggravated voice was a low, deep growl.

"Never." She clenched her teeth and closed her eyes to the pain that hammered inside her head. His weight pressed her into the bed. She felt trapped and helpless—both of which pissed her off to no end. No, she wasn't done yet. He might have the advantage right now, but he had no idea who he was dealing with.

She opened her eyes and came face to face with her captor's quicksilver gaze. Recognition clicked in, and her sudden inhale was involuntary, an error the pirate noted immediately.

"You," she hissed.

"Nice to see you again too."

Other *Leisure* books by C. J. Barry:

UNLEASHED
UNRAVELED
UNEARTHED

UNMASKED

C.J.BARRY

LOVE SPELL NEW YORK CITY

This book is dedicated to the Purple Pens:
Chris Fletcher, Molly Herwood, Lisa Hilleren,
and Carol Lombardo. For the friendship,
laughs, and love of words.

LOVE SPELL®

June 2005

Published by

Dorchester Publishing Co., Inc.
200 Madison Avenue
New York, NY 10016

ISBN 0-505-52574-7

The name "Love Spell" and its logo are trademarks of Dorchester Publishing Co., Inc.

Printed in the United States of America.

Visit us on the web at www.dorchesterpub.com.

ACKNOWLEDGMENTS

I'd like to thank my editor, Chris Keeslar, and everyone at Dorchester Publishing; my fearless agent Roberta Brown; the CNY Romance Writers; my dedicated critique partners Patti, Joyce, and Stephanie; the Romance Writers of America; the Lollies, and every one of my loyal readers.

Special thanks to Lisa Hilleren for her amazing powers of critiquing, and Robin D. Owens for her generosity.

And as always, I am grateful to my wonderful family: Ed, Rachel and Ryan.

Chapter One

"Engine core meltdown in thirty-two minutes," the ship's computer said in a synthesized female voice.

"Words every captain wants to hear first thing in the morning," Torrie muttered. Lying on her back, she yanked open the panel door above her. The primary circuits flashed furiously inside the cabinet. No wonder it wasn't responding: the entire system was overloaded. She'd never be able to circumvent the problem from here.

Swinging out from under the engine banks, she hit the deck running. As she sped through the empty corridors of her dying ship, she pressed her personal comm unit. "Howser, where are you?"

Her first mate responded. "In the shuttle bay, loading the crew into the transport ship. When are you getting here?"

"I'm not." Torrie leapt onto the third rung of the gangway ladder and climbed to the upper level.

"What? The ship is going to blow up in—"

"Thirty minutes, I know," she finished, pulling

1

herself up to the main deck. She ran past the flashing alarm lights toward the bridge. "You take the crew and get the hell out of here."

"If you're staying, so am I," Howser replied. "Your brother didn't put me on your maiden voyage to skip out when things got bad."

Torrie jumped through the bridge hatchway. "And Carmon didn't make you captain on this freighter, either. So get your ass in that ship and take care of my crew, or I'll jettison the lot of you whether you're inside or out. And don't even think about staying behind. I already sealed the air lock."

"Dammit, Torrie."

She shimmied into the command chair. "You better move before you lose the force-field barrier. I don't need to tell you what happens to an unprotected body in deep space."

She punched up the systems, but they responded sluggishly. For some unknown reason, the engine core temperature was still rising steadily into the red zone, and nothing she'd tried so far could stop its slow march to detonation.

"We are launched," Howser said over her comm. The shuttle bay holocam confirmed that the small transport carrying Howser and the rest of her five-man crew was pulling away from *Ventura2*. She closed the shuttle bay doors in case Howser decided to play hero.

"Jump to hyperspace now. I want you as far away as possible."

He grumbled something that she didn't quite catch and probably didn't want to hear anyway, but her scanners verified the transport's jump— out of visual, and out of danger if she failed. Then she remembered something and glanced around the bridge. "Do you have Nod with you?"

"Yes, of course," Howser griped. "He's flying around here, asking everyone if he can help. Really, can we reprogram him? Doesn't he have another line?"

Despite the dire situation, Torrie smiled. "If we ever get out of this mess, I'll try again." Then she added a heartfelt "Thank you, Howser."

"Don't thank me. I'm the one who's going to have to tell your mother and the rest of the family that you went down with the ship for no good reason."

The lights on the bridge flickered off, leaving only the control console lit. *Wonderful.* Torrie decided not to tell Howser.

"I don't plan on letting my ship explode. There has to be a way to cool the core." She tried manual shutdown of the engine drives, but they wouldn't obey. She tried rerouting all activity through the primary channel so she could cram a shutdown command through the secondary systems. No go.

Frustrated, she repeated an earlier order, hoping it would get through this time. "Computer, Priority One command: Shut down engines immediately."

"Unable to comply," it responded, as it had to all her previous requests.

She banged on the console. "Why the hell not?"

"Last command unclear. Please rephrase question."

Torrie gritted her teeth. "Computer," she began with all the self-control she could muster, "why can't you comply to Priority One shutdown?"

"All previous commands are in wait queue."

"Then move my commands up in the queue," she told it.

"Unable to comply."

Torrie mimicked the computer's patent response. "Computer, if you can't multitask, I'm changing you

3

to a male." She pushed a tangle of hair out of her face and hit her comm. "This doesn't make sense, Howser. It's like they are all overloading at once. The more I try to clear a channel, the more locked out they become."

"We did get that strong energy surge right before the circuits went crazy," Howser noted.

"Core meltdown in twenty-three minutes," the computer recited.

"Computer, you can shut up now."

Torrie leaned forward and worked the controls again, trying everything her years of practicing in emergency simulation exercises had taught her. Systems were freezing up, leaving her with fewer and fewer options. In the back of her mind, she began to wonder if maybe Howser was right. If she couldn't find a way to gain control of the core, she'd be vaporized with the rest of the ship.

"All systems are now offline. Onboard computer shutdown imminent," the computer said.

Torrie watched helplessly as the entire control panel went dark, plunging her into the pitch-black of the deep space surrounding her. Outside of the panoramic viewport, a billion stars pierced the endless universe. The silence was painful.

"Damn."

"What happened?" Howser asked.

Torrie closed her eyes and accepted her fate. "We're dead."

"That's it, I'm coming back for you."

"You know it's too dangerous to drop out of hyperspace prematurely. Besides, I have no power. I can't open the shuttle bay door."

"What about the manual air locks? You could put a suit on and get out—"

"And then what?" she interrupted. "I couldn't get

4

far enough away from the ship to make a difference. And even if by some miracle I could, you don't have an air lock on the transport to bring me aboard."

"We could hail a nearby ship," Howser pressed.

"You know there isn't another ship in the vicinity. And even if you found one, do *you* want to inform them we're going to blow into a billion pieces shortly?"

For once, Howser was silent. He knew she was right. She rubbed her arms, her tank top offering little protection as the bridge grew markedly colder. She should grab a jacket, but what was the point? How long did she have? Twenty minutes? Not much time to tie up one's life.

"I guess you were right after all," she admitted. "This wasn't one of my better ideas."

It took a few moments before he replied, and he sounded choked up. "I'm going to stay with you until the end, Torrie."

She smiled sadly. She knew he would, too. Howser had always been there for her, teaching her, encouraging her. He'd worked for her family's merchant shipping business for as long as she could remember. His confidence in her abilities was one of the reasons Carmon had let her have her own run—a run she'd fought for her entire life and finally won. And now lost.

She stared into the stars, and her heart ached in her chest. This is where she belonged: among the vastness of space, free to spread her wings and fly. Her family called her the wild one, but she knew exactly where she was going. Even if the journey ended up killing her.

She pushed fear aside, blocking it from her mind. She wasn't going to spend the last minutes of her life feeling sorry for herself. If she had a choice on how to die, this would be it—quick, painlessly and with her ship.

Howser interrupted her thoughts. "You can record a message over the comm, and I'll deliver it to whoever you want."

She swallowed. "Good idea." She should leave her family a message. Torrie gathered her thick, disheveled hair in her hands and began to braid it blindly, trying to decide what to say to her mother. After watching Torrie's father die just a few short months ago, Nevica Masters would be devastated by another loss, especially that of her only daughter.

Torrie recalled their last conversation, and her final agreement with her mother. *If this run doesn't work out, I promise I'll stay on Dun Gali and help run the business.* She'd never once expected that she wouldn't succeed. Well, at least she wouldn't be stuck in the office for the rest of her life. Or worse, married to some money-hungry man her family thought would keep her safe and dormant and out of trouble.

And she wouldn't have to listen to six older brothers gloating that they were right all these years—she couldn't handle her own run. She preferred death to that.

Her fingers stilled in hair that felt heavy. Hope flickered. She stood up in the silence of her lifeless ship, and took a few tentative steps around the bridge.

"Howser, if we power-out, shouldn't the artificial grav be down, too?"

"Well, yes."

"It's not. And the stabilizers are still functioning. Otherwise, I'd be listing by now." She moved around the bridge, blindly accessing anything she could get her hands on. "Something's not right. Computer, are you there?"

No response.

Howser asked, "Can you tell if the core is still roasting?"

"No. None of the monitors are functioning." She stared at a pinprick of light on the wall panel in front of her. "But we have juice somewhere."

"Auxiliary?" Howser asked.

"If auxiliary were on, I'd still have computer access. It should be the last system to go."

A slight movement outside her viewport caught her attention. She looked up and concentrated on the spot where she thought she'd seen it. Nothing but black, black and more black. That's when she noticed the billions of stars were gone. A shadow passed in front of her. *A ship.*

Impossible. Her scans would have picked up a vessel this close.

"Tor—" Howser's message was cut off in a blast of static through her comm. ". . . Nod detects . . . activity near—" More static. Torrie turned down the volume. The transmission wasn't getting through: someone was blocking it.

The ship's consoles suddenly came to life. Torrie reached out and accessed the closest one.

"Systems locked out," the computer said, startling her. When had the computer come back up?

"Locked out by who?" Torrie asked.

No response.

"Security override. Voice confirmation: Torrie Masters," she told the computer.

"Invalid access."

"I'm definitely changing you to a male," Torrie muttered, and checked the ship's stats. The engine core temp was within the normal range. In fact, all

C. J. Barry

her systems were normal. They just were no longer under her control.

She knelt under the main console and started loosening the fasteners on the panel. If she couldn't get in the easy way . . .

"Shuttle-bay door activated," the computer announced.

Torrie raised her head over the console, and watched in disbelief as the shuttle bay holocam showed a midsized ship entering and setting down. It wasn't Howser.

"Pirates," she whispered in loathing. It all made sense—the power surge, the mysterious systems malfunctions and the false core burn. They set it up so the crew would have no choice but to abandon ship. Then they'd steal the ship, register it under a new ID, and sell it for whatever they could get.

Her family had lost hundreds of freighters to ruthless pirates. But they wouldn't lose this one. No way. The pirates might have taken control of her systems, but there was no way she was giving up her ship to a band of cowards and thieves without a fight. She turned and sprinted down the main corridor. They'd head for the bridge first, and there were only two routes—the access ramp to the cargo bays and the gangway ladder she'd just come up from the engines. Unfortunately, they were located at opposite ends of the freighter. She could cover one, but not both.

As Torrie approached the gangway hatch, she drew her twin pistols and slowed, silencing her footsteps. After a few seconds, she detected no sounds or movement on the ladder below. They must be coming up the back ramp.

She moved stealthily toward the rear of the

8

freighter and heard voices. At the top of the long ramp, she pressed against the wall and listened over her pounding heart. There were two voices, maybe three—all male and moving closer. She'd fire the first round over their heads. Hopefully, they'd believe the ship was manned and ready to be defended, and they'd leave. If not, she'd shoot to kill. She'd heard her brothers' stories. Pirates could be vicious and bloodthirsty with their victims, and she had no intention of becoming their day's entertainment.

She raised her pistols and drew a deep breath. Then she rolled around the corner and unloaded a barrage of laserfire over three shocked men's heads. They shouted and scattered for the cover of the ramp's structural ribs.

Torrie ducked back as return fire pelted the wall behind her. So much for getting the hint.

"Okay, boys," she whispered. "Playtime is over."

Torrie came out blasting with both pistols, pinning the three men to their cover. Her laser shots sprayed the ramp. The intruders returned fire in a torrent of light, and she was forced behind cover. The barrage stopped, and she peered around the corner just in time to see two of the three men moving up the corridor from rib to rib. Eventually, they would reach her. She'd need to retreat to a more secure location.

Then she felt the poke of metal in her back.

"Drop them, lady." The voice was soft and husky, but deadly serious.

Damn, he must have come up through the engine room. Torrie gripped her pistol handles, and felt her foe's gun tip jammed into her back.

"Now."

She let her pistols fall just as the first of the other

men rounded the corner to face her. He was wearing a black wrap around his face, and only his eyes were visible. With arms the size of turret cannons, he looked like a giant. He would be the muscle of the group.

His thick eyebrows rose. "Nice little surprise," he said over her head. Two more men appeared behind him, both wearing masks. They were smaller and rougher-looking—the freight handlers.

Torrie twisted to look at the man with the gun in her back. Quicksilver eyes watched her through a slit in his black head covering, and a shiver ran down her spine at the intensity and sheer concentration in them. Calm, serious and deadly—this one was the leader.

Slowly, Torrie turned her head back to face the giant. He'd holstered his gun, as had the other two, who had moved to either side of her. That left one weapon trained on her. She could see the collective amusement in their eyes. Apparently, they didn't view her as a serious threat. *Bad move, boys.*

Without warning she spun around, kicking the rifle to the side with her boot. She hop-stepped forward and caught the pirate with a direct hit to his unprotected solar plexus with her other boot. He gave an *oomph* and doubled over.

The pirate on the right made the next move, and she took him out with a straight jab to the nose, dropping him in his tracks. The one on the left made a grab for her. She blocked his attack and delivered a quick succession of strikes to his head. He howled and clutched his face beneath its covering.

Torrie sensed the giant close in behind her, so she turned and nailed him with an old-fashioned hard uppercut to his jaw. His head snapped back, but his feet didn't even move. Pain stung Torrie's

10

arm, and she watched in disbelief as his head lowered, his angry gaze drilling into her. Moving faster than she thought possible, he lashed out and cuffed her biceps with a steel grip. She wrenched her body around, but not quickly enough. He grabbed her other arm and twisted her to face the man who had recovered his rifle, which was now aimed at her again. She tried to reach the giant's groin with her heel, but he was too tall. When she went for his kneecap, he squeezed her arms together behind her until they felt like they'd break.

As the other two pirates shook off their injuries, the leader watched her. He was dressed in black, from his well-worn boots to loose pants that wrapped narrow hips and cinched a flat abdomen. His shirt shimmered as it moved around broad shoulders and rolled over pronounced biceps.

He stepped up to her, his eyes hard, the silver in them coming alive like metal shards glinting in the light. His singular focus riveted Torrie for a split second as an uninvited awareness thundered through her. She squelched it with visions of the man lying dead on the floor with a laser hole in his head.

She raised her chin, challenging him even though she knew she was essentially helpless.

"You will never get away with this, you filthy pirate," she growled.

Chapter Two

Qaade ignored the throbbing pain in the center of his chest and tried to draw a full breath as he considered his captive's remark. She might very well be right. He eyed his latest misadventure as she struggled to no avail in the massive arms of Sly. This encounter was as unwelcome as it was entertaining.

The woman was fighting mad, her burnished red hair partially covering her face and blazing green eyes. But what held his attention was the sexy sneer her full lips formed as she glared at him.

Equally distracting were nicely shaped breasts that pushed against the thin fabric of a black tank top. Her muscled torso clenched as she struggled; her shoulders and arms were well developed yet attractive. And he could personally vouch for the strength of her legs, concealed though they were under light blue fitted pants, a pair of thigh holsters wrapped lovingly around each. There was something intriguing about a woman who wasn't afraid of her own power. Even if she used it against him.

"This is my ship, and if you think I'm going to give it up without a battle . . ." she grimaced and tried to twist away from Sly, "you're dead wrong."

Her ship, Qaade thought. According to his source, the captain was supposed to be a man named Howser. He hated when his source was wrong.

Beneath his face wrap, Qaade's burly crewman chuckled. "We got a live one here. Too bad we have to kill her."

The woman froze in Sly's grip. Her head shot up, and Qaade caught the full impact of those green eyes, wide with anger.

"Bastards. I haven't done anything to you," she hissed.

Qaade shrugged. "We pirates like tying up all loose ends. For good."

Her eyes narrowed to slits of green ice. "Why don't you and I settle this like uncivilized people—fight it out? Or are you afraid that losing to a woman would improve your reputation?"

Qaade grinned. Considering the gunfight she'd put up, she would be an interesting adversary. He'd have his hands full. He considered her thin tank top. Might not be such a bad thing.

"What? You don't like *me*?" Sly asked with a chuckle. The woman threw her head back, hitting him squarely in the chin with a solid whack. Then she shook her head in pain, while Sly bellowed with laughter.

"That's enough," Qaade cut in. He tucked his rifle under his arm, keeping it close in case their captive escaped Sly's grip. He wasn't taking any more chances with this one. "Why didn't you abandon ship with the rest of your crew, Captain?"

"There is no crew, just me."

He smirked. "Then what about the transport that left?"

Her green eyes widened. "If you touch my crew, I'll—"

He raised a hand to stop her. "I have no interest in them."

"You just want my ship."

"Actually, your cargo. This time," he added.

She glared a hole in his head. "You simulated a system malfunction to make it appear the core was overheating. Why?"

Smart lady, he thought. Even more intriguing. "It's much easier to board a ship and collect the cargo without a lot of people in the way. *Most* captains have the common sense to abandon ship when every single one of their systems fails." The strategy usually worked for him, leaving the ship unoccupied. A pity if it wasn't. As he'd said before, he couldn't afford to leave witnesses behind.

His captive said, "This ship and its cargo are my responsibility."

"Believe me, I need your cargo more than you do. Besides, I'm sure Masters Shipping can absorb the loss," he snapped, trying to control the bitterness that seeped into his voice. He gave her a long once-over. "Unfortunately, now I have to figure out what to do with you." He didn't want to kill her.

She lunged at him, but Sly pulled her back against his chest. The giant warned, "If we let her go, she'll send InterGlax after us."

Seeing the sheer determination in the woman's eyes, Qaade had no doubts that sector law enforcement would get a call from her. "In that case, we have a serious problem."

He could almost see her mind working as her tongue slid along her top lip. His mind, however, was definitely sidelined as he watched her lips glisten. Seemed a shame to waste such perfection. Finally the woman said, "I won't notify InterGlax."

Qaade laughed heartily. "Lady, I trust you about as much as you trust me."

Her eyes grew desperate beneath the veil of contempt. "Please," she begged, her gaze steady. "I'm just trying to make a living."

He studied her. She was a danger to his operation; he shouldn't let her go. Then again, she was simply a paid employee. No one should have to die for that. It's not like she actually *owned* the wealthiest shipping company in the galaxy. She was one woman, captaining a common freighter— probably the most boring job in the universe, aside from the occasional pirate boarding. How much trouble could she possibly cause?

"Are you willing to give me your word on that?" he said, not really expecting her to do so. He'd outrun InterGlax before. He just needed a head start. Still, he didn't want to let her go without a bargain. What kind of pirate would he be?

Her eyes widened marginally, and he could see the thoughts there. It surprised him that her word obviously meant something to her. She studied him to see if it would matter if she gave it or not. But those green eyes were clear and honest. This woman would keep her promise.

"My word," she agreed.

Qaade studied her for a long moment. "Put her in restraints and lock her in the engine room."

Sly blinked beneath his mask, "Are you sure that's a good idea?"

"No, but do it anyway." Then Qaade moved closer, brought his face inches from hers, and watched her pupils dilate. He could feel the warmth of her breath on his face and the heat from her body. A wave of tension flooded through him at the unexpected intimacy.

In a soft voice, he said, "Don't break your promise, lady. You won't live to regret it."

"My first run out, and I get boarded by damned pirates," Torrie muttered as she lay on her belly in the engine room and struggled behind her back with her wrist restraints. Two more bound her ankles. The magnetized rings rolled around each other and wouldn't release without the right demagnetization code, which she didn't have. She'd have to cut them off. "Computer, are you there yet?"

"Systems are initializing."

"Bring up the ship comm first. They took mine."

She shimmied over to a storage cabinet and activated the door with a hard kick of her boots. It popped open, and inside lay maintenance tools for the internal systems. While she fished out a pair of cutters, she thought about her next move. The pirates had let her live, but her cargo was gone and that was *not* going to happen.

"Communications functional," the computer said.

" 'Bout time. Hail Howser."

She activated the cutter behind her and tried to calm down enough to work on the wrist restraints. It wouldn't do to cut herself and bleed to death *before* she murdered the pirate.

"Torrie, you're still there. Thank the stars." Howser's worried voice filled the engine room.

She twisted around for a better viewing angle as the cutter sliced into the metal cuffs. "I'm here. Wish I could say the same for our cargo."

"What happened?"

"Pirates. They took control of the systems to get

rid of the crew, boarded us and grabbed our cargo." One of the restraints let go. She sat up, pulled her arms around in front of her, and shook them.

"Are they still there?" Howser asked.

"Long gone by now." She started cutting the second restraint. "I'm happy to report that I was a big surprise. Unfortunately, I couldn't protect the cargo. Too many of them."

"Did they hurt you?"

"Just a few bruises. Although, I did have to beg for my life, which someone is going to pay for. They were good. Experienced and efficient. I got the distinct impression they do this a lot. I'm going to run their descriptions and tactics through the archives to see if I can figure out who they are."

"The holo-recorders would have picked them up."

"I'm sure they deactivated the monitoring equipment. Besides, they all wore black face wraps and generic clothing. But don't worry, I'd recognize them again."

And she would, too. The big one would be an easy make because of his size alone. The other one . . . she paused, remembering the sharp, silvery eyes that had watched her through the slit in his mask, the impressive physique under the loose shirt and pants, and a voice that was branded in her mind forever. She shook off the whisper of curiosity that curled in her belly and concentrated on the wrist restraint. It clattered to the floor, and she bent forward to work on the ankle binders.

"Ghost Riders," Howser said in a reverent voice.

"Hardly ghosts," she replied in a huff.

"No, I mean the Ghost Riders of the Dead Zone. They are the most daring and elusive pirate force operating in the quadrant, wanted across the galaxy for stealing ships and cargo. Very smooth, very good. And they always wear black masks."

Torrie rolled her eyes. "Pirates all wear black, Howser. And these are nothing but common thieves preying on hard-working, legitimate shippers. It's people like you who perpetuate silly legends."

"I'm just telling you what Macke told me," Howser replied, sounding put out. "He fought off a similar attack last quarter. As a matter of fact, I think his computer system crashed as well."

Great, Torrie thought. Now she'd never hear the end of it from the family. She'd spent her life listening to her brother's grand stories about battling pirates and making daring runs, about ruthless pirates who left a trail of dead bodies in their wake. Just once, she'd like her own stories of success to tell.

"Well, I'm still alive and those pirates didn't get this ship, did they? They only wanted our payload, and I can't help but wonder why. There's nothing wrong with this bulk freighter. It's worth a hundred times more than anything we're hauling. So either they are the stupidest pirates alive, or they know something about our cargo that we don't."

"That bothers me as well. Did they take it all?"

"They were here long enough to. As soon as I lose these restraints, I'll go back and check."

There was a short, potent pause. "What is Carmon going to say? This was supposed to be your trial run."

She clenched her teeth. Growing up, her father had staunchly refused to allow her a run. She'd finally got her chance after he died and her oldest brother took over. Unfortunately, Carmon was almost as bad as their father. If he found out about this, he'd never give Torrie another chance.

"We aren't going to tell my brother, Howser. In fact, we're not going to tell anyone in my family."

"Uh, Torrie, don't you think they will get a little suspicious when number one, we don't show up at our destination, and number two, Client 151 starts screaming for his shipment?"

The ankle binders fell away, and Torrie rose to her feet. "Well, *I* won't tell them, and if you do I'll shoot you."

Howser snorted. "Not likely. I taught you everything you know, girl." It was true, and they both knew it. Howser was a small, wiry man over thirty years her senior, but she'd seen him take out a man twice his size in sparring exercises.

"You let me worry about Carmon." She made her way to the cargo bays. Empty corridors echoed with her footsteps and her failure. Everywhere she turned was a reminder of the legacy of Masters Shipping. With over 30,000 freighters and 100,000 employees, it was the largest, most successful merchant fleet in the sector. Her father had built the empire single-handedly, and it remained a solely family-run business. No pirate was going to humiliate her at the dinner table.

"What's your ETA, Howser? The systems are cold-starting so I can't pick you up."

"About two hours, full tilt. Did you notify Inter-Glax yet?"

She rounded the corner and walked down the ramp to the rear of the ship. Laser scorch marks scarred the walls and it smelled of singed metal. "No, and I'm not going to."

There was a clunk on the comm that could only be Howser falling off his chair. Seconds later, he came back. "Are you crazy? Pirates boarded our ship, mistreated you, and stole our cargo. Why wouldn't you call law enforcement?"

"Because I gave my word I wouldn't. In exchange, they let me go."

"Well, screw that," Howser said, his voice rising to a fever pitch. "They're pirates. Who gives a damn?"

"I do," she told him. "Besides, how long do you think it would take Carmon to find out I filed a complaint with InterGlax?" She walked past the blown-out cargo door control panel and into the cargo hold. It was dead quiet, and upended containers littered the floor. She walked over and kicked a container. It was full. "We still have cargo. This makes no sense."

"Then why did they board us?"

She moved between containers, trying to figure out what was missing. "They must have taken something, but I don't think they planned on taking it all. Their ship wasn't very big. It's like they knew exactly what we were carrying . . . ." Halfway across the bay, she found a bare spot. "The medical supplies are gone," she muttered.

"Damn," Howser said, sounding disgusted.

Torrie shook her head. "Why would they execute a surgical strike to steal common medical supplies that are available everywhere?"

"Maybe they *are* stupid," Howser said.

Remembering how they'd dismantled her ship, she muttered, "We should be so lucky. The good news is that they took the containers also . . . with my trackers."

There was silence, and then Howser said, "Now Torrie, don't go getting any crazy ideas. Just because you designed your own system—"

"For this express reason," she interjected.

"—is no reason to—"

She grinned. "In case my shipment was pirated."

"—think you can just—"

"Track it?" she finished with a smile. "Why do you think I developed this system, Howser? Carmon laughed at me and said it wasn't worth the investment to line all our containers with the trackers. I think this is an excellent way to test my invention."

"We can test it some other way—"

"Too late." She turned and headed back to the bridge. "Move that cruiser, Howser. I'm getting my cargo back."

There was a long suffering, frustrated sigh on the other end. "I was afraid you were going to say that."

Chapter Three

"I have a bad feeling about this."

Torrie glanced from her controls to her first mate. Howser stared out over the activity surrounding their ship, which was docked in a common area at the Wryth Spaceport. He wore a look of perpetual worry on his face that made him appear older than his true six decades. Short, white-shot brown hair covered his head, framing a pair of bulging blue eyes and generous lips.

"Howser, you always have a bad feeling about everything," she noted.

"Yes, but I have a justifiably bad feeling here. We aren't exactly blending in, Torrie."

She was well aware of the amount of attention they drew from the locals. Her clean, sleek ship looked sharply conspicuous in the monotonous gray of a docking area in which she would normally never be caught dead. No legitimate commercial shipper stopped here.

Howser muttered, "What a blackhole this place

23

is. Your pirate certainly has some interesting friends."

"Interesting friends," Nod parroted in an exact imitation. Torrie smiled and lightly tapped the little orb hovering in midair next to her.

"We aren't here to make lifelong friendships, you two. Only as long as it takes to find those pirates."

"Can I help?" Nod chimed in cheerfully.

"Actually, you can. Use your wireless to remotely access this space station's schematics. I need a floor plan to integrate into my datapad."

"Processing," Nod responded. "Overlaying memory."

"*Now* we're in trouble," Howser grumbled.

Torrie concentrated on the signal coming from the embedded tracker that would lead them to her cargo. "He'll be fine."

Howser leaned toward her. "You think? He's overlaying his memory. You know what that means. He won't remember something really important. Like who we are, or why we are here."

She whispered, even though she knew Nod could hear her with his sensors. "It's not his fault, Howser. I didn't build enough memory into him."

Howser was silent. He knew Nod's limitations as well as she did. Lightballs were a relatively simple technology functioning as autonomous light sources. But she'd inserted a computer and sophisticated sensors into the housing, giving this lightball special capabilities. He was her first effort, a prototype wedding gift for her brother Zain and his new mate. Unfortunately, she'd underestimated some of his components, memory being one. She herself seemed to be one thing he never forgot, though.

24

Howser moved on to another topic. "I've been thinking, they must have been waiting for us when we dropped out of hyperspace to navigate the Bearing region."

"They were expecting us."

"And they knew our cargo, too," he added. "Doesn't that worry you just a little?"

"More than I care to think about."

"Schematics downloaded," Nod said. "Integration into your datapad completed." He paused. "Greetings, Howser. When did you get here?"

Howser rolled his eyes. "Why is it always me he overlays?"

Torrie watched her tracker signal blink. "The signal is coming from the next bay over. I'm going to see if it's our pirate."

Howser turned to her with clear concern, then pointed a bony finger out the viewport in accusation. "You aren't going out there alone."

She pushed up from her seat and walked to the back of the small transport ship with Nod tagging along. "I seriously doubt the pirate will deliver our cargo back to us, Howser. So yes, I'm going. Alone. You need to stay here and make sure none of the locals take any more interest in our ship. I don't trust my security systems after what happened onboard *Ventura2*."

Howser sprang out of his chair and followed her. "Forget it, I'm coming with you. Wryth is the most dangerous spaceport in Sector 28. Every criminal in the quadrant calls this place home."

She turned to face him as old, familiar frustration filled her. "Are you implying that I can't take care of myself?" She pulled two pistols from a rack and flipped them into her thigh holsters. "Because if you are, then you are going to have to listen to the same damn speech I've been giving my family for years. I'm getting pretty sick of proving myself over and over again." She strapped a loaded weapons belt around her waist and let it settle low across her hips. "And I'm truly tired of all the men in my life trying to shackle me to a nice, safe place where I can't hurt myself." The datapad holding the spaceport's floor plans went into a pocket.

"Why are you doing this?" Howser asked. "Even Carmon has been boarded. The company expects losses."

Torrie looked him in the eye. "Because I can recover at least some of it. None of my brothers has ever done that. And it'll give us a second chance with Carmon."

Howser shook his head slowly. "Your pride is going to be the end of you."

"It's not pride," she snapped. "It's business."

"Call it whatever you want. It's still foolish, and you shouldn't be going alone. It's not good *business*," he said.

She gritted her teeth and pulled a long, gray duster over her black tank top and pants. The coat would cover her arsenal of weapons and give her some protection against the unsavory elements of Wryth. *Foolish? No, foolish would be coming this close and then turning around and leaving.*

She took a deep breath to center herself, and said, "Let me see exactly what we're up against. Once I have a plan, I'll contact you." She smiled at him. "Deal?"

"Torrie, my job is to make sure nothing happens to you. Carmon trusted me—"

She held up a hand. "Carmon can't shoot his way out of a carbon bag. I've had training, remember?"

He ran a hand through his sparse hair. "You've plenty of training. In a simulator and with me, but nothing to prepare you for what's out there. You aren't ready for real combat."

It took all the willpower she possessed to let that one slide. Howser was her best friend, even if he was a pain in the ass sometimes. "I'm willing to take that chance. Besides, you know I'll draw a lot less suspicion solo. *I* can blend." That implied that Howser couldn't, and he didn't deny it.

"We could call the spaceport authorities," he suggested.

She raised one eyebrow and gave him a cavalier look. "And what do you think they will do?"

Howser sighed. "Probably confiscate our cargo from the pirates and keep it for themselves."

"Exactly." She stood in front of him, her hands on her hips. "We're burning starlight, Howser."

He still didn't look happy. "Fine. But take Nod with you. He's not much, but at least I can track your progress through his comm."

Torrie could live with that. "Time for a little adventure, Nod," she said as she snagged the lightball out of the air and slipped him into her duster. She headed for the exit. "And Howser, don't you dare come after me unless I expressly ask for help. You know how much I hate that."

"I'm telling you, we shouldn't have let her go," Sly murmured as they wended their way along a crowded promenade. Most of the other patrons on the Wryth Spaceport parted like a sea for Qaade and his giant crewman. "That woman is trouble. I could smell it on her."

"She doesn't deserve to die just because she's too stubborn to leave her ship," Qaade countered quietly. The woman's memory surfaced. There were plenty of female captains across the sector, but this one was different. And not in a bad way. "Did we ever get a name on her?"

"According to her ship's logs, it was Captain Sheri Maullet. But I couldn't find much more on her. Very sketchy background for a captain with a legitimate shipping outfit."

Interesting, Qaade acknowledged grimly.

They turned down a side alley, past the bellowing vendors and myriad shops that made up the spaceport. Stale, dank air ripe with rot and sweat assaulted his senses. Aliens, humans, and animals alike scurried in the shadows, vying for survival in this place of perpetual night.

The dim lighting served a purpose, as buyers and sellers huddled in corners bartering for products not found anywhere else. Wryth welcomed all thieves, pirates, and worse with open arms—and a hefty tax on all transactions struck. In return, the authorities made sure law enforcement looked the other way as ships came and went with their ill-gotten gains.

Qaade should have felt perfectly at home here but he never did, even though his black face wrap blended in with those of all the other souls who wished to remain strangers to the galaxy. He doubted anyone here could even remember their real name anymore. Identities changed hourly, credits flowed freely, and lives were snuffed out for one wrong move.

He and Sly wove around hover carts and boisterous traders shouting prices for their wares to anyone who could hear them.

"Did you give Horg the manifest?" Qaade asked.

Sly's head bobbed up and down. "Besides being highly entertaining, that last raid was a pretty good one."

A spark of unease flickered through Qaade. On that ship, he'd finally found the Phellium medical supplies he'd been looking for. His sources had come through for him as usual, and other than running into a striking female captain, the heist had gone perfectly. So why did he feel so jumpy?

They passed a malevolent-looking man dragging a small woman behind him. Instinctively, Qaade watched her eyes. Her vacant stare looked through him. She was a slave. He had learned long ago how to pick them out of a crowd. But before he could track her, she disappeared in the swell of human and alien traffic. Anger and frustration rose in him. He'd failed to save another one.

Renewed determination energized his perpetually exhausted body. "Sell everything except the med supplies. That should give us enough credits to keep operating for one or two complete circuits."

Sly nodded. "Got it."

As they neared their meeting location, Sly took the lead and Qaade fell behind him as the subordinate. It was a tactic they'd used for years to protect Qaade's true identity. Even among thieves, he wasn't safe.

They stopped at a security door and waited while surveillance units studied them. Then a light flashed above a small box into which Sly recited a password sequence. After a few seconds, the security door slid open. Qaade and Sly passed into a small foyer containing two heavily armed guards who stepped forward and roughly searched them, relieving them of their weapons. It was all standard procedure when doing business with a man who had so many enemies.

Disarmed, Qaade and Sly were escorted into Horg's inner sanctum—a shabby office in a dimly lit room. A lone table sat in the middle. No chairs, no welcome sign, no friendly faces. Qaade would not expect them from one of the most notorious traders on Wryth. He and Sly took positions around the table where they could see each other as well as the two guards.

Horg made his entrance with a bold strut through a side door. His slicked-back hair gleamed under the dim light, and he was dressed in a garnet suit that made his white leathery skin look downright sickly. Qaade clenched his teeth. He hated dealing with Horg, but options were limited.

"Greetings," the man boomed. He stopped on the other side of the table, his eyes gleaming above a cheater's smile. He looked directly at Sly, ignoring Qaade altogether. "Make yourself comfortable. We're all friends here."

Qaade scowled. Friends? He knew the trader would like nothing better than to see the men beneath the black face wraps. *Unlikely.*

Sly replied, "Business, Horg."

The trader grinned and threw up his hands. "Just being a good host."

"If you want to be a good host, give us a fair price for the manifest," Sly said.

"Ah, yes. The manifest. Excellent selection. Don't suppose you'd care to give me your supplier?"

Sly chuckled. "I could, but then he'd have to kill you."

Horg roared with laughter.

Qaade said quietly, "How much, Horg?"

The man glanced over as if he'd just realized

Qaade was there. Then he turned back to Sly. "Three hundred marks."

Qaade crossed his arms, giving Sly his response. He knew how much he needed, and 300,000 credits wasn't enough.

"You call that fair? I could get more than that on the street," Sly blustered.

Horg shrugged his shoulders. "You can try."

Qaade slid four fingers over his biceps.

Sly understood and leaned forward across the table. "Three-forty."

The trader narrowed his eyes. "I'm in a generous mood today. Three-ten."

Qaade removed one finger.

"Three hundred-thirty," Sly countered. "Or I call some of my more generous friends."

A few quiet moments passed while Horg went through his usual expressions of consideration. Finally he said, "Three hundred-thirty marks. I'll send my men to pick up. After they verify the manifest, the funds will be transferred to your account."

"The goods are at Bay 2-1343. We'll be waiting for you."

Horg smiled. "Always a pleasure doing business, gentlemen."

Qaade fought the urge to tell Horg how he really felt about their little encounters and turned to leave. A commotion behind him stopped him. The side door opened, and a burly man entered carrying a body over his shoulder. He deposited it unceremoniously on the table.

Dread filled Qaade. He recognized her instantly, even though a mass of red hair hid most of her face. Blood smeared the duster she wore. Her top had shifted and the slope of an ivory breast was revealed.

Qaade watched her shallow breathing and wrestled to control his fury. She must have followed him; that was the only explanation. He wasn't sure who he was angrier with—himself for not seeing her, or this woman for being brazen enough to chase him into a hellhole like Wryth.

"What's this?" Horg asked his guard.

"I caught her sneaking around the back entrance, so I stunned her for you." The man gave a wicked smile. "She's not local, boss. No brands, no ID, no embeds." His eyebrow lifted. "Virgin stock."

Horg circled the table, checking her out. "Well, well. It's a shame she trespassed on private property. I guess that means we get to keep her."

His blatant leer made Qaade's blood run cold. Hatred, deep and raw, surged through him. He reached for his weapon and found an empty holster. Sly moved next to him and narrowed his eyes in silent question. Qaade made the only decision he could.

"We'll buy her from you."

Horg tore his gaze from the woman to look at Qaade. "What?"

Sly stepped forward. "I said, we'll buy her from you. How much?"

The trader eyed him suspiciously. "I didn't think you boys moved bodies."

Sly shrugged. "Slaves. Cargo. We move it all. How much for the woman?"

Greed morphed Horg's face into a twisted smile. "I don't know. She's prime. First-class, good breeding, clean. Untraceable. And my buyers love redheads. She'd do well at auction."

"Horg," Qaade warned softly.

The trader grinned. "Fifty."

Qaade pursed his lips. They didn't have fifty

thousand marks to spare. But he wasn't leaving her with Horg, even if she was a fool to follow him. He knew what her future would be like. Qaade ran through his options while Sly remained silent, waiting for an answer.

"The meds," Qaade whispered to Sly's back.

His crewman tilted his head slightly, and Qaade knew he was surprised. But he said to Horg, "We have a four-by-four shipment of Phellium. Even trade."

That got the trader's attention, and his smile faded. "Phellium, you say? That wasn't on the manifest."

Sly shrugged. "Didn't think you'd give us a decent price."

Horg dropped his gaze to the redheaded woman, and Qaade held his breath. If Horg wouldn't sell, she'd vanish into the slave system and he'd never find her again.

But he needn't have worried—greed always won. The trader turned away and said, "She's all yours."

Chapter Four

Torrie heard a groan through the fog she was drowning in. A painful stab followed, consciousness trailing in its wake. She clung to it, pulling herself to the surface one excruciating degree at a time.

"You okay, lady?"

She paused, unsure of the voice. But he sounded worried. A good sign. She fought toward him, breaking through the fog. White lights blinded her, and pain ricocheted behind her eyes. Gentle hands held her down while her head spun in crazy circles.

"Easy, girl."

She blinked and focused on the face of an older man she didn't recognize. His nose was visibly crooked, a scar ran the length of his cheek and another lined his forehead. Red and white hair covered his head, and he wore a blue flightsuit that was too big for him.

He smiled. "Welcome back. How do you feel?"

Run, screamed her mind. She closed her eyes and

waited for her head to rejoin her body. What had happened? Where was she? Why was her brain insisting she was in danger? She reached a clumsy hand for one of her pistols. That's when she realized her hands were resting on her belly—in restraints. She lifted them and then looked accusingly at the old man.

He shrugged. "Sorry. Not my decision."

Then who the hell's decision was it? She grasped at scattered snippets of memory. Landing on Wryth. Locked out of the pirate's hanger. Saw the pirate leader leaving with the big, bad one. Tracked them deep into the spaceport. Tried to get closer. Someone hit her from behind. No, must have stunned her. That's why her brain was on fire. But what had happened after that?

The old scarred man watched her. Had *he* stunned her? She checked his hands. No weapons. *Good.* She moved her gaze around the small room. Metal walls. Probably a ship. Not hers. *Not so good.*

She tried to raise her head, but pain ripped across her skull.

"I wouldn't do that for a while, dear," the old man said. "You took a full charge. Gonna be at least a couple of hours before any part of you is in the mood to dance."

"Who are you?" Torrie asked, her words sounding disconnected.

"My name's Lapreu. At your service."

"Glad to hear that, Lapreu," Torrie joked. "You can remove the restraints now."

He gave her a genuinely sympathetic look. "I wish I could."

Okay. Change of tactics. "Where am I?"

"Ah," he answered, his eyebrows rising. "I'm afraid I'll have to leave that question up to Cap."

36

Lapreu wasn't a very helpful guy. "Cap?"

"The boss 'round here," he replied as he tucked a blanket around her. "Captain of the ship. He'll be along shortly."

And apparently the captain was the one who'd put her in restraints, Torrie thought.

The old man gave a grunt and wobbled to his feet. "You rest, dear. I have a feeling you'll need it."

She watched him shuffle to the door. It opened into a nondescript hallway, then closed behind him.

Strange little man, she thought. Speaking of strange little men, Howser was probably having cerebral overload right about now. Since he wasn't hovering over her, she had to assume he couldn't get to her. He'd never let her live this one down.

She licked her lips and encountered a crusty mass. Gingerly, she touched her lower lip with her fingers. *Blood. Lovely.* Wonder who gave her that. What a stellar day this was turning out to be. She was zero for two in the combat department. Either she wasn't as good as she thought, or no one was playing by the rules except her.

Her senses returned slowly. She was on a full-sized bed in a fairly large room—a bigger setup than your standard ship's quarters. Shelves lined the walls, along with a padded bench, a chair, and a table. Spartan, but based on the scattered personal mementos, someone lived here. She definitely didn't want to know who.

Despite Lapreu's warning, she struggled to one elbow and waited for the room to stop swaying. The pain in her head was more bearable than the fear in her heart. Regardless of how nicely Lapreu had treated her, she was in an unknown place under dangerous circumstances, injured, unarmed and wearing restraints. He hadn't removed them, and that said it all. Obviously, whoever shot her must have brought her here. No wonder her brain was screaming *run*.

She dragged her heavy legs over the edge of the bed and sat up. Oh damn, that hurt. But other than the bloody lip and her throbbing head, the rest of her felt more or less normal. Her pistols were nowhere in sight. Neither was her duster, which contained Nod. Hopefully, the lightball was recharging and not in trouble. If he woke up here, he'd be even more confused than usual.

Gone too was her wrist comm unit, replaced by restraints. She studied them. It took her a minute to realize they were the same type the pirate had bound her with. What? Did someone have a sale?

She took a deep breath and forced her muscles to move. After an uneven start, she was able to stand. She scanned the room for anything that could be used as a weapon. A glint of metal on one table caught her attention. She staggered to it and found a leveler tool—long, sharp and pointed. *Perfect.* Using the furniture for support, she reached the door. She turned around and squared her shoulders against the wall. The room faded in and out before slowing to a stop. There. That wasn't so bad.

Her head had cleared enough for her to realize just how much trouble she was in, imprisoned on an unknown vessel by unknown captors. The first order of business was getting a real weapon. Second, losing the restraints. Third would be an escape off the ship itself.

Settled on a plan of attack, she gripped the tool with both hands. Now, if she could just stay awake long enough for Cap's impending visit. . . .

* * *

"The credits will be enough to get us supplies, food and fuel at Delta Port for a complete circuit," Brilliard said. Through the holo comm, Qaade's operations chief appeared more harried than usual. He rubbed his bald head absently as he sat in the ops center of the ship *Freeport*, the heart of Qaade's freedom network.

"But we really need that Phellium. I'm still processing the last thousand slaves you brought in and most of them need treatment."

"I should have it in two days," Qaade offered.

Brilliard winced. "That'll have to do. But I won't be able to hold up traffic through *Freeport*. I'm out of space as it is. I've been dropping off the treated ones at the primary stations as fast as I can, but Slipstream's tributaries can handle only so many at a time." He sighed. "And with no Phellium, I'll be forced to send untreated slaves through."

Next to Qaade, Sly leaned toward the comm. "Maybe we can send some of the supply down through Slipstream to catch up with those people."

Brilliard replied, "Perhaps. But you know we probably won't reach them once they pass through the secondary tributaries to the safe havens. They will be given fresh identities and acclimated to new homes. I'll never be able to track them after that. Hell, the conductors can barely keep up with them, and they are the ones doing the relocations."

Qaade frowned. The woman he'd saved had cost him dearly. "Do the best you can and log anyone you miss."

Brilliard gave a half-hearted laugh. "That would be most of them. The percentage of scrubbed slaves is increasing. They come in here like lost children. No idea who they are or where they belong. I have entire families who don't even realize they are related. It's criminal. The only hope they have is the Phellium dose. At least then their minds can start to build and hold new memories again."

"Hold back the families for now," Qaade said. "Send the singles through Slipstream. We'll treat them later."

"Will do," Brilliard replied. "Good luck, Qaade. Out."

Qaade watched the holo dissolve and rubbed his hands across his face. "Damn."

Sly eyed him. "Two days? How are you going to manage that? We don't have time to locate another shipment, or to make another raid to get enough marks to buy the shipment we gave Horg. Even if we did, you know he wouldn't sell the Phellium back to us."

"Captain Maullet is the key," Qaade said simply, pushing away from the table and looking at his first officer. "How did she find us, Sly?"

He shrugged. "No idea. She sure as hell didn't follow *Exodus*."

"What about her cargo?"

Sly shook his head. "I detoxed the cargo myself. I *know* there was no tracker. Maybe she just got lucky."

"I don't think so. She followed us directly to Wryth, and I'm betting she followed her cargo." Qaade tossed a datapad on the table. "I found this in her coat along with a dead lightball and assorted weapons."

Sly turned the unit over in his hands. "Have you tried to access it yet?"

"Locked up tight. But I think that's the tracker. And if she did it once, she can do it again. Horg hasn't shipped anything in the past three hours she's been here. The Phellium is still on Wryth."

Sly handed the datapad back to Qaade. "Hell, you're going to steal it? Have you seen Horg's warehouse lately? We'll never find it in there, let alone get to it. And even if you did, his men carry real guns with real ammo and everything."

"I'm not going to take it out of the warehouse. Security is too tight." He looked at Sly. "We'll wait until they move it."

"And how will you know when that will be? I don't think Horg is going to send out a bulletin."

Qaade smiled. "That's why I need the woman. If she wants her freedom, she'll give me access to this unit."

Sly rubbed his chin. "It's a hell of a risk."

Qaade shrugged. "I can deal with a few guns."

"Who's talking about guns? I'm talking about the woman."

"I can handle her, too."

Sly laughed. "Not that one. She's like playing with live ammo."

"I'll survive. Okay, here's the plan: I want you to leave Wryth in *Exodus* to keep Horg off our tails. Once we are out of sensor range, I'll backtrack using *Umbra* and pick up the Phellium. Then, I'll rendezvous with you."

Sly shook his head. "I don't like it, Qaade. *Umbra* is a fast ship, but it's small, with limited firepower. What happens if you run into trouble?"

"I already ran into trouble," Qaade noted. "She's down the hall." He lifted his gaze to the door as Lapreu entered and limped across the office, then settled gingerly into a chair.

"Our lovely guest is awake."

Sly leaned his hefty body back in his chair. "She's a feisty one, eh?"

Lapreu nodded. "And very curious." His gaze met Qaade's. "She be lookin' for her guns, and I think she means to use them on you."

"I've already seen her shoot, and believe me, I'm not letting her near a gun," Qaade said. "Why do you think I restrained her?"

Lapreu grinned. "Haven't you ever heard that putting restraints on a beautiful woman will ruin any future romantic opportunities?"

"Don't worry. Future romantic opportunities aren't likely."

The old man frowned. "How long does she have to wear the restraints?"

Qaade glanced at his loyal deckhand, and the man's scars from former injustices gleamed in the overhead light. The old man hated restraints for a good reason. The best reason.

"I'll take them off as soon as I can trust her," he said.

Lapreu gave him a dubious look. "Don't you need her help? Leave those cuffs on, it may be a while before she trusts you."

Qaade didn't doubt that. In fact, it might not be a bad idea to talk to her *before* she recovered all her faculties. "She's the one who followed us to Wryth to begin with," he defended.

Lapreu shrugged. "She didn't do anything wrong 'cept come after what were hers."

"I don't feel bad for Masters Shipping," Qaade said firmly, tension filling his body. "They don't give a damn about the slave trade. And they don't give a damn about us."

"They will when one of their captains comes up missing," Lapreu pointed out. "InterGlax doesn't need another reason to be huntin' you, Cap."

Qaade cast Lapreu a serious look. "She cost me

the entire load of Phellium! I'm not going to let my people suffer for that."

The old man shook his head. "She won't help you."

"She'll have to, or I'll sell her back to Horg and let him do what he wants with her."

Lapreu's eyes widened. "You wouldn't."

Qaade clenched his teeth. No, he wouldn't. "She doesn't know that." He glanced from Lapreu to Sly. "And no one is going to tell her, either."

"Don't you think she'd be more cooperative if she knew why we needed it?" Sly asked.

"She obviously has too much loyalty to her employer," Qaade replied. He placed his elbows on the table and stared at his two crewmen. "No one can know about Slipstream, boys, especially someone on the other side."

"We're saving slaves here," Sly said in frustration. "She can't have anything against that."

"And we are also pirating shipments all over the sector. Since her ship was one of them, somehow I don't think she'll consider us justified. Either way, I'm not taking any chances. As far as she knows, I own her and she's my slave. The deal is, she helps me get the Phellium and she's a free woman. She can go back—no harm done—and work for Masters Shipping forever for all I care."

Lapreu set his jaw stubbornly. "I'm not treating her like a slave."

Qaade took a calming breath. "I'm sorry, Lapreu. You have to. It's for her own good as well. If Inter-Glax finds out she's been hanging out with the most wanted men in the sector, she'll be in more trouble than she ever imagined. So, this is what we are doing."

He watched the pair nod glumly, and he rose

from his chair. "Sly, get us off Wryth. I don't want you around if there's trouble. If they ever tie *Exodus* to me stealing back the Phellium, we'll never be able to operate out of here again."

Sly scowled. "I'm coming with you."

Qaade relented. "Fine. Lapreu, you and Urwin are in charge in our absence. I'll be in my quarters if you need me."

Neither Lapreu nor Sly spoke as Qaade snagged his facemask from the table, left his office and headed to his cabin. He hated treating anyone like a slave as much as they did, but even they realized the consequences. All it would take was one person to ruin his network. No one was going to jeopardize Slipstream. He pulled the face covering over his head. He'd staked his life on it.

Chapter Five

Torrie's eyelids were heavy, begging for rest, but surprise would be her only advantage and she couldn't afford to lose it.

She swallowed back her fear and tried not to think about what these people had in mind for her. Of course, having her six brothers show up and rescue her held even less appeal. She could hear them now. Carmon would bellow like her father while Macke launched into his standard pirate lecture and Cahill laughed his ass off. The others would just sit back and enjoy the show. The only person on her side would be her mother, and even then, as always, her mother would do whatever was best for the family. Which meant Torrie would be in the office forever and ever. No, she was going to save herself.

Echoing footsteps breathed energy into her weary body. She focused. They were coming down the hallway, drawing closer: one set of heavy steps.

A man. *Cap.* He stopped on the other side of the door.

Adrenaline flooded Torrie's veins, a welcome ally. She gripped the leveling tool and rallied her body to action. The door breezed open beside her. A black facemask came into view, and she attacked her captor midstep.

The tool sliced through the air, ripping toward his neck with her full body weight behind it. He turned fast, deflecting most of the impact, but she felt her weapon contact flesh and saw a flash of red. The man twisted, throwing her balance off just enough to make her stumble past him.

Damn the drugs. She was never this clumsy. Having her hands bound wasn't helping either, shortening her reach and putting her at a serious disadvantage.

She recovered, slashing at the closest body part of her enemy, which happened to be his shoulder. Shirt fabric tore as she nicked it but missed her intended target. She gripped her weapon for a return pass, but a steely hand closed around her wrist. Pain seared her arm, robbing her muscles of strength. Pressure exploded in her head from the physical exertion as she kicked, clawed and slashed at him. Her foe blocked each move, squeezing her wrist until she could no longer hold the tool and it clattered to the floor.

He spun her around and pushed her toward the bed. She fell face-first and rolled onto her back a split second before his entire weight landed on top of her, pinning her arms beneath him.

"Bastard!" she yelled, trying to throw him off her by arching her body.

"Are you almost done?" The aggravated voice was a low, deep growl.

"Never." She clenched her teeth and closed her eyes to the pain that hammered inside her head. His weight pressed her into the bed. She felt trapped and helpless—both of which pissed her off to no end. No, she wasn't done yet. He might have the advantage right now, but he had no idea who he was dealing with.

She opened her eyes and came face-to-face with her captor's quicksilver gaze. Recognition clicked in, and her sudden gasp was involuntary, an error the pirate noted immediately.

"You," she hissed.

"Nice to see you again, too."

Anger energized her body. She tried to roll right—no go. She bucked left, her elbow connecting with his chest, and got a grunt for her efforts. He lifted off her and shifted, trapping her thighs between his legs. With one hand, he stretched her arms over her head and pinned them. Then he lowered his face to hers.

"*Now* you're done."

She couldn't move, forced into submission as he regarded her with annoyance and impatience.

She gathered her rage and enunciated every word clearly. "I want my damn cargo, pirate."

The corners of his eyes crinkled. "Possession is ninety-nine percent of the law, woman."

"And a big gun is the other one percent. If I get my hands on one, that ninety-nine percent isn't going to save you."

He had the nerve to laugh in her face. When he recovered, he moved closer—a hairsbreadth away from her. "I guess I don't have to worry about it, since I no longer possess your cargo."

No! "What did you do with it?"

"I sold it to buy you." His gaze traveled from her eyes to her mouth. "I own you."

A roar erupted inside Torrie. "Go to hell. No one owns me."

"They do now. And if you ever want to be free again, you'll help me get my shipment back."

She gaped at him for a split second. "*Your* shipment? That's *my* shipment, and I'm not helping you get your grubby hands on it again."

"Then I'll sell you off, and you can spend your life enslaved."

She tried to remain indifferent to his threat, but panic was creeping over her. This couldn't be happening. He couldn't be telling the truth. Somewhere deep in her mind, an old memory surfaced. She'd seen one slave in her life, a long time ago. Nausea welled in her belly, and she shoved the memory aside in self-preservation.

"Do you have any idea what it's like to be a slave, Captain?" the pirate asked. He leaned closer until his mouth was within a centimeter of hers. "It hurts," he whispered. She saw bitterness in his eyes. "Every day is a reminder that your life doesn't matter. You are nothing but a possession. And a body to be used in any way your owner desires. Don't kid yourself, woman. You were an expensive purchase, but I can easily get more for you than I paid."

"You filthy, despicable animal." She seethed with rage and horror.

"The choice is yours. That's more than you'll get from another owner. Trust me, most slaves never have a chance for freedom."

"Then why are you giving me one?"

His expression calmed and he eased off her slightly, giving her entrapped body some relief. "I want that shipment. Specifically, the Phellium you cost me. And since you had no trouble tracking it to Wryth, you should have no problem finding it again. Am I right?"

Shock and disbelief took hold as she processed what he'd said. "What the hell are you talking about? What Phellium?"

He laughed. "Playing innocent won't work, lady. Every captain knows what they're hauling. Especially one working for Masters Shipping."

"I wasn't hauling any Phellium. It's prohibited by the company," she told him.

His eyes narrowed dangerously. "Then I guess you need to screen your clients more carefully."

She blinked. He was lying. Phellium was a legal, but highly sought-after drug used to help the brain heal itself, explicitly in the areas controlling memory. It was worth a small fortune on the black market, which is why Carmon would never allow the company to carry it: It was simply too tempting. But a niggling voice in the back of Torrie's mind kept bugging her. Was that why her ship had been targeted by pirates? Could this be the something they knew that she didn't? The client she was delivering for was one of their oldest and most trusted, despite the fact that he ran his shipments from point-to-point, drop-shipping everything. But if he had been trafficking Phellium, would they know it?

"How did you track it?" the pirate asked slowly.

She wanted to tell him to go to hell. She wanted to tell him that she could buy her freedom a hundred times over whatever he paid for her. But if Masters Shipping was hauling Phellium, she needed to know.

Steely resolve stole over his expression at her silence. "If I send you back, they'll scrub your memory. You won't remember who you are, let alone recognize anyone. That includes your mate, your children, and your family. You won't know enough to ever want to escape. You won't *exist*." He said the last word with stark emphasis.

A sick and elemental fear trembled in her belly. She'd heard of scrub drugs, capable of wiping short- and long-term memories and turning the victim into a mindless, memoryless shell. "You wouldn't."

She could see him smile beneath the mask. Detestable scum. He would. No, she didn't want that. She didn't want to forget about the pirate who did this to her. And she needed to know about the drug. Besides, he would have to free her hands if he wanted her to help him.

Once she located the shipment again, she'd have a chance to check it for herself, and maybe even steal it away from him. If it was Phellium, she wanted it for evidence. If it wasn't, she still wanted it back—if for nothing else to prove to her family that she could hold her own against pirates. But she wouldn't give Cap her tracking system to do it. It would keep her alive, at least until he had what he wanted.

"Fine, but *I* do the tracking," she finally said.

One of his eyebrows went up. "And?"

She narrowed her eyes. "If you are waiting for my undying love, you can kiss my ass, slaver."

"Maybe later. If you do anything stupid," he moved closer and darkness filled his eyes, "like try to double-cross me. Again. In fact, I'm not sure I can trust you at all."

"And you expect me to trust you—a pirate and a slaver? Not in my lifetime."

"You gave me your word before," he added. "Obviously, it doesn't mean much."

"I didn't call InterGlax," she snapped. "That's all I promised you."

He stared at her for a few long seconds. "Does Masters Shipping know that?"

At the mention of the family business, she stilled. Oh, damn. She was a Masters. He must not be aware of that. Otherwise, they wouldn't be bartering for her freedom. With her family's fortune, she was worth much more than any slave. He could ransom her for millions. Losing one shipment would pale in comparison to her family's bailing her out of this situation. Well, that certainly reprioritized things in a hurry.

Straight-faced, she replied, "They won't be happy if I don't come back with it."

"So you decided to recover it on your own? How noble of you. Do they pay you enough to risk your life?"

She snarled at his mockery. "It's an honest living, which is more than you can claim."

He chuckled. Then he released her and stood up. She tried to move, but her arms caught on something. She looked up to find he'd anchored her cuffs to a lockdown clip. No matter how hard she yanked, they didn't give.

"You'll only hurt yourself," he said casually as he bent down and picked up the leveler she'd dropped. He turned it over in his hand, then shifted his scrutiny to her. A trickle of blood had run down his neck and stained his shirt from the inside out.

For the first time, she felt truly vulnerable as he moved around the room, gathering various objects. All she could do was watch. He was choosing items that were potential weapons. He wasn't as stupid

51

as she'd hoped. While he stowed them in a secure cabinet, it occurred to her that she must be in his quarters. And in his bed. This just kept getting better.

When he was done, he settled into the chair across from her. He leaned forward and steepled his fingers in front of his face. For a long time, he studied her stretched across his bed. Real panic gripped her, her powerlessness getting the best of her. She could only imagine what he was thinking. She didn't give a damn if he owned her or not, she wouldn't let him touch her. Her legs were still free and she could use them to—

"How long have you been working for Masters Shipping, Sheri?" he asked.

Torrie blinked, caught off balance. He knew her name. Well, her false name anyway. The one she'd adopted so that no one knew she was a Masters, which would be a problem. In this case, a really serious problem. But for now, she was safe. "A few years. And since you seem to know all about me, what's your name, pirate?" she asked with a superficial smile.

He slid back in his chair, lazily sprawling out his long body with a contemptuous look. His fingertips tapped lightly on the chair arms. "You can just call me Cap." He squinted at her. "But we have a problem." He cocked an eyebrow, and added, "Sheri."

"In case you hadn't noticed, *I'm* the one with the problem," she said.

He continued in a slow drawl, "If I take those restraints off you, I get the distinct impression that you'll try to kill me."

"Really?" She tugged on the restraints from a different angle. They rattled loudly. "Now, where would you get an idea like that?"

"Just a hunch. I'd like your word, Sheri."

She glared at him. Howser was right. Why should she give her word to a pirate?

When she didn't answer, he took a deep breath. "You're lucky I was there when they brought you into our meeting." His gaze focused on her with a mix of disdain and cocky arrogance. "Horg was ready to put you on the auction block."

"What are you talking about? *Your* men captured me."

"Wrong. Horg is the meanest trader this side of Goldrick Gap, and you trespassed on his property. On Wryth, that's enough to get someone executed. You weren't so lucky." He stood up, taking command of the room, and walked over to her. "If I hadn't been there when they brought you to him, you'd be standing on a block with a discipline flake in your head and no memories to call your own."

"That's a lie," she said, unable to believe he'd "rescued" her.

Cap folded his arms and stared at her without blinking. He wasn't mocking her. He wasn't even gloating. Could he have really *saved* her? In irritation, she realized that would explain the kind old man. And if Cap's men had shot her, then he wouldn't have needed to buy her in the first place. He'd still have her shipment, and she probably wouldn't be alive right now. Well, hell.

"Your word, please," he repeated.

She seethed at the indignity of it all. "Fine. I won't kill you. But in return, I want your word that you will let me go after I locate the shipment."

He took a long time replying. "My word."

She wondered just how much that was worth.

Chapter Six

Fahlow stood beside her owner and his game. Chauvet walked around the center holostage, admiring his creation. He stroked his chin, deep in unspeakable thoughts. Dark, demented and unstable he was—she'd learned to expect nothing good from him. Her gentle world had not prepared her for such a monstrosity of a man.

The inner sanctum held her, its familiar walls like the bars of an exquisite cage. Elaborate laser etchings covered their every surface, gleaming magnificently for their young, angry owner who would never concede their splendor over his own. Four graceful, pointed arches framed the square chamber, with alcoves that led to double doors and that were flanked by windows with a view of deep space.

Despite all the majesty of the orchestral accompaniment, it was the image on the center holostage that captivated Chauvet's sick mind. In a way, Fahlow was glad to have his attention diverted from persecuting her. But as she secretly studied the images of ships and stations in the hologram, her heart sank. She would give her life to save the man Chauvet was about to destroy. He was the only man who could save them all, including her people who were enslaved and scattered across the sector. The man was unknowingly about to enter a deadly game.

Chauvet stopped his pacing and zeroed in on her with such utter dominance, Fahlow braced herself for the worst.

"So what do you think of my game, Princess?"

Fahlow suppressed her anger at his use of the honored title her people had placed upon her. "I do not think, My Lord."

He chuckled. "Of course you don't." He paced around the holo-image again. "It's perfect. The Slipstream circuit—*Freeport, Exodus*—all mapped out. Every detail of his operation is within my grasp, along with the *laghato* himself." He spread his arms wide. "The savior of slaves everywhere. But he hasn't saved *you,* has he?" Chauvet added with a smirk. "And he won't. Your faith and the faith of fools like you is wasted."

Fahlow lowered her eyes to avoid his stare. So much bitterness in so young a man, as if he'd been hoarding it since birth, guarding it like a terrible, monstrous treasure.

"You think I don't know what you hold in your heart?" he continued. "The name you whisper to the others in the shadows?"

She stiffened her slight frame. He had taken everything from her, but he would never see into her heart or comprehend the strength of her soul.

"Your dreams are futile," Chauvet sneered with a deep bitterness.

A soft chime echoed between the arches, followed by an announcement. "Sir, I have Urwin on the comm for you."

Mercerr's lively voice soothed Fahlow, bringing the only comfort she'd found in her long three years here. Even though he was Chauvet's second in command, he was a good man; kind to her if only through his smiles and concern. But that was the limit of his power.

"Put him on," Chauvet ordered.

Seconds later, a raspy voice said, "Urwin here."

Fahlow's heart stilled. *The traitor.*

"Report," Chauvet said, locking his hands behind him as he stared at Fahlow. She could feel his gaze peeling away the thin layers of her gown.

"Qaade has taken the bait," Urwin said. "But there's a problem."

Her owner's expression morphed into displeasure. "What kind of problem?"

Urwin cleared his throat. "Apparently, he traded the drug for a slave. She's aboard *Exodus* now."

"Who?" Chauvet demanded.

"The captain of the Masters ship. Her name is Sheri Maullet. She followed her hijacked shipment to Wryth. However, Qaade plans to steal the shipment back from Horg. What are your orders?"

For a long time, Chauvet stared into the holo-image, his face frozen in blue light. "We wait. If laghato isn't good enough to get the shipment back himself, he isn't worthy of the game. Contact me when he has it. Out."

Chauvet stepped over to her. Fahlow saw his hard black eyes look at her, vacant of empathy or decency or anything even remotely human. His gaze traced a line down her throat between her breasts. Her stomach twisted, knowing what was to come next. She would have preferred the hard edge of his hand, but the discipline flake embedded in her spine guaranteed her capitulation. As he stepped close, she concentrated, disassociating her body from her mind in self-preservation. Pulling deep inside herself, she felt the world around her change to a watery blur. But it never faded enough for her to escape completely. She could still see Chauvet's face.

Qaade sat in the subdued light of his office and scrolled through the latest docket from Brilliard. It listed the steady stream of slaves beginning their journey to freedom through his nomadic spacebase—*Freeport.* Among the names were the Unknowns: scrubbed so clean, they didn't even know their names.

"Not many Unknowns in this batch," he told Brilliard.

The man nodded through the comm. "Those were the lot you picked up on Kettering Crossing. I was able to match their genetic signatures to our ID-Net and then back to their families. Someone raided their entire region, taking mostly the men and young girls. Unfortunately, the remaining family members are refugees in their own land. If I send these slaves back, they won't receive the medical treatment they need."

An undercurrent of anger kept Qaade's despair at bay. After all this time, he'd learned to balance his emotions.

Brilliard added, "And the region is still volatile, with regular slave raids. Slavers are harvesting people faster than you can free them."

Qaade looked up from his pad. "It's not hopeless, Brilliard."

The man sighed deeply. "It just feels like a never-ending battle." His tired eyes met Qaade's. "No matter how good you are, or how fast I hustle them down Slipstream, we'll never save them all. It's getting worse, Qaade. I don't know why, but activity is really picking up. Something's shifted. Someone is pushing the flow."

Qaade pursed his lips. He knew that. His network of contacts kept him informed when a shipment of slaves was being transported. For fifteen years he'd boarded those ships, rescued the people held there, and sold the slaver ship to pay for their treatment and relocation. But lately the traffic was increasing at such an alarming rate that he couldn't hope to keep up.

"We need another ship besides *Exodus*," Brilliard said. He raised his hand. "I know you don't like that, and believe me, I realize how hard you are working. But we aren't even making a dent in the traffic, and you know it."

Qaade tossed his datapad on the table and leaned back to regard his old friend. "Can't do it. I'm not about to risk any more of my crew. Raiding those slavers is too dangerous. Besides, if any head is going to roll, it's going to be mine. *Freeport* and Slipstream are my operations. My creation."

"You are going to have to let go sometime. You can't continue to run yourself ragged, Qaade. If the slavers or InterGlax don't kill you, your schedule will." He moved closer. "What if you get caught?"

Qaade replied, "I won't. Not unless I'm dead. Sorry, I know you mean well, but I'm not letting anyone else raid slavers. And I won't trust this operation to just anyone. Besides, *Exodus* is a custom craft. Fastest ship in the Dead Zone. We don't have the credits to buy another. You're stuck with me."

His ops chief gave up with a shrug. "It was worth a try. We both need a lot more sleep than we're getting." Then he grinned mischievously. "Speaking of sleep deprivation—I hear you bought yourself a personal slave."

Qaade scowled at the joke. "Temporarily. She's going to lead me to the Phellium."

Brilliard eyed Qaade's throat. "And did she give you that?"

Qaade touched the bandage on his neck. "She didn't take kindly to discovering she was a commodity."

Brilliard gave a rare laugh. "I'll bet. You really think she's going to help you steal her own shipment back?"

"She'll have to if she wants her freedom." After a moment Qaade added, "I'm going to send you a gen-sig scan on her. I want you to run it through your ID database."

"You don't know who she is?"

Qaade crossed his arms. "She told me her name, but I'm sure it's false."

"Can't imagine why. You being such a gentleman and all." Brilliard smiled. Then his expression softened. "Speaking of gen-sigs, no one in that last batch of slaves matched your genetic signature."

"I noticed."

"The chances of finding your mother and sister are very small, Qaade."

"You are a fountain of optimism today, Brilliard."

The man chuckled. "Sorry. I'm a little tired. I just don't want you to get your hopes up. It's been thirty years. Anything could have happened since your family was enslaved and split up."

"They're still alive. I can feel it," Qaade said softly.

Brilliard nodded. "Then they must be." He looked at something to his left. "I'm moving *Freeport* through Quadrant 115 now, but skipping the next scheduled stop on the circuit. There's some unusual activity in this region lately."

"What kind of activity?"

Brilliard frowned, the skin on his bald head bunching. "Just a lot of little things that are making me nervous. Or maybe it's just my lack of sleep. Anyway, if you need to drop some slaves off, check our coordinates. We're running a little ahead of the timetable right now."

"Got it. And Brilliard . . ." His old friend raised his gaze, and Qaade gave him a smile. "Thanks."

"Hey, we're in this together," the man replied, suppressing a yawn. "For as long as it takes. Now get some sleep. Out."

The holo comm went dark, and Qaade rubbed his eyes. Sleep would be nice. Unfortunately, he had a Phellium shipment to steal. He shoved his tired body out of the chair, grabbed his captive's duster and exited his office for his quarters. She should be rested enough to give him the information he needed. Maybe she'd attack him again. That had been . . . stimulating.

A small smile touched his lips at the thought of her body beneath his. She was a beauty, no doubt about it. But the fire—he nearly growled—that fire could burn a man alive. Not a bad way to go. He'd never met a woman so fearless. Touching her had been like igniting a rocket: fast, lethal, burning out of control.

He supposed he could try to ignore the red-hot beauty and her effect on him. But she'd be gone soon enough and, frankly, it had been a long time since he'd found anything that could ignite his own flame and help him escape the grueling, end-less responsibility of running Slipstream.

He stopped in front of his quarters and pulled his mask on. The door slid silently out of the way. Framed in the doorway was his bed with Sheri sleeping in it. He stepped through silently and tossed her coat on a table. The door probably closed behind him but he didn't hear it. All his senses were tuned in to the woman.

She was stretched across his bed, her face tilted away from him. The rest of her, however, was right up front. She still wore the tight black tank that stretched across and just below her breasts. A band of ivory skin showed off a trim waist. Her pants hugged her hips low and outlined strong thighs and calves. From head to toe, she was tightly bound with muscle and strength, was a woman built for speed. He'd rarely seen such a strong physique in such an electrifying package. It was a miracle Horg had sold her at all. Luckily, he hadn't gotten a good look at her.

Qaade tempered his wandering imagination and waved the scanner over her body. Her genetic signature registered, along with her vital stats, which looked healthy. He finished at her head and mass of fiery red hair. It suited her with its bold intensity.

Qaade reached out and touched a lock, brushing it from the woman's face. Green eyes blinked open and then widened when she saw him. He studied them. Beautiful, like the rest of her, they were equal parts fire and ice—either of which could be deadly under the right conditions.

She was sitting up a split-second later. "What the hell were you doing?" she snapped.

He grinned. "Now, is that any way to treat your owner?"

"Drop dead," she said, her eyes scanning the

room—for a weapon, no doubt. He'd have to keep a *very* close watch on her. Oh, the hardship.

"I'm just checking to make sure you don't have any injuries. You're fine." He pocketed his scanner and crossed his arms. "Time to locate my shipment."

Her green eyes turned to killer slits. She might have given her word, but he still didn't trust her. There was something she wasn't telling him, something that meant a great deal to her. He couldn't help but wonder why an ordinary space-ship captain would go to such risks for a cargo whose value her company could easily recover through insurance.

He leaned back against the table and waited.

He was bigger than Torrie remembered. Unwelcome curiosity reared its ugly head, and she squelched it quickly. She didn't give a damn about who this was, where he came from, or what he wore to bed.

He said, "Horg hasn't moved any of his cargo yet, so the Phellium is still on Wryth—but not for long. So, what's your secret?"

She clenched her teeth. Her secret? The private tracking system she'd designed herself. A system so unique, only she and Howser knew how it worked. If she told this pirate how to find it, then what would he need to keep her alive for? How would she resteal it from him? And how would she ever take it back to show Carmon?

"I'll lead you to the cargo myself," she said.

One eyebrow kicked up beneath the ever-present face wrap. "You realize it would be much safer for me to get it."

It was her turn to smile. "I wouldn't want anything to happen to you. At least, not until we locate it."

63

He laughed—a deep rumbling that curled in her belly. Then he muttered something she didn't catch. To her surprise, he pushed off the table and came to her. Their eyes locked, and she fought the urge to look away from the fervent stare with its sensual undertone.

He tugged her from the bed and pulled her into him. Every muscle in her body tensed as hot hands wrapped around hers. Instinctively, she yanked back. His eyes narrowed slightly. She'd never seen such wise, sad eyes. As if he'd seen it all. As if he'd lived too much. As if nothing she could do would faze him.

"I can't remove the restraints if you don't let me touch you."

He grasped her hands again, and this time she curbed her automatic reaction. Warm, strong fingers slipped over her skin. She had no idea how he worked the restraints when he didn't take his eyes off her, but he took his sweet time.

He slid his fingers around her wrists and slowly, with maddening deliberation, slipped the shackles off. Her hands were free, but the rest of her was held hostage by his steady gaze.

Then he reached into his pocket and withdrew her datapad. Her heart leapt. She had a comm in that unit.

He handed it to her and said, "Let's see what you can do, lady."

She took the unit, trying not to look the least bit excited. Before she could access it, he moved behind her. She sidestepped away without looking at him when he brushed against her shoulder.

"We already removed any standard locators or transponders," he noted.

"I know. Mine aren't standard."

"Custom?" he said. "Interesting."

"It's a hobby."

He stepped closer, and she could feel his body heat burning her back.

"If you keep that up, I'm going to embed this data-pad in your forehead," she said, focused on logging in instead of on the way he jumbled her concentration.

He leaned near her ear. "I just want to make sure you don't call your friends. Kind of like you're trying to do now."

Damn. Who'd have guessed pirates were so smart? She closed the comm layer she'd opened and accessed the tracking section. The signal appeared on a small floor plan. She flipped the data-pad closed and turned to face him, slipping the unit into her back pocket. "All of *my* cargo is still on Wryth—three levels below us."

"Then it's still in Horg's warehouse. They will probably ship it with the next regular delivery in seven hours." Qaade reached around her with a grin and retrieved the datapad from her pocket while she scowled at him. He put it back in her hands. "Set it to notify you in case the cargo moves before that."

She snatched the pad away and set the alarm. Then she pushed it into him.

He looked distinctively triumphant and activated his comm. "Get my ship ready. Captain Maullet and I are leaving shortly."

Torrie recognized the responding voice as that of the pirate giant. "You sure about that?"

Cap kept his eyes upon her. "Positive." He closed the comm and handed Torrie her duster. "After you."

Torrie pulled her coat on and surreptitiously patted the pocket. Nod was still there, still recharging. If she could keep him quiet after he woke up, he could report back to Howser.

She gave the pirate a smile and breezed by him.

Chapter Seven

The pirate's personal transport was smaller than the one he'd used to board her ship, and a lot smaller than the craft he'd just walked her through, which she'd been held captive inside. That was a sizable Emmeron cruiser—a ship known for its speed and armaments. Everything was well maintained and top of the line. No wonder these guys were so good.

She moved from the rear cargo compartment of the personal transport to the claustrophobic front cabin, and frowned. Very small. Two single bunks were folded up end-to-end along the right wall of a narrow corridor. She moved past the bunks, lav and galley on the left to the cockpit with two seats, and she scanned the ship's console. Standard controls. She would have no trouble flying it. All she had to do was get rid of the pirate.

"Make yourself at home," Cap said as he squeezed past. She held her breath at the brush of his body against hers. He was doing that on purpose; she was sure of it. Just to shake her up. Well, Torrie Masters didn't quake for any man.

He turned to face her, his expression grim. Then she felt the cool, hard grip of restraints around her right wrist and tried to pull back.

"No," she snapped. Too late. Her other hand was shackled a split second later. She held the restraints up, and with real feeling said, "I *hate* you."

He pushed her into one of the cockpit seats and grinned. "I can't have you molesting me while I fly."

She grunted while he slipped into his seat beside her. "The only thing I'd molest you with is a pistol to your groin."

"You don't get many dates, do you?"

"I don't need any more men in my life, thank you."

Cap maneuvered his ship smoothly out of the shuttle bay into space. "No men? What are you afraid of?"

"I'm not afraid of anything," she told him as she watched Wryth Spaceport appear in front of them. "Why did we leave Wryth, only to go back again?"

He shrugged. "I prefer to keep a low profile."

She stared at him as it dawned on her. "You don't want the thieves knowing you're a thief."

His silver gaze swung around to her, dangerous and solemn. "You can save the morality lesson, lady. I'm well beyond redemption." The look in his eyes was guarded but almost rueful. Torrie turned away, suppressing any notion of guilt. He was a slaver. He didn't own a soul to suffer with.

He contacted Wryth for landing clearance, and she watched him pilot the ship, noting every maneuver, every procedure. If she got a chance to take control of the vessel, she would. Security lockout would be a problem, but not an unworkable one. She could hotwire ships twice this size given enough time.

Thirty minutes later, they landed in a dingy, littered private bay. Cap released his harness and stood up. "We're less than fifty meters from Horg's warehouse, one level below us. Close enough to move when my shipment does." He helped her out of the chair and to her feet before turning toward the back of the ship. As she watched, he pulled his shirt off. Her senses clamored with both fear and approval. "What are you doing?"

He wadded up his shirt and deposited it in a side bin, his back to her. "Bedtime, lady. I don't know what sleep schedule you are on, but I need a few hours."

The first distraction, of course, was his bare back, tightly muscled and beautifully sculpted. Then she remembered that he had spoken. Had he said *bedtime?*

He moved around the ship, locking down cabinets and doors. When he turned around, she was still in the same spot.

"Do you plan on sleeping standing up?" he asked, putting his hands on his hips. Unfortunately, his torso was as nice as his back. Well-defined muscles packed an impressive chest. A fine sprinkling of curly hair drew her gaze down to his waistband. She raised her eyes to his face and realized he was smiling at her behind his damn mask. She'd love to rip it off his face, expose him for what he really was.

Anger, embarrassment and dismay mixed into her venomous response. "I'm not sleeping in the same bunk with you, if that's what you're thinking."

"Lucky for you, I'm a very tired owner."

She glared at him as he lowered both bunks from their berths in the wall.

He looked at her. "Pick one."

"The restraints?" she reminded him, showing him her bound wrists.

He shook his head. "Improvise. I don't plan on falling asleep and never waking up."

"Coward," she muttered under her breath, and scooted up on the bunk closest to the front. Covertly, she glanced over to where her datapad lay. As soon as her captor was asleep, she would . . .

"Lie down," he ordered softly. She turned her head to find him facing her as she sat on the edge of the bunk. Their eyes locked in a war of wills. He had no idea who he was messing with. She'd grown up with older brothers. She'd learned not to flinch. The problem, however, was that he wasn't one of her brothers, and he had a way of looking at her that undermined her best efforts to stay aloof.

He leaned in. "Would you like some help?"

"Would you like a broken nose?"

Amusement blossomed in his voice. "I love it when you talk tough."

She clenched her teeth and lay down on the bunk. She managed to ignore his substantial body beside her until she felt him pull her hands over her head.

"What—" Her restraints clicked into a connection on the wall. She turned to him with murder in her eyes as he moved to his bunk. When her foot just missed him, he chuckled.

"Sleep well." He stretched out on the other bed, threw an arm over his eyes, and went to sleep.

Torrie checked the strength of the latch. It didn't budge. The datapad lay three meters from her in clear view—infuriatingly close. She blew out an aggravated breath.

Bastard.

His captive wriggled around for ten minutes before falling asleep, no doubt trying to escape. That was one determined woman. Too bad she wasn't on his side. Qaade could put all that restless, uncontrolled energy to good use.

He adjusted his arm over his eyes, trying to give his body the sleep it so desperately needed. His body, however, had other ideas, which was his own fault, depriving it of female company for so long.

He'd lied to her. He might be tired, but he wasn't *that* tired. In fact, he had plenty of energy to burn. But there were more important matters to deal with than sex, or his lack thereof. He couldn't believe he had just thought that, but it was true. He needed every ounce of energy he possessed to keep his slave rescue op running. And one feisty, albeit tempting woman wouldn't alter that goal. There were too many lost souls depending on him.

Torrie woke after a short, unproductive nap. It took her a moment to remember where she was.

Cap was already up, leaning back in the pilot's chair with one booted foot on the console, trying to access her datapad. The muscles in his bare torso bunched in the glow of cabin light. And from the deep furrow between his eyes, he wasn't having much luck circumventing her security lockout.

"Problem, pirate?" she said, and leaned up on one elbow.

His silver gaze transfixed her like a spear. "You need to learn a little respect, woman."

She grinned. "Didn't sleep well, did we?"

He abandoned the datapad and rose to his feet. He walked over to her, and she curbed the urge to shrink back when he braced both his hands against the edge of her bunk. He leaned in, blocking out the ship. She swallowed and tried to ignore the fact that he wasn't wearing anything except his black mask and pants.

"No, I didn't sleep well," he said with deliberate menace. "Too much pent-up energy."

She trembled involuntarily under the force of his gaze—a direct contradiction to the softness of his voice. Raw sexual tension radiated from him. And, much to her dismay, she reacted to it instantly with a quickening of her heart. She tried to escape to a safer distance, but the restraints attached to the wall stopped her. "If you have so much energy, why don't you go somewhere and work it off? I'll be happy to watch the ship for you."

His shoulder muscles corded as he moved closer. "Actually, I had something else in mind."

The rasp in his voice unnerved her, and the look in his eyes reminded her that she was his. "Forget it, pirate. I'll never surrender *that* to you. I don't care how much I cost you. You might as well just shoot me now." The hoarseness of her own whisper surprised her.

For a long time, he just stared. Then he reached a hand out, and she braced herself for retribution or worse. Instead, she heard the click of the demagnetizer. The restraint released. Surprised, she watched as he opened the other. He pushed away from her bunk with a solemn look. Then he walked over to a wall cabinet and withdrew a shirt.

No reaction. No emotion at all. She'd pushed him pretty hard and nothing. His restraint was impressive. But she had to remember that he was keeping her alive to find her shipment. That meant she'd be pretty much worthless to him afterward. Disposable.

It all fit. That's why there was no retribution. He was planning on executing her after she found the shipment. Which only reinforced her plan to take it from him. That load belonged to her client, and she would deliver it. Even if it was Phellium. It wasn't her job to reprimand customers for breaking the company rules.

The pirate turned and threw her a black object. She snagged it out of the air. It was a facemask like his.

"You wear masks so other thieves don't recognize a Ghost Rider of the Dead Zone?" she asked.

He hesitated for a split-second, long enough for her to know she was right. Then he tossed his clean shirt on the bunk. He nodded at the mask. "So you don't become the most wanted woman in the sector. Masters Shipping might have a problem with that."

"You're concerned for my future well-being? I'm touched," she said, dropping the mask behind her. "Do all slave owners worry this way?"

His silver eyes narrowed. "If I treated you like a real slave, you'd learn what fear meant."

Her eyes narrowed, too. "So how many slaves have you had, Cap?"

He drew a long P5-Eight pistol from the cabinet above him. "I deal with them every day."

"Animal," she murmured.

He looked up from checking the pistol's charge. "Since when do you, or anyone else, care about the plight of slaves? Or is it because you are now one that suddenly it matters?"

Torrie clenched her fists at a rush of annoyance.

Don't act rash, she told herself. *He has a gun in his hands.*

"No one should have their freedom taken from them. It is the most basic of all rights," she said, her words measured. "And anyone who takes another's freedom should pay with his own liberty. Or life. In your case, I'd choose life."

The pirate's movements stilled and he watched her. "I don't see you or Masters Shipping doing anything about it. Slavery is legal in half the sector. If you cared so much, you'd do something about that."

His bitter words cut through her, feeding her anger. How dare a common pirate pull this holier-than-thou act with her? She *did* care. Slavery was a horrible, detestable part of reality. It wasn't her fault societies were still bent on perpetuating it. She sat up and swung off the bunk to stand in front of him. "There are laws and law enforcement to impose them. Unfortunately, it's people like *you* who keep slavery alive."

The pirate gave a sardonic laugh. He holstered his pistol and stepped up to her. She glared at him as he invaded her space. "Is that what you think? Law enforcement is handling it? It's easier that way, isn't it? You don't have to get your own hands dirty."

She pushed her face in his. "Most of us live within the law. What would happen if we *all* became renegade vigilantes and self-proclaimed judges? InterGlax is around for a reason. They—"

"They don't do a damn thing," he cut in with a low growl. "After all, what's the incentive? What do poor, powerless slaves have to offer them? Nothing. The slavers pay InterGlax to look the other way.

There is *no one* to stop their ships from crisscrossing this sector every day." He leaned closer and whispered, "No one will save you. How does it feel?"

Fury tore through her, and she delivered a blow to his chest. He grunted and blocked the fist she threw at his face. Still, she managed to rip his mask off, which distracted him long enough for her to reach for his pistol. The pirate deflected her hand and wrapped it in his. He captured her other hand and spun her around, pinning her flat to the wall with his unyielding body.

She called him every nasty name she could think of as he stretched her hands to each side and pressed against her hard enough to steal the air from her lungs. His heat and anger radiated through her clothing. Mid-flail, she heard his harsh words: "Do that again, and I'll make sure you never get out of those restraints."

She laid her head back against the wall and looked into his unmasked face for the first time. He was older than she'd originally guessed, maybe forty standard years. His eyes were even darker now, piercing and unforgiving. His hair was short, thick and light brown. But it was his mouth that riveted her—full, firm and formed by blatant rebellion and cynicism.

"I'd rather die," she said, seething.

"That can be arranged."

"I'm not afraid of you."

"You should be, woman. I hold the keys to your freedom."

"I hope your choke on them."

Their eyes locked, but Torrie refused to flinch even from the growing intensity of his gaze. Seconds passed, and she became acutely aware of the hard muscle and bare skin searing against her. She was nearly as tall as he was, their bodies molding well, but he had her in the brute strength department. Steamy heat built between them, subverting her anger with something far more dangerous.

He made no move to ease away, instead wedging himself even closer. The pirate's eyes became slits as he lowered his head the few centimeters it took to meet her gaze. She could feel his breath on the sensitive surface of her lips. She shuddered at the thought that he might try to kiss her—brand her. Then he tilted his head, nudging his face into her hair. He inhaled deeply and made a low, throaty sound that spoke to her primal side. She thought she felt his lips skim her neck just below her ear. Or maybe it was the caress of his hot breath. Whatever it was froze every muscle in her body.

"Are you afraid of me yet?" She felt more than heard his rasped question. He moved around to her throat, never quite touching her but sending shivers rippling across her skin. The realization of his power over her galvanized her strength, driving resolve deep.

She said, "You disgust me."

He chuckled softly. "Could have fooled me." She felt the brush of his short hair skim the tender skin under her jaw. "You're awfully hot for a disgusted woman."

A chime indicating a comm link broke the moment. The pirate pulled back from her, ever so slowly. The cool look he gave her nullified the heat of his body. He was toying with her, because he could. Because she let him.

"Comm on," he said aloud.

"Qaade, you're there."

Torrie's eyes widened. So, the pirate had a name.

The voice continued, "How are we doing on our Phellium?"

"I'm working on it as we speak," the pirate responded, his gaze never leaving Torrie's. She tried to shift positions, but he held her fast. "Any word on the identity of my new slave?"

She sneered at him, and he grinned wickedly.

The man replied, "Sure do. That's why I'm calling. You aren't going to believe this. Her name is Torrie Masters. Yes, I said Masters, as in Masters Shipping. Her family owns the business, now into its second generation. She's the youngest of seven children and the only daughter. You better be careful with this one. She could be major trouble for us."

Torrie watched as the pirate's arrogant smile turned into a cold, merciless mask, and her stomach clenched. He knew now. There would be no saving her. She could just imagine her family's response to a ransom. Her entire career would be ruined, along with all her hopes and dreams.

"Are they looking for her?"

"I found no reports, which seems a little strange. She might not be missed yet."

Qaade replied softly, "It's only a matter of time." He squeezed her wrists marginally, making her grimace.

"Oh, and you better not let her see who you are. She'll be able to ID you."

His jaw muscles clenched. "Too late for that."

There was a weighted silence. "Oh, damn. Is she there? Can she hear me?"

"She's here," Qaade said roughly, the edge of his voice striking true fear in Torrie's heart. "Thanks for the information. I'll contact you as soon as we get the Phellium. Comm out."

He closed in on her, nose-to-nose. "You lied

about your identity . . . Torrie Masters."

She held on to her anger to keep her growing unease at bay. "So did you . . . Qaade. We're even."

"That's not exactly the way I see it. Let's get one thing straight. You make one false move out there, and I'll make sure Masters Shipping pays handsomely for your safe return."

"You promised—" she started.

"To give you your freedom," he said, his voice just about a snarl. "And I will. What it costs is up to you."

A thumping sound from the front of the ship captured his attention. They turned their heads to see her duster bouncing around.

Torrie's heart sank. *Bad timing, Nod.*

Qaade released her and approached the duster. As he lifted up the corner, the lightball flew out and bobbed in the air in front of him.

"Can I help?" it chirped in a childlike voice. Qaade's eyebrows rose as the lightball executed tight circles with fresh energy.

"It's okay, Nod. We don't need your help just now," Torrie said.

The pirate glanced at her, and then back at the lively orb. "I'm Qaade. Nice to meet you, Nod. I've never met a talking lightball before. You must be very unique."

"I am Nod, Torrie's computer. She created me."

Qaade eyed Torrie. "Is that right? What do you do for Torrie?"

"Nod—" she warned, but too late.

"I access artificial intelligence systems and download data to my memory for reference. I can communicate with every known computer in the sector," he responded proudly. "I also house several sensors."

"That's enough," Torrie warned.

Qaade captured the ball gently with one hand and carried it over to Torrie. He held it up to his ear. "Communications. How interesting that you didn't mention this little guy before."

"He's harmless. My pet."

"Oh, I think he's a bit more than that." Qaade set the ball free between them. "And if you want your freedom and his, you'll keep his communications functions quiet. Or I will put him in a container for the duration of the mission."

Their gazes met over a happily bobbing Nod. Qaade's eyes were unforgiving. Now Torrie would have to not only save herself, but Nod as well.

"That won't be necessary," she said.

"Glad to hear it. But just to be sure, Nod rides in *my* pocket from now on."

Chapter Eight

From behind a large container, Qaade watched Horg's men move cargo out of the warehouse to one of their transport ships. He had a pistol in one hand, and Torrie in the other. He wasn't about to let her loose, especially since she was now officially "trouble." Keep your enemies close, he'd learned a long time ago. Torrie and Masters Shipping qualified as the enemy as far as he was concerned.

He didn't give a damn how many times she'd claimed to care. She didn't. They didn't. They were the largest, wealthiest, most successful commercial transgalactic shipper. All they were concerned about were their profit statements. Anger burned inside him. With slavers and InterGlax chasing him for all these years, how ironic would it be if the most apathetic business in the galaxy would be the group to bring him down? He wouldn't allow it. He'd worked too hard to fail now.

Torrie tried to slide farther from him, but he

squeezed her arm in warning. She flinched, and gave him a glare that he ignored.

He knew Horg shipped daily, and he also knew Horg would move the Phellium as soon as he found a buyer. It was too valuable to sit on for long. From their cover, he measured the distance between the warehouse to the waiting transport.

Three men were handling the loading operation—two movers hauling cargo and one loader securing it in the transport. A single armed man stood guard, watching the proceedings with supreme boredom. His day was about to become real exciting. Their most vulnerable point, and Qaade's best chance, would be when the men were stretched the farthest apart.

"Status," he asked quietly.

"Nothing since the initial move to the staging area," Torrie replied, barely civilized, through her mask. He would have liked to rebuff her blanket condemnation of him, but she didn't know who he really was or that Slipstream even existed. And he would keep it that way, despite his pride. Lord knew he'd swallowed enough pride in his life. This was nothing.

"Tell me the second the Phellium changes position," he said after pressing close enough to smell her hair. The desire to slide closer yet was overwhelming, and he cursed his weakness. But no matter how much he tried, he could not wipe her scent, the softness of her skin, or the way her body felt against his from his memory; they now belonged to him as much as those from the long years at the hands of an owner. Only these memories would be much more pleasant. Uncomfortable, he admitted, realizing how aroused he'd become on the ship, but still more pleasant. Unless she blew his op. Then things would get very ugly.

He felt her lightball bounce in his pocket. *Communications.* Just what he needed. He cast her a quick glance as she concentrated on her datapad. She'd fashioned her dark red hair into a loose braid that lay over her right shoulder. Beneath, she wore the long duster that concealed a very tempting body. Quite on its own, Qaade's mind flashed back to the ship and the heat. It took superhuman effort to drag his thoughts back to the present.

"It's moving," she announced, and glanced up from the datapad. Piece by piece, Torrie's cargo of medical supplies was hauled across the warehouse and loaded into the waiting freighter. Qaade held his breath, hoping that Horg hadn't already sold the Phellium. To his relief, the pair of meter-long, half-meter-diameter cylinders containing the drug appeared on a hover cart. As the cart was drawn across the bay, Qaade raised his pistol.

"What about me?" Torrie asked.

"If you think I'm handing you a weapon, you are dead wrong. Stay here."

"And what if I don't?"

He gave her a hard look. "Then you risk getting shot . . . by me."

Her cool green gaze drilled into him. He shook it off and slipped between the tall containers. When the Phellium was exactly midpoint, he made his move. His first shot stunned the armed guard, followed by the loader. The two movers had a split-second to look confused before he shot them and they crumpled to the floor in quick succession. Qaade stepped from cover to scan the area. It was clear, but it wouldn't take long before someone noticed that loading had stopped.

He sprinted to the Phellium, now sitting unguarded on the hover cart. He felt Torrie's presence behind him as he checked to make sure the drug was still inside. He activated the digital screen on each cylinder, which displayed the contents—thirty tightly packed tubes lay neatly inside.

"How do you know it's Phellium?" she demanded with a frown. "It looks like any other drug."

He deactivated the screens and gripped the hover cart's handle. "Sensor scan. You should try it sometime."

Watching for Horg's men, Qaade pulled the cart behind him toward the exit to the access tunnel where they'd left their ground shuttle.

"I don't believe you," Torrie said. "My family scans all shipments. They would have found it."

"Maybe they did and they just didn't give a damn."

"You'd love to think that, pirate, but I assure you—" A laser shot spit between them as an angry shout rang out. Two men raced past the downed movers, firing on the run. Qaade pushed Torrie in front of him.

"Go!"

He caught her longing look at the rest of her shipment.

"Leave it," he yelled, and shoved her toward the door. He pulled the cart behind a bulky container. Laser fire pelted around him. The bay would be swarming with Horg's men in a matter of seconds. He lifted the containers of Phellium off the cart and balanced them on his shoulders. Only one problem; he couldn't use his pistol worth a damn. More heavy fire pinned him behind cover.

"Hell," he muttered. There were at least three

men moving toward him. He glanced at the exit door, which was twenty meters away—with a lot of wide open space in between. The heavy containers dug into his shoulders. They would slow him down, but there was no other choice. The hover cart was too slow, and he wasn't leaving this bay without the Phellium.

He gripped the containers with his pistol in one hand. Activating the trigger unleashed a salvo of laser fire in the general direction of his assailants. The siege stopped momentarily, and he ran, pumping his legs toward the door. Laser fire streamed around him, striking one of the containers. He tried to return fire, but he couldn't shoot behind him.

Just when he thought he'd made it, Torrie appeared in the doorway—with a pistol. Alarm rolled through him. *She wouldn't.* She aimed at him and fired. Lasers flashed over his shoulder, and he twisted around to see one of the guards drop. As he raced past her she continued to cover him, running backward until they'd reached the waiting shuttle.

He tossed the Phellium containers in the open back and hopped in. Torrie swung onto the passenger seat, her pistol spitting laser fire long after he got the vehicle rolling. He took a quick glance behind him as they sped out through the complex network of byways.

"They're coming after us," Torrie announced when she finally turned and sat in her seat. She grabbed a support bar. "Either we have to outrun them or outwit them. I vote for the obvious: outwit."

"Don't count on it. Horg's men might not be the brightest and the best, but they are effective." He spared a glance at her pistol. "Where'd you get it?"

"Knocked out a passerby and stole it." Her green

eyes pinned him through his mask. "I figured I could just blame it on you pirates."

He swerved the shuttle into a side alley. "I thought you were going to shoot me."

She twisted around to look behind them. "Don't think it didn't cross my mind. But then who would carry the cylinders?"

He smirked at her logic until she added, "We have company."

Qaade checked the proximity scanners. Two shuttles were on their tail. He exited the alley and merged into a chaotic grid of traffic on this space station that never slept. He moved into the lane that led to the upper levels where his ship was docked. Laser fire peppered the air above them, and a chorus of shuttle alarms went off in protest. Damn, that was fast.

Torrie ducked behind her seat with her pistol ready. "I can't shoot. There are too many people in the way."

Qaade knew they had to lose the shuttle they were driving. Even a station as lawless as Wryth wouldn't put up with a running gunfight for long. And although this lane was moving fast, it would still take too long to get up to the next level. He turned the shuttle into a tight side alley and parked it halfway down, blocking the alley to buy them some time.

"We're on foot from here on." He hopped out and hefted the Phellium containers onto his shoulders. They settled heavily.

Torrie noted his grimace. "Are you sure you can carry those? We aren't exactly close to the ship."

"I'll make it," he ground out.

Torrie exited the shuttle, and they ran the length of the alley. Behind theirs, the other two shuttles pulled up, and Horg's men jumped out, guns flashing, just as Qaade and Torrie cleared the alley into a wide pedestrian street.

"I hope you know where we're going," she said, eyeing the heavy containers he lugged.

He winced. "Not exactly."

"Great," she grumbled. "Stop for a second."

"Not good timing, Torrie," he grunted, continuing along.

She huffed. "Never mind. I'll do it myself."

While they ran, he felt her hand inside his coat and fumbling through his pockets. *Now* she wanted to fondle him?

Torrie withdrew Nod, and tossed the lightball into the air. The lightball glowed and floated along with them. What was she doing?

"Can I help?" Nod chirped.

Torrie said, "We need the fastest route back to Qaade's ship. Download the station schematics and find it."

Precious seconds passed as they weaved through the pedestrian traffic. Then Nod said, "Data accessed. Route mapped."

"Lead the way."

Nod zipped ahead of them. Qaade followed with Torrie bringing up the rear, her weapon ready as she scanned the vicinity. They turned down an alley, then another, cutting between main streets.

Qaade turned a sharp corner and stumbled a little. From behind him, Torrie yelled out, "Are you going to make it?"

"I'll make it," he snapped. "I just hope your lightball knows where he's going." In the dim light, Qaade noted that Nod's light wasn't all that bright. "Is he running full strength?"

Torrie answered, "Unfortunately, yes. He's been up for quite a while . . . Oh, no."

In the alley ahead, Nod had stopped. His light flickered, then faded completely. He dropped to the floor with a solid thud.

Qaade halted forward motion beside him and looked down at the now-black ball. "What happened?"

Torrie scooped Nod up and pushed him into a pocket. "He powered off."

Qaade looked at her incredulously. "Now? Why?"

Guilt registered on her face as she looked at him. "It's not like he can control it. He doesn't have enough energy capacity or memory capacity. When he runs out of power, he just stops functioning."

Qaade couldn't believe it. "That's why you call him Nod. Would have been nice if you'd told me he was defective!"

"He is not defective," she snapped, and pulled out her datapad. "Don't worry, we still have a map." Torrie studied the datapad for a moment, pulled out her weapon, then took off running. "Keep up, pirate."

Qaade could see their bay entrance fifty meters away. He had to admit, Torrie had done it despite the faulty lightball. His shoulders were burning, his arms ached and he would be damn glad when he could drop the cylinders safely in his ship.

"Run ahead and initiate the start-up," he told Torrie. "Access code Delta Five-Two-Five." Torrie sped up as he hobbled behind her.

He was nearly at the door when he heard, "*Laghato*," in a small whimper of a voice. He turned at the sound and at the name the freed slaves had bestowed upon him. The name that meant "libera-tor."

A frail woman wearing a long cape huddled in a doorway. He slowed to a stop in front of her with-out replying. It could be a setup. The black hair, round black eyes and smooth olive skin were mired with filth and hopelessness. She clutched two ragged children to her legs.

"*Are* you laghato?"

If it was a setup, it was a damn good one. Too good. "Yes."

The woman smiled sadly and then her eyes darted around, fear clouding her delicate face. She gently shoved the two girls forward. They peered up at Qaade, lost. "I know you will take care of them. I can't. Please. *Please*," the woman whispered, the desperation in her voice tugging his heart.

Qaade glanced the length of the empty corridor. He thought about Horg's men on their tail. This wasn't a day of good timing. "I'll take you all. Fol-low me."

Ignoring the protests of his body, he sprinted the final meters to his ship, where Torrie waited in the hatch.

"What took you so long?" she asked.

He dropped the containers at her feet. "A small problem." He looked back at the bay door. Where was the woman and her kids? Was she hurt?

Torrie eyed the Phellium reverently, and Qaade hesitated. He couldn't trust Torrie with the Phel-lium, and he couldn't leave the woman and chil-dren behind. He looked back up at Torrie standing in his ship. "I have to go back for something. Don't leave."

Her gaze moved from the containers to him. He

could see the determination and resolve. "Your word, Torrie. You won't leave until I get back."

For a few seconds, she just stared at him, and then very coolly she replied, "My word."

He paused, torn, but there was no real choice. Then he ran back out of the bay to where he'd left the slaves. The two children were huddled together, alone, but otherwise the corridor was empty. He sprinted a short distance looking for the woman, but she was gone. Obviously she didn't want him to find her. She'd simply left her most precious possessions.

He tugged off his facemask and knelt down before the frightened pair of children. They had black hair, like their mother, and the largest brown eyes he'd ever seen. "Your mother asked me to take care of you. But you have to come with me." He moved closer, and they cowered in unison. Regardless of how afraid they were of him, he needed to get them in his ship before Horg's men arrived. He scooped the two little bodies into his arms and headed inside.

Horg's thugs appeared just as he passed through the archway. Laser fire ricocheted around him. He kicked the bay door controls with his foot, dropping the rusted metal shield between him and them. Hopefully, it would last long enough to make their getaway.

Then the sound of his engine thrusters firing up stopped him in his tracks.

Torrie brought the ship's systems up as quickly as she could. He'd given her the access code, the Phellium and then left. Even Nod was here. She couldn't ask for better luck. The fact that she'd given her word only nudged her conscience a little. Screw him. He'd bullied her, enslaved her and heavens knew what he was going to do with her now that he had his Phellium. She was getting out of here while she still could. The comm announced she'd been cleared for lift-off by the Wryth controller.

She primed the lift engines and reached for the release. That's when she saw him, unmasked and standing a short distance from his ship that was now trembling with harnessed thrust. In each arm, he cradled a small child, filthy and ragged, their faces buried in his chest. Is that what he'd gone back for? More slaves? No. She wouldn't be a party to his slave operation. Her hand hovered over the execute control. She wanted to press it, wanted to free herself of him. But there was something about the way he held the two children—protectively and gently—that gave her pause.

Their eyes locked. His were angry, but beneath that rage was a look of despair and burden. She fought the power that shook her to her soul. He was a good-for-nothing, lying, stealing pirate and slaver. He had no redeeming qualities. He . . . mouthed the words: *You promised.*

She willed her hand to initiate lift-off, thinking of all the good reasons she should leave him behind, but failed. She had given her word. And no matter what it cost her, a Masters never went against her word. It was what separated them from scum.

Besides, if she left Qaade now, the children would suffer. Anger surged through her from a source she couldn't name, resurrecting a dark memory she didn't want to recall.

She backed off the launch sequence and un-sealed the rear hatch. She pulled out her pistol, and then thought better of it. It wouldn't take long for Horg's men to track them here. Number One priority was getting off Wryth in one piece. After that she'd deal with the pirate.

Torrie exited her seat and met him halfway. He handed her a waif of a child and deposited the other gently on his bunk. "Secure the girls as best you can without scaring them any more than they already are. I'll take the helm."

He brushed by her, leaving two pairs of huge, anxious eyes watching Torrie. Fear filled their meek expressions. Dirt marred their cheeks, covered their clothes. They smelled of hunger and human waste. The older one, maybe five standard years of age, peered at Torrie with such a look of hopelessness and submission that Torrie nearly crumbled.

She took a step back, unsure what to do next and wanting nothing more than to run from those needy eyes. *Slaves.* The past rushed over her, swamping Torrie. The little girl who'd lived next to her when she was a child. Zoe, with her ever-present marks and sad brown eyes. Guilt wracked Torrie's conscience from an old regret that had never been rectified.

Qaade's ship lifted off, reminding her that they would be launching into deep space momentarily. The two children nestled together, gripping each other, and Torrie's heart ached. Broke.

"Secure them, Torrie," Qaade barked. She moved, galvanized by his sharp order, and gently positioned the girls against the wall where she clipped them into flight harnesses.

The ship was just clearing the shuttle bay door into space when a voice echoed over the comm. "Hailing Vessel A55E-1CC. Return to port by order of Wryth SSC. You are under investigation for illegal activities. If you do not surrender voluntarily, you will be fired upon until such time as you surrender—"

Qaade muted the message. "Illegal activities," he muttered. "Nice try, Horg. Torrie, you need to come up here with me. We are about to have a rough ride."

She looked at her seat in the cockpit next to Qaade, and then back at the two terrified little girls trembling in their harnesses. A hard laser blast rocked the ship, and the interior lights flickered.

"I need your help, Torrie," Qaade insisted over his shoulder. "Five interceptors are on us."

She clenched her fists as the girls whimpered pitifully. Then she grabbed a blanket and tucked it around them. "You will be safe here," she whispered. "I won't let anyone hurt you." She gave the girls a little smile and headed to her seat.

Qaade spared her a quick look as he pounded the console controls. "I hope you know tactical. I need to get us far enough away from Wryth for a hyperspace jump."

Torrie checked the small ship's heavy armory. "Nice weapons system."

"Comes in handy more often than I'd like," he grumbled. Laser fire crossed their viewport, and Qaade wrenched the ship right. While he orchestrated some impressive maneuvers, Torrie concentrated on slowing their attackers down with a spray of cannon fire.

Qaade checked their coordinates. "Almost there. Give me another thirty seconds."

She did, taking out two of the five ships before she felt the welcome tug of the hyperdrives. Then they were away.

As they jumped into hyperspace, Qaade relaxed for a blessed moment against his control panel. When he finally raised his head, he found the barrel of Torrie's pistol in his face. Over the sight, her green eyes were fierce and wild.

"What are you going to do with those girls?" she asked.

He moved his hands a fraction, and her index finger tightened on the trigger. She said, "Don't even try, pirate. I will shoot you where you sit."

She would, too. He could see the tension in her body, and the glassy look in her eyes as her pupils grew huge.

"You promised you wouldn't kill me," he reminded her.

The muscles in her jaw worked. "I'll find a way to live with myself. What are you going to do with those girls?"

Interesting. The woman wouldn't break her word for herself, but she would murder for two children she didn't know. Or maybe not. Maybe she was just looking for an excuse to get out of her oath.

"Would you be willing to trade your freedom for theirs?" he asked.

Her eyes narrowed dangerously, and Qaade watched fresh anger rise red in her face. Adrenaline radiated off her in waves. He'd gone too far.

"I would be willing to do whatever it took to stop you from stealing another soul," she said through clenched teeth. Her finger squeezed the trigger.

Qaade inhaled. "I plan to save them."

Chapter Nine

His softly spoken words barely penetrated all the layers of fury that raged in Torrie's blood, uncontrolled and reckless, unlike anything she'd felt before. She was ready to pull the trigger to keep him away from those babies, willing to rip him apart with her bare hands, to die for them. She wouldn't be stopped by gutless deceit.

"You lie," she hissed, and raised her pistol to her eye-level.

"It's true. I rescue slaves."

The weapon trembled in her hand with burning tension. "Coward. You'd say anything to save yourself."

"If you shoot me, you will be responsible for the deaths of thousands of slaves. My operation needs me." He hitched his head back at the girls. "And you don't want them to witness a murder. They've already been through enough."

She frowned at him through the pounding of her heart, trying to make sense of what he was saying.

"I don't believe you. You bought me. You said you *owned* me."

He pursed his lips. "I didn't buy you. I bought your freedom. I only let you think I was a slaver to protect my operation. And to get your cooperation to track the Phellium."

The Phellium. Her resolution faltered. The drug that restored memory. For scrubbed slaves? Is that what he needed it for? It couldn't be. Phellium was a valuable commodity in the underworld. His world.

She regripped the pistol. "You deny that you are the Ghost Rider of the Dead Zone? That you raid merchant ships for your profit?"

"I don't deny it," he said with a shake of his head. "But my profits go into my operation. And the Phellium is to help ex-slaves."

"You steal ships that are never seen again," she insisted.

"Most of them are slavers' ships. It's the only way to ferry so many bodies to safety. After they are transferred into Slipstream, I resell the ships to fund their relocation."

Her hand wavered. "Slipstream?"

"The network I use to place former slaves in new homes."

She narrowed her eyes. "I never heard of it."

He smirked. "That's the idea. If everyone knew about it, I'd be out of business. Not that they haven't tried. Between InterGlax and the slavers, we're lucky to make a complete circuit without detection."

She studied his silver eyes, which had mellowed and softened as he talked. Gone was the angry man, the one who'd bullied and harassed her. He spoke calmly, quietly. Behind her, one of the girls whimpered and he turned to them. His compassionate glance wiped away the last of Torrie's anger.

"They need to be cleaned and fed," he told her. "I could use your help."

Not yet, she thought. Not until she was positive without a doubt that he wasn't going to turn back into slave master extraordinaire. "Prove to me that this Slipstream exists."

He pressed his lips into a thin line. "I need to access the comm."

"One false move—"

He held up a hand. "I know. Believe me, you look very comfortable with that pistol. Computer, open a channel to *Freeport* and hail Brilliard."

Seconds later, a familiar voice said, "Brilliard here. Please tell me you have our Phellium."

Qaade's gaze stayed on Torrie. "I have it."

"Best news I've had all day," the man said, sounding thoroughly relieved. "If you get it to me in the next fifteen hours, I can treat the group destined for Swayk Drop."

"I'll be there in ten. And I have two girls for you that I lifted from Wryth, probably three and five. Can't tell if they've been scrubbed."

Torrie's eyebrows rose at the blistering language before Brilliard finished with, "Poor things. We'll assess them when they get here."

"Sounds good. Calculate a ten-hour rendezvous point and feed the coordinates to my ship."

"Got it. Anything else?"

Qaade watched Torrie. "How many slaves do you think we've run through Slipstream this circuit?"

"In the past sixty days? All fifteen drops? I don't know. Probably ten thousand. We've been busier than usual. Why?"

"Just curious. Thanks, Brilliard. Out." The comm blinked off, and Qaade leaned back. "Believe me now?"

Torrie lowered her pistol slowly. "Maybe."

"Close enough. I need to check the girls. I promised their mother I'd take care of them."

"Where is she?" Torrie asked.

He betrayed a flash of sadness. "She stayed behind. The girls are mine to care for now, and that's what I plan to do," he said and shoved himself from his seat.

Torrie blinked after him, trying to defuse the adrenaline that coursed through her veins. Her mind would take longer to come around. Could it be that the pirate had a heart after all? She had to admit, it made sense. He hadn't treated her like a typical slave as far as she knew, although he'd definitely tried to intimidate her. But everything he'd done had been to get the Phellium.

She rubbed her hand over her forehead. Could he really be telling her the truth? If so, then she was relatively safe from him. And so were the girls. But what about her cargo? He was still a pirate; he'd still stolen it from her. How could she trust him at all?

Confused and rattled, she got up and followed him to the rear bunk. He was skimming the girls with a scanner device, and the children watched him with fear in their eyes.

"You're scaring them," she said, giving him an accusing glare.

"I have to neutralize any embeds they may be wearing."

"Embeds?"

He reached around and scanned the girls' backs. "Trackers embedded in their bodies so their owners can locate them if they try to escape. Discipline flakes to keep them in line. Explosive units that detonate if they pass a perimeter."

Torrie swayed with horror. Good lord. Who would do such a thing to another human being?

He pocketed the device, looking satisfied. "Fortunately, both of them appear to be clean. Removing an embed is a pretty nasty procedure." He turned to her. "I'm going to make them something to eat. I need you to wash them up. Check to see if they have any conditions that need medical attention."

Torrie took a step back. She had nieces and nephews around thanks to her brothers, but she'd never bathed them or tended to them. She'd been too busy learning how to fight and fly. For some reason, being captain of her own ship and crew was far less frightening.

"Just because I'm a woman doesn't mean I automatically know how to take care of children," she warned him.

Qaade cocked an eyebrow as if he already knew that, and added, "They will probably trust a woman more than a man." His gaze dropped to her hand. "Without the pistol, of course."

He was right. For the girls' sake, she slipped the pistol into a thigh holster. Qaade nodded with obvious approval, then headed to the galley.

From his seat, Qaade glanced up from his datapad to where Torrie was coaxing the girls to sleep in a bunk. The same woman who a few hours ago was prepared to fry his brains was now soothing with the gentleness of a mother. Qaade counted his lucky stars. Again. One of these days, he was going to run out of stars.

She'd surprised him, though—both with her protectiveness of the girls and the fact that she hadn't left him behind on Wryth when she could have. Especially after he'd given her every reason. His treatment of her hadn't been the kindest, even if he had taken the worst of their physical clashes.

He watched her interact with the children. Where before there had been only panic, the girls now peered up with curiosity and trust. Torrie smiled at one of them and said something soft. It was the first time Qaade had seen her smile, and he froze, mesmerized by the flash of white teeth beneath full lips.

With surprising intensity, his body responded to the memory of her pressed against him, a recollection of the sizzle she suppressed. He'd bet she'd be an incredible lover—committed, tenacious and focused—a gratifyingly dangerous combination with a body like hers. The ache in his groin reminded him that he had been alone too long.

She flicked her gaze to his for a split-second. Then her smile slipped as she studied him. She was probably still trying to figure out how to get the Phellium back.

He turned around to the ship's controls. Even if she had helped him get it and escape Wryth, he couldn't let her have the Phellium. He needed it more than any client she had.

He knew he was in trouble the moment she'd found a weapon. He'd never get it away from her now without losing something vital. Not that he would try. She knew about Slipstream, and with that knowledge, she was bound to him whether she realized it or not.

No one outside his operation knew of Slipstream. Oh, there were rumors of the shadow of a man dubbed *laghato*, who shuttled slaves to safe havens. However, most people believed he was more myth than man, and that's just the way Qaade preferred it. But now there was an outsider involved. What he was going to do about it was a huge question.

She was a Masters—wealthy, successful and spoiled no doubt, used to getting whatever she wanted. What could he give her to keep her quiet about Slipstream? He couldn't pay her off; he didn't have that many credits. Besides, she had a pride streak a kilometer wide; if he suggested a bribe, she'd have his head for sure. Threatening her wouldn't work. At least, it hadn't up until now. He could ask for her word again, but he couldn't count on that forever, especially once she was back in her own world. So what could he appeal to?

He glanced back and was surprised to find her watching the girls with a look of sadness, the blood drained from her face. Gone was her smile, replaced by raw, heartrending emotion. She wiped perspiration off her upper lip with a shaky hand before sliding stiffly off the bunk. Without a word, she disappeared into the lav.

What was that all about? She looked downright frightened. It reminded him of the look on her face when he stood outside the ship with the girls. Was she afraid for them? Was that why she hadn't left him? Did she think she could save them from him? The thought intrigued him. If so, then she did have a weakness, one he could exploit to save Slipstream.

He hailed *Exodus*. Sly answered immediately, his broad smile filling the holo image. "You survived."

Qaade kept his voice low. "So far. She keeps me awake just wondering what she's planning next.

We picked up the goods on Wryth and two children that need immediate attention."

Sly's expression sobered. "Where do you want to rendezvous?"

"I'm heading directly to *Freeport*. Meet us there."

His crewman's eyebrows rose. "Any particular reason?"

"I want to show Torrie Slipstream."

Sly's mouth dropped open. "You what? Brilliard told us who she is. You are letting a Masters see our operation? Why?"

Qaade tapped his fingers on the panel. "To keep her quiet."

"So, in order to keep it covert, you are going to march her through the whole damn thing? Are you sure she didn't drug you or something?"

"I'm going to appeal to her nurturing side," Qaade told him, enjoying Sly's flabbergasted expression.

"Nurt—" The man stopped and shook his head. "I've seen that woman in action. Trust me, she doesn't *have* a nurturing side."

Qaade cast a look toward the back of the ship. "She does for some things."

Sly ran both hands through his hair. "Whatever you say, boss. My bet is that she'll haul ass to InterGlax so fast we won't even see them coming."

"Let me worry about that."

"Fine. See you on *Freeport*. If she doesn't nurture you to death first."

The holo image disappeared. Qaade rose from his seat and walked over to where the two girls slept, curled up together. Torrie had bathed and dressed them in two of his clean shirts. Nod was wedged between them like a favorite toy. They looked like angels. Motherless angels.

102

He bowed his head when he thought about the woman who had entrusted them to a man she knew only from legend. How desperate could she have been to never see her children again? Even though he'd witnessed such sacrifices countless times, the horror of it never lessened. It was such horror that drove him to work day and night to save a few souls. The hard part was thinking about all the ones he missed, and there were many. For every slave he saved, a hundred thousand were doomed.

A noise came from the lav. He stepped up to the door and listened, and heard sobbing. Was she ill? "Torrie?"

He waited. No reply.

"Computer, release lav door."

The door slid aside to reveal Torrie huddled on the floor, head down, shoulders shaking.

When he entered, her head came up in surprise. The split-second of painful anguish she'd permitted was quickly exchanged for annoyance.

She wiped a hand across her wet face. "Get out."

"Are you all right?" He reached out a hand. She glared at it like it was on fire.

"Leave me alone. I don't want your help or your pity."

He withdrew his hand, grateful that it was still intact, and leaned a shoulder against the wall in the narrow space. *Huh.* "Then what do you want?"

"For you to leave me the hell alone."

He surveyed the lav. "I kind of like it back here. It's cozy."

"Were you put in this universe just to aggravate me?" she retorted and rose to her feet. He snagged her arm as she tried to get by, effectively pinning her between him and the sink. Fierce anger and profound sorrow melded in her expression. She opened her mouth to say something, a short inhalation followed, and then her chin trembled with the effort to hold herself together. Qaade watched her tough façade falter, leaving behind bare torment.

"What happened, Torrie?"

She whispered, "They were whipped." Her fists were clenched white, her body tightly tensed. "When I bathed them . . . their little bodies are scarred . . . ."

So that's it, he thought. Now she knew. "Physical abuse is common for slav—" He stopped, realizing that her face was twisted in agony as if she were feeling every mark she had seen. Qaade had the strongest urge to reach out to her, despite his better judgment. Torrie wasn't the kind of woman a man touched without express permission. In writing. And notarized.

She turned away from him and used a wet towel to wipe her face. "How could anyone do that? They're babies." A breath shuddered through her.

Qaade shoved his hands in his pockets to keep them from trouble. He wasn't expecting such a strong reaction from her over the girls. It surprised him as much as when she'd argued against slavery earlier, a feat he didn't think possible of a Masters. On the other hand, she hadn't agreed to hand her Phellium over to him yet either.

She looked at him over her shoulder. "Where did you get the girls from? I want to go back and find the bastard that did this."

He smiled at the return of her ferocious spirit. "I don't think even you could track them down. It's not like anyone broadcasts they own slaves. On Wryth, no one asks."

She faced him and rubbed her bare arms. "So what will happen to the girls?"

"We are heading to *Freeport*. The medics will take care of any injuries they can. After that, we'll find good, safe homes for them somewhere along Slipstream."

"Swayk Drop?"

"Probably not. Too soon. They need time to acclimate and heal. And feel safe again."

"Any chance of finding their mother?" Torrie whispered.

He wished he had a happier answer. "No."

Her green eyes studied him for a long moment. "How do you stand it? How do you do this?"

He tasted bitterness as he told her, "Because the alternative is leaving them there. At least I'm doing something."

She looked unsteady. He should pounce now, guilt her into giving him the Phellium freely and keeping silent about Slipstream. Embarrass her and make her pay for all the times people like her ignored the plight of those less fortunate. Now would be the perfect time.

But as she gave him one final fragile look and exited the lav, he didn't say a word. Qaade exhaled. Why didn't he do it? After all, Slipstream was at stake. Everything he'd worked for and sacrificed for was exposed. He'd done worse to protect his operation—lied, cheated, stolen, even killed.

As he followed her out, he realized the reason: this time, his heart hadn't been in it. And he couldn't help but wonder why. He turned the corner to find Torrie staring at the one empty bunk. The other was occupied by the two sleeping children.

"I suppose you are going to want to restrain me,"

she said. And then she swept her gaze to his. He was still dealing with the ramifications of the sleeping situation. He hadn't even gotten to the restraints yet.

He tried to act noncommittal and shrugged. "I won't kill you if you don't kill me."

A fledgling fire lit in her eyes. "Why would you kill me? Just because I know who you are?"

Qaade turned and pulled a blanket from a wall bin. "Because you know about Slipstream."

She put her hands on her hips. He grinned and waited.

"And what, exactly, would I do with that information? I don't know where it is. I don't know what it looks like." She pointed at him. "In fact, I have no concrete proof it even exists."

He threw the blanket over the bunk. "You will. Tomorrow we visit *Freeport*." He patted the bunk. "Hop up."

She frowned at him. "Why do I get stuck on the inside?"

He pulled his shirt off and tossed it in a bin. "Just because I'm not restraining you doesn't mean I trust you."

"Fine." She climbed up on the bunk, fully clothed, and plastered her back against the wall.

"Computer, lock down all communications systems," he said, which prompted a glower from Torrie. He grinned and slid onto the bunk beside her. While he stretched out, taking up most of the bunk and making himself comfortable, she watched him with icy green eyes. So much for all the compassion and caring. He'd be lucky if he didn't freeze to death tonight.

But he knew he wouldn't. Already he could feel the heat of her body seep into his. And his responded with marked—and visible—interest. He closed his eyes and tried to pretend he was sleeping alone, just like most nights. But even without the aid of his eyes, he could see her in his mind. He couldn't even remember what his *ship* looked like with this much detail. He inhaled her scent—spicy and rich. He listened and heard her steady breathing in his ear.

Maybe he should be the one wearing restraints. He shifted, rolling over onto his side with his back to her. As risky as that was, it was still safer than her seeing a fully aroused man next to her.

He stared at his ship. Torrie's heat burned into his backside. It was going to be a long night.

Chapter Ten

Chauvet stood with his back to Fahlow, his black ensemble a sinister silhouette against the iridescent blue holo of his gameboard. Urwin's voice filled the sanctum.

"Qaade has the drugs back. Stole them out from under Horg's nose and escaped Wryth Station somehow. I heard it was quite a show."

Fahlow allowed herself a small, careful smile, knowing that laghato had succeeded where Chauvet thought he wouldn't.

"Alone?"

"No. The woman helped him. Not sure if it was voluntary or not. They have a kinda strange relationship. I think she thinks she's his slave, but Qaade would never own one. Regardless, no one is talking. Oh, and I have a name now. Torrie Masters of Masters Shipping."

Fahlow detected the slightest twitch in Chauvet's right shoulder. "Another player," he murmured as he stepped around the holo image. "Now why would a respectable shipping captain be willing to work with a pirate to steal drugs?"

"Maybe she doesn't know the shipment contains drugs."

Chauvet stiffened. Fahlow could feel his wrath from where she stood. "I do not expect a response from you, Urwin. Your job is simply to report moves."

There was a pause. "Yes, sir."

"Where are they now?"

"Heading to *Freeport*."

Chauvet nodded. "What is their next stop on Slipstream?"

"Twel Station, in eleven hours."

"And *Exodus*?"

"Will rendezvous with *Freeport* in about eight hours."

"I want an update then, Urwin. Out."

Fahlow shivered in the silence. At least when Urwin was speaking, she felt connected with the outside worlds. Worlds she might never see again.

Chauvet strode around his gameboard. "Computer, add another piece, a woman designated Torrie. Link to Qaade piece and move them to *Freeport*. Put *Exodus* there in eight hours." As he spoke, the computer made the requested alterations to the holographic ships and stations on the board that comprised Iaghato's enterprise. "Move *Freeport* eleven hours from Twel Station."

When all the pieces were placed, Chauvet stopped and studied the images thoughtfully. Fahlow's heart squeezed in anguish. She'd been with him long enough to know that whenever he pondered, people died.

For years now, she'd watched Chauvet build his

game, piece by piece, meticulously planning and plotting, consumed with vengeance. Vengeance for one man, and his one unforgivable mistake.

Torrie awoke with a start, sprawled across the bunk—alone—after a restless night of trying to ignore her firebrand of a bunkmate. Her eyes focused slowly on Qaade leaning against the corridor wall and watching her. His thick, short hair was still wet, and his face clean-shaven. For a moment, she just stared. He looked too sexy to be real. And then she looked at his eyes and sat straight up, driven by the seriousness in his expression and the fact that he was wholly fixed on her. How long had he been there?

"I'm not giving you back the Phellium," he said abruptly.

She shook her head, trying to function after too few hours of sleep and enter a conversation that had obviously started without her. He moved forward and braced his hands on the edge of the bunk. "I need it."

"Can you at least wait until I'm alive?" she said, brushing her hair into some form of order.

"I don't want you thinking there's even a chance you'll get it back."

She narrowed her eyes. She hated waking up to a problem. "You know, just because you are saving slaves doesn't give you the right to steal, loot and lie, Qaade. There are other ways."

He gave her the Devil's smile. "Really? You tell me how I'm going to take all those slaves from their owners or the slavers who capture and move them. You think if I ask nicely, they'll just hand them over?"

Anger laced her words. "Have you even *tried* to ask InterGlax for help?"

Her words produced something she hadn't planned on: his entire demeanor turned dark and stormy. It took all the courage she had not to back away from his quiet, tightly leashed wrath.

"I did. Once. They boarded my owner's ship when I was ten. I told them I was being held against my will. They laughed at me and left. After which, my owner beat me so badly, I couldn't walk for days."

Torrie stared at him in disbelief, speechless. Even if she had words, they wouldn't be worthy. The brutality of it weakened her to the bone. She knew he was telling her the truth, because it finally made sense. Every fiber of his being was driven by passion, and now she understood why. He'd lived the life he was trying to save others from.

"I'm sorry," she said.

His jaw muscles clenched, and he pushed himself away. "Sorry doesn't save people. I do. And I'm not going to stop, not for you or anyone else." He pointed toward the sleeping girls. "Their welfare depends on it."

"I know that," Torrie snapped. "Did you think I wouldn't care? That I could be so heartless as to ignore human suffering? How dare you? How dare you dictate my response? You have no right to steal that choice."

He gave her a look. "Well, here's your chance. Give me the Phellium."

"You are going to take it anyway. What's the difference?"

"It matters to me," he said. "I want you to give it to me."

And then she understood. He was testing her, to see if she was as heartless and greedy as he thought.

Well, screw him. She wasn't heartless or greedy, and she knew it. Besides, she still didn't know for sure there *was* Phellium in those canisters.

"It's not mine to give. Even if it was, I wouldn't condone your stealing my cargo or anyone else's."

"That's what I thought."

"If you want help, InterGlax can—" she started.

He cut her off harshly. "InterGlax would sooner have me executed than see me rescuing slaves. Don't you get it? Slavers pay InterGlax to keep off their asses. Every InterGlax depot in this sector is corrupt from the top down. You want to know why slavery is so rampant in the Dead Zone? Because InterGlax is *helping* slavers instead of stopping them."

She knew he was right about the corruption, because she'd seen the worst when a traitor in InterGlax set up her brother, Zain. But she'd also see them at their best when they cleared Zain. There were bright spots in InterGlax's armor.

"They aren't perfect, but I know one man you could—"

"Forget it," he growled. "And forget I even asked. Kiss your shipment good-bye."

"So this is *Freeport*?" she asked a little while later, watching the old freighter loom large in their path. Somehow she'd been expecting something more . . . impressive. It was nothing more than an ancient deep-space hauler that had seen one too many runs. Its hull was patched and bore no markings. Boxy and enormous, it was as plain and benign a spacecraft as any she'd ever encountered.

"That's *Freeport*," Qaade replied as he piloted their ship toward the shuttle bays at the rear of the vessel. She heard the pride in his voice, despite the fact that he was trying his best to ignore her. She must have really pissed him off. The thought prompted a smile.

"How does your operation work?" she asked, just to make him talk.

Qaade didn't look up from his controls. "*Freeport* runs a continuous loop through the sector. We drop off the slaves we pull from slaver ships. They get processed and treated at *Freeport,* and released along the route to whoever can take them."

She blinked in surprise, because he'd actually told her. "Then what happens?"

"Conductors route them through the tributaries of Slipstream to safe houses, and then to their final destinations."

"New homes?"

He nodded, and looked up at the shuttle-bay opening. "And new lives. Most of them are starting over again."

She stared at him for a moment. "Why are you telling me all this?"

"You asked."

"Ha," she said with a laugh. "Unlikely. Why are you risking all this information with me? You said it yourself, you don't trust me."

He turned and settled his silver gaze on her. "I want you to know what it's like in my world." He hitched his head back to where the girls were safely harnessed, watching Nod perform loops for their enjoyment. "Their world."

"I already know," she said. She didn't need a reminder of what those girls had endured.

Once they touched down, Torrie took one of the children while Qaade lifted the other. A lanky, balding man met them at the ship's hatchway. His blue eyes lit up in his face when he saw them. "Welcome to *Freeport*! I'm Brilliard." He gave a quick bow. "You must be Torrie Masters."

"I am. Pleasure to meet you, Brilliard. I have the deepest respect for anyone who works for this dictator."

The man laughed heartily. "I can see I'm going to enjoy this."

Qaade exited behind her. "Don't encourage her. This is Nod, Torrie's computer."

"Can I help?" Nod gave his normal greeting.

Brilliard stared at the lightball. "Now there's a first."

"I'll get the Phellium." Qaade handed off one of the girls to Brilliard, who took her with a big smile.

"Greetings, sweetheart. Do you have a name, too?"

The girl didn't respond, only looked at him with intense worry.

Torrie's stomach clenched. "No name," she said. "I don't think they speak Basic. They haven't said a word since we took them off Wryth."

Brilliard's smile softened. "Well, we'll handle that. There's a whole room of orphans waiting to meet them."

Torrie's heart sank. The knots in her stomach squeezed as uninvited memories surfaced. Zoe's face flashed into her mind with unnerving ease, along with the guilt and the nights she'd cried, missing her best friend. She had never developed another friendship like that again.

She jumped when she realized that Qaade was staring at her intently. She hated when he did that; it made her feel transparent.

"Follow me," Brilliard said with a wave of his hand. He bounced the girl on his hip while he headed for the exit. Qaade had put the two Phellium

115

canisters on a hover cart behind him and stepped up beside Torrie. They entered a long corridor with Nod zipping back and forth in front of them, prompting a smile from the child Torrie carried.

"You want me to carry her?" Qaade asked.

"No, she's fine," Torrie replied tightly.

"And what about you?"

She cast him a quick glance. "I'd be a lot better if you weren't stealing my cargo in front of me. Tell me, if it's not what you think, do I get it back?"

"It's Phellium. My source has never let me down," he said firmly.

Brilliard led them into a major concourse buzzing with activity. It spanned the full length of the freighter. A string of entrances on both sides spouted workers and carts.

"Did your source also tell you when and where my ship would drop out of hyperspace so you could ambush us?"

He hesitated. "Different source."

"Lovely," she muttered. Who would have access to her itinerary? Masters Shipping was very careful with their flight schedules for security reasons. It had to be someone on the inside. The thought worried her. Is that how the pirates also knew what she was hauling?

They turned into a side corridor and directly into an infirmary that was a hive of activity. One hundred meters deep, it was filled with beds, equipment, medics and patients. Torrie began to realize just how big Qaade's operation was. The credits to keep this place running—how did he do it all alone?

A portly woman with gray, tightly bound hair looked up from a patient lying on a bed and gave them a cheeky smile. She patted the man lying in front of her and made her way over to Brilliard.

"We have babies," she said, and clapped her hands together. Torrie's fears diminished as she watched the easy way the woman welcomed the girls.

"We've been expecting these darlings." Without hesitation, she took the child from Brilliard's arms and swung her around. It was clear she'd done this many times, taken in orphans. Torrie looked down the long row of occupied beds with unease. She didn't need to see the suffering. She knew it existed. Maybe Qaade and Brilliard could do it on a daily basis, but she really didn't need to be here.

Qaade leaned toward her. "Coreana is our head medic and resident warden."

The woman swatted Qaade on the arm. "Stop that. You'll scare her."

"Not possible, trust me."

Coreana passed the child off to one of her assistants. "You must be Torrie. I hear you saved these two babes from that hellhole." She gave Qaade a chastising look. "Despite the fact that *someone* led you to believe you yourself were a slave."

"It got you your Phellium," Qaade said with a wry smile.

Coreana shook her head and took a loud breath. "One of these days, that kind of thinking is going to be the death of you, child."

As Coreana talked, Torrie watched her shipment be taken away by another medic. *Kiss it good-bye,* she thought. How could she stop it now, when it was so evident how much they needed it?

Coreana reached for the child Torrie held, breaking into her thoughts. She held the girl a little tighter. "Will they be all right?"

The woman looked surprised. "Of course, they will."

"But they haven't spoken—"

Coreana's warm hand wrapped around her wrist with strength and confidence. "They will be fine, dear."

Torrie finally gave her charge over to the total stranger. Before she knew it, the girls were swept away in a sea of excited medics and patients—embraced just like family, she thought. But when they were well, who would take care of them? Who would make sure they were never hurt again?

"Ready for a tour?" Qaade asked.

She couldn't look at him. If she did, then he'd know just how close she was to tears.

She spun on her heel. "Let's go."

Qaade drove the cart through the main corridor of Level One with a silent Torrie next to him. He didn't like it when she was quiet. It meant trouble; he just didn't know what. At least when she was making verbal swipes at him, he knew what she was thinking.

She remained expressionless as he pointed out the crew quarters, rec centers, commissary, engines and common areas. He was beginning to think *Freeport* wasn't as remarkable as he thought it was.

"You aren't impressed," he observed as they passed beneath tall archways from the rear of the freighter toward Free Quarters.

Her gaze swung to his in surprise. "Why would you think that?"

"You haven't said much. Still upset about your Phellium?"

She didn't even bite. "No." Then she took a deep, controlled breath. "If it is Phellium, you can keep it."

Now, his face held shock. "And what will you tell Masters Shipping?"

"I'll think of something." She shifted in her seat, distinctively uncomfortable. "This is a huge operation. You can't possibly fund it yourself, even if you are pirating ships."

He shrugged. "I do okay. And some of my funding and supplies come from private sources."

She turned to him. "Private? Who?"

He gave her a cynical look. "No one you would know. It also helps that most of my people are volunteers and former slaves themselves. They are just looking for a safe place to call home."

She was silent for a long time, but Qaade could feel the subtle tension in her body. She was thinking too much. He wasn't sure he wanted that.

"And when will you stop?"

The question surprised him. Qaade turned the shuttle into the atrium. "When every slave is free."

"Won't happen, Qaade, unless you find a way to change the laws. If you keep this up, one of your raids will go bad, and InterGlax will catch you."

He pulled into Free Quarters, stopped the cart and turned to face her. "Don't forget the slavers who have a bounty on my head big enough to buy this freighter ten times over. I know the risk, Torrie. And I'm willing to take it." He swept a hand across the expanse of the atrium. "For them."

She gazed up through the corridor atrium at the four levels of housing. It looked like an artificial canyon with balconies that lined each level, currently jammed with people. The common area before them contained a peaceful setting and play area for the children.

"What is this place?"

"Free Quarters. Once a former slave is in our custody, we call them Free People. They come here to recover after Coreana's medics have treated them and before they are sent down Slipstream." He jumped out of the cart. "Level One houses the orphanage. Level Two accommodates families, not that we get many intact. Level Three holds the free folk with special needs, and Four is for re-education just before we funnel them through Slipstream."

As he came around her side, Qaade noted the paleness in her face and stiff posture.

She stared straight ahead and said, "I don't need to see this."

He squinted at her, trying to figure out her problem. "There's nothing dangerous here."

"I'm not worried about danger," she snapped, and glared at him. "Why are you doing this? You already have what you want. You don't need me, don't need to be nice to me. In fact, I've *paid* for my freedom. When do I start?"

He saw it then. Beneath the fierce anger and stoic wall was vulnerability. Fear. No, not fear. Understanding. He'd finally gotten through to her and in a big way.

"It won't go away if you ignore it."

"I'm not ignoring it," she replied harshly. "My family gives millions of credits away to charities every year."

He laughed. "Really? You think they'd give some to me?"

"If you were legitimate, they would."

He leaned toward her. "If I were legitimate, this operation wouldn't work. Do you know how hard it is to prove that a ship is carrying slaves? By the time we get through the regulations and legal ramifications, the ship is long gone, docked and those slaves disappear. The system doesn't work, Torrie. It never will."

"I don't believe you," she countered stubbornly. "There has to be a way to change the laws to make it easier—"

"And don't forget the fact that slavery is legal in some places." He narrowed his eyes. "Like Dun Gali."

He noted her sharp inhalation at the mention of her home planet.

Her voice was rough. "Not everyone has indentured servants there."

"Legalized slavery."

She paled. "I'm not the one who makes the laws."

He gave her a hard look. He hated it when people like her hid behind their laws. "But you can change them."

"It's not that easy," she said, frowning.

"Neither is *this*," he snapped, his anger rising to the surface.

The comm squawked. "Qaade, you there?"

He patched in. "I'm here, Brilliard."

"You need to come down to the infirmary. Real important. And you might want to bring Torrie along."

Why did Brilliard want Torrie? They'd be in big trouble if her cargo wasn't Phellium. "On our way."

Chapter Eleven

Torrie rode beside Qaade to the infirmary, thanking the stars for the timely reprieve. But it had come too late. The damage had been done. She'd never be able to shake the memory of the vacant stares and condition of the former slaves she'd seen. This might be Qaade's triumph, but it was her nightmare. She couldn't have imagined such a devastating and sad world. All these people were rescued from a fate she couldn't bring herself to think about. How did the volunteers do it day after day? How did Qaade? Her hands were shaking at the mere thought of so much human suffering.

His accusations cut deep, and she couldn't deny them. Slavery was legal on her planet, regardless of what they called it. But what could she do about it? She wasn't a politician. Yes, her family had money and they had clout, but not *that* much. Not enough to make a difference.

Her thoughts sank into stifling depression. In fact, this whole damn place was depressing. She had to get out. She felt suffocated at every turn by the vicious nature of man.

The shuttle pulled up next to the infirmary, and Torrie followed Qaade through a side door into a laboratory. Sitting alone, Brilliard glanced up from one of her shipping containers opened on the counter, his expression grim.

"What's wrong?" Qaade asked. "Isn't it Phellium?"

Brilliard pursed his lips and looked from Qaade to Torrie. "It's Phellium all right. High grade, too. Some of the best we've ever gotten. That isn't the problem. *This* is the problem." He held up a slender tube. "I found it buried in the package of Phellium."

Torrie frowned. What was it?

Qaade took the tube and studied it. "What's inside?"

Brilliard pushed away from the counter and handed the datapad to Qaade. "You aren't going to like this."

The speed with which his body tensed was Torrie's only warning, and when he turned his murderous gaze to her, she braced for the explosion.

She scowled at him. "What? What is it?"

"Ricytin," he said in a low, deadly whisper. "You were transporting scrub drugs."

Torrie's mouth dropped open. Her words came out in a hush. "That's impossible."

Brilliard piped up. "I tested a bunch of samples. It's pure. There's enough of it here to scrub a few hundred thousand people."

"It can't be. We'd never transport illegal drugs."

Qaade took a step toward her, his face a mask of fury. "Just like you didn't know about the Phellium? How convenient." He pointed out the door.

"Do you think if you tell those people out there you're stupid, they will forgive you?"

She held her ground. "I don't care what else you believe about me, I'd never traffic illegal drugs."

He took another step, and she had to back up to keep from being run over. "You'd haul anything that made you and your family credits. It's people like you who make my job impossible."

She pointed to the open container. "I don't know how that drug got in there or how it made it into our shipment, but I assure you that Masters Shipping scans everything we haul."

Qaade leaned close. "Then you have a security problem. And a bad client."

Their eyes locked, and despite all her protests, Torrie knew he was right. Somehow, the drugs had gotten through their detection scans. "We can't open cargo that's been sealed by the client," she told him. "Privacy laws prohibit it. They are required to full disclosure of the contents."

Qaade broke into a short, cynical laugh. "Well, that makes it okay then. We wouldn't want to stomp on your clients' privacy. Tell me, if a client handed you fifty slaves and told you they were free souls who liked to wear chains, would you believe them?"

"Go to hell, Qaade," she said, trembling with frustration.

"This *is* hell," he replied. "Thanks to you."

Brilliard held up a hand. "Qaade, really—"

Qaade ignored him. "Is that why you don't want to see our refugees? Because it makes you feel guilty?"

She pursed her lips, trying to come up with another explanation. "Maybe the Ricytin is for some other use."

"There is only one use for scrub drugs, Torrie. To destroy lives." Qaade handed Brilliard the datapad. "*Exodus* will be here tomorrow. We'll transfer over and drop you at the nearest port. I'm sure you can find your own way home from there." And then he walked away.

Torrie was still rattled as Brilliard walked her to crew quarters. Questions and anger roiled in her head with dizzying confusion. She needed to kick something, to lash out and release the pent-up energy of helplessness.

All she had were weak words. "I didn't know, Brilliard."

He cast her a quick glance. "I believe you. Qaade knows it also. He's just too stubborn to say so. This is his operation. He started it fifteen years ago, working night and day to build what you see today. He *is* Slipstream."

She agreed there. He was single-minded and driven, and let nothing stand in his way. And if it wasn't for the fact that she was squarely in his path, she might even respect that. Right now, she just wanted to get the hell away from him. Tomorrow couldn't come soon enough.

Brilliard stepped up to a nondescript door, and it opened for him. He ushered Torrie into standard-issue crew quarters with a bed, small table and chair. "It's not much, but it does have a private lav."

She smiled at him. "I appreciate that."

He stood awkwardly in front of her for a brief moment. "Don't feel too bad, Torrie."

Right. She was transporting illegal drugs that scrubbed the memories of innocent people, basically stealing their lives. But she shouldn't feel bad about it.

"We won't ship for that customer again. What else can I do to fix this?" she asked.

He scratched his head. "I wish I knew. Frankly, I'm surprised the Ricytin went through your company in the first place. Despite what Qaade says, I know Masters is an upright place. Why would a customer take the chance? There are plenty of independent shippers who would kill for that haul." He shrugged. "Maybe your client isn't very experienced."

This was a customer they'd had for years. Number 151. Of course, the customer's funds were good and their credentials solid, but what else did Masters know about them? They only ran dock-to-dock drop-ships. As far as she knew, no one in the company had actually met or spoken to them.

"But I can tell you one thing," Brilliard said. "The timing couldn't be worse."

"Why do say that?"

He frowned. "We've been busier than usual in the past few cycles. I've seen a big surge in trafficking, and I can't explain it. It's like it's . . . organized."

"Is that possible?"

"I suppose. Never happened before." As if realizing he was doing all the talking, he clapped his hands to his thighs. "I better get back. If you need anything, you can reach me on the comm. Just address the computer, and I'll answer." He turned to leave and then paused. "I have to keep you confined to quarters."

She gave a short laugh. "Qaade's orders, by chance?"

He grimaced. "Sorry."

After he'd gone, Torrie sat down on the single bed

in the room. For a long time, she stared at the opposite wall with her hands clenched into tight balls, trying to mentally diffuse the furious energy coursing through her veins.

Bolting from the bed, Torrie walked a tight circle around the room. How had this happened? There was no denying the company's detection equipment had failed. Either that, or someone inside was tampering with shipments. Carmon would burst a major artery when he found out.

She buried her face in her hands. What had they done? The vacant stares—could they be her family's fault? How long had this client been concealing scrub drugs in his shipments? Were they dealers or users? Had they sold it to someone else? Were they having it shipped from another source?

Whatever the reason, the client was the key. And they needed to be stopped, whether they were going to use the drug or were dealing it. As soon as she got home, Torrie was going to tell Carmon . . .

"Oh, hell," she muttered as the situation registered. If she told Carmon, he'd bring in InterGlax. When word got out that they'd shipped Ricytin, the damage to the family's reputation would be irreparable. And she would be the reason why. Forget another run. She'd be lucky to be sitting at the dinner table.

No. This would have to be done quietly, without bringing Carmon or InterGlax into the picture. At least, not until she could finger the client. So how could she go after the client by herself? Returning to Dun Gali was out of the question. She'd have to explain the missing shipments and face certain grounding. That wouldn't help her investigation.

Besides, she wasn't leaving until she proved to Qaade that she wasn't the naïve, uncaring person he thought she was. All she required was a ship, access to Masters Shipping records, and time—none of which she possessed at present.

She let out a groan of frustration and began to pace. There had to be a way, but she was too wound up to think clearly. No matter how many laps around the tiny room she made, she couldn't shake her restlessness. If she were home, she'd go for a long, hard run down the windy roads that led to the sprawling Masters estate. Or she'd spar with Howser for a few hours until she was spent. She glanced around her prison and remembered something Qaade had shown her on his tour.

"Computer, please hail Brilliard for me."

"Hailing," the detached voice replied.

"Brilliard here."

Torrie said, "I was wondering if I could use your gymnasium for a while."

"Sure, I'll be up to escort you. Give me about twenty minutes. You'll find some clean clothes in the wall cabinets. Help yourself to whatever fits."

"Thank you," she said, feeling better already. She smiled. "Qaade could use some of your people skills."

"Don't I know it," she heard the man mutter.

Qaade looked up from his monitor as Brilliard walked into his office and took a seat opposite him across the table. And he had that look on his face that meant only one thing.

"I don't want to talk about her," Qaade said as a preemptive strike, and tried to concentrate on Slipstream's dismal finances instead. He heard Brilliard's chair ease back.

"She didn't know, Qaade. And she feels terrible about it."

129

Qaade gave a soundless growl. So much for pre-emptive. "It doesn't matter. The damage is done."

"Well, you are right about that. So, let it go. You should talk to her."

Qaade glanced at a man with no fear. "She won't get my forgiveness or pity, Brilliard. I'm damn sick of killing myself for indifferent people who hide behind their ignorance. If you want to make her feel better, send her home where she belongs."

Brilliard started chuckling. "It must be hell being perfect day and night. But you gotta give us mere mortals a break." He performed a mock prostration. "Forgive us, we're all sinners."

Qaade couldn't help but smile, although he did his best not to. Brilliard was like a brother in every sense and knew him better than anyone else aboard. They'd argued and butted heads more times than he could count, though they'd die for each other in a heartbeat.

Brilliard locked his hands behind his head. "This is all new to her. Yeah, maybe she knew the slave trade existed, but she's never had to deal with it head-on like we do. You can't tell me you don't see that in her eyes."

Qaade didn't want to tell him that he hadn't been concentrating on her eyes for the past few days. He shoved away from the monitor, giving up on work. "I noticed she's feeling guilty, that's all. Whether or not that will change anything is yet to be seen."

"She's changed, I'm certain of that, and you can bet she'll do something," Brilliard said with a nod. "That's one strong woman."

Qaade rubbed his stiff neck. "As long as she doesn't tell anyone about Slipstream, I'll be happy enough. Nothing else she can do will make a difference."

Brilliard gave him a wry smile. "I wouldn't be too sure about that." He tapped a finger on the table for a few seconds. "You look pretty stressed, Qaade. Maybe what you need is some exercise."

Chapter Twelve

Qaade walked through *Freeport* carrying his sparring gear. Maybe Brilliard was right. A hard workout was just what he needed to loosen up after too many hours in space. And the woman whose image haunted his every step had absolutely nothing to do with it.

Maybe she hadn't known about the scrub drug, but hell, if her family didn't check their damn shipments, how would the trafficking ever stop? Did he have to do everything himself?

He entered the gymnasium to find the place packed with a quarter of his male crew. Since when had so many of them decided to take up exercise? He could barely get them to step foot in here except under direct threat. Not that any of them appeared to be working out. Instead, they were three-deep to the holo-ring and cheering at whatever contest was being played out. From the level of noise, someone was putting on quite a show.

He made his way to the front of the raucous

gathering to find . . . Torrie battling a much larger sparring partner in the holographic ring.

Qaade frowned deeply, and scanned the spectators. Brilliard manned the ring controls, and he gave Qaade a mock salute before turning back to the action.

You need some exercise, my ass, Qaade thought. Obviously, Brilliard had set him up. But as he watched Torrie, it was kind of tough to complain.

Sweat dripped from her body as she lashed out with a no-nonsense, street style of fighting. Fierce green eyes peered between the combat gloves she was using to protect her face. Her bare arms and legs bore red marks, but her opponent looked much worse. They exchanged blow after blow until finally he moved one step out of position. Torrie's foot connected solidly with his unprotected midsection.

Qaade winced in sympathy as the man dropped to the floor in agony and dissolved back into the computer from which he'd been summoned. The crew roared approval. Torrie gave them a smile, and wiped perspiration from her face.

"Again!" the chant went up. Apparently, she'd already taken out a few virtual opponents tonight, and no wonder. The blue two-piece suit she wore hugged a long, hard body capable of amazing speed, strength and grace—it was a natural weapon. But despite her fighter's build, he couldn't help but remember how soft she'd felt. In fact, it was pretty much burned into his nerve endings.

A woman like her should be a warrior leading a battle. Freeing slaves from slavers. Instead, she wasted her time and energy hauling cargo. That disappointment bothered him even more because she had the ability and funds to do whatever she wanted. And she'd chosen shipping.

Torrie nodded to Brilliard, and that's when she noticed Qaade. He could tell by the icy mask that covered her features. Her eyes narrowed to slits of steely resolve. Surprise, she wasn't happy to see him.

Another virtual opponent appeared, blocking Qaade out. Before the man could even set himself, Torrie attacked with a vengeance, and a flurry of vicious strikes dispatched him in less than a minute. As he disappeared into oblivion, she glared at Qaade. That victory had been for him. Their eyes locked amidst the roars and yells for more.

Qaade spoke up. "Let's pack it up, boys, unless any of you are here to get a workout yourself."

Just as he figured, the place was empty in five minutes. Torrie relaxed, hands on hips, breathing hard while the grumbling crowd dispersed. Even Brilliard slapped Qaade's shoulder as he exited. "Your turn to watch her," he said with a knowing smile.

Qaade hopped up onto the ring. "I don't think you have to worry about any of my crew asking you to share a quiet evening."

"I needed to vent some energy," she replied coolly. "They wouldn't give me a gun."

"Lady, you don't need a gun."

She crossed her arms, unamused. "Where's Nod?"

"Asleep. I think. He crashed on the floor in my office," Qaade said. "Doesn't he give you any warning before he powers down?"

She raised her chin defiantly. "It's part of his charm."

"Uh-huh. And he forgets as fast as he learns. I had to tell him who I was . . . again. Is that also part of his charm?"

A shadow passed across Torrie's face. "I admit

that Nod's not perfect, but he's mine. So you better be taking good care of him."

Interesting, Qaade thought. "He's safe enough."

A few tense moments passed before Torrie glanced down at his feet on the holo-ring floor. "If you don't mind, I'd like to run through a few more rounds."

"Actually, I was hoping to use the ring myself. Why don't we save some virtual lives and work out our frustrations together?"

She squinted. "Are you serious?"

Qaade pulled off his shirt and tossed it aside, leaving his compression shorts on. He pulled on his headgear and gloves. "I'll be gentle."

Fire lit her eyes, and he knew she wouldn't reciprocate. She backed up and began circling him—wound tight and ready to spring. He mirrored her footwork as they faced off. She struck out so fast, he nearly caught a foot to the head. He blocked a quick succession of strikes, but a few managed to get through. He shook off the blows while Torrie grinned.

"Had enough? I wouldn't want to hurt you."

"Oh, yes, you would," Qaade said, keeping a watchful eye on her.

They circled silently, each searching for an opening, a vulnerability. Qaade took the offense this time and delivered a direct strike to her shoulder. Torrie spun around from the blow and surprised him with a flying kick to the side of his head that had him seeing stars for a second. But he managed to snag her wrist in the exchange, and yanked her around with her arm bent between them. She threw her head back and butted him in the face, which hurt like the blazes but he didn't let go.

He wrapped her up with an arm under her chin, locking her head beside his. Her steamy body, wedged against his, went very still. "Had enough?" he asked. "I wouldn't want to hurt you."

"Don't worry, you won't." She shifted quickly, and with more power than he thought possible, rolled him over her shoulder. He hit the floor with a thud. A split second later, she was on him—knee to his chest, her eyes ablaze.

She ripped off her headgear and leaned down to his face. "I did *not* know about that scrub drug, dammit. If I had, I never would have transported it. I'm not a heartless, soulless, greedy person. Do you hear me?" she yelled.

Qaade twisted, knocking her off his chest and onto her back. He covered her body with his. She didn't try to struggle, didn't fight him; she just lay there with that determined look on her face. He could tell she meant what she said. Torrie didn't pull any punches. She didn't lie, didn't go against her word, and she felt hot as hell between his legs.

"I hear you," he said. "But I'm tired of cleaning up the mess you people leave behind."

"I want to help."

Her admission stunned him, and he shook his head. He must really be tired. "What?"

"I said, I want to help. And I have an idea."

A noise at the entrance to the gymnasium brought Qaade's head up. One of his crewmen was standing there gawking, red-faced with embarrassment and shock. It occurred to Qaade that he was on top of Torrie in a most compromising position.

The man backed out the door. "Sorry, Cap." He fled.

"Oh, great," Torrie muttered. "How long will it take that to get around?"

"Seconds," Qaade conceded. He looked at her. "What idea?"

"You want to get off me first?"

He scanned her prone body beneath his. "Maybe."

Her green eyes narrowed. "Don't make me hurt you."

He chuckled but slid off. She sat up, and he was glad to see her pull off her gloves. Then she corralled her tangled mane of hair and proceeded to rebraid it—a simple gesture that mesmerized him.

"I want to go after my client," she said.

He rested his arms on his knees and stared at her. What trick was she pulling? "What happened to client confidentiality?"

Her expression hardened. "They broke our agreement when they shipped illegal goods through our business. I want them arrested and convicted."

Well, well. Maybe Brilliard was right. "And how do you plan to do that?"

"Depends. I have to find them first." She took a breath. "They do all their business electronically. No one in our company has ever met them. Their shipments are dock-to-dock in sealed containers."

"I wonder why," he muttered.

She finished with her hair and swung the heavy braid down her back. "I need a ship."

"You have a ship," he reminded her.

"No, I need a different ship."

He didn't like where this was going. "Why?"

She laced her fingers in front of her. "Because I can't bring this investigation home. It would damage the business."

So that was it. She didn't want to hurt the Masters' good name. He leaned toward her. "I'm not giving up one of my ships to save your damn company."

She scowled, hard. "You said it yourself, the only use for Ricytin is to scrub slaves. So the client must be a dealer, or they wouldn't risk shipping the product. My guess would be they've been doing this for a while, or at least for the few years since they set up their account. Which means they are selling a fair amount on a regular basis."

"All that does is incriminate Masters Shipping," he noted.

She had the grace to wince, but she kept talking anyway. "And Brilliard told me that the traffic has been getting steadily worse."

Damn Brilliard.

"He thinks it's organized," she continued with a thoughtful look. Then she turned to him. "And he's right. You're dealing with a slave *ring*."

Her statement worried Qaade beyond measure. The only thing keeping Slipstream afloat was the fact that slavers weren't neighborly. He didn't even want to consider what would happen if they united. "Slavers work for themselves and no one else. They wouldn't organize if you paid them."

"Then how do you explain the increase in activity? Or the Ricytin shipment through Masters?"

"You're sloppy," he said.

"No. These guys are smart. They know we won't breach their containers. In fact, they figured out we're the perfect hauler. Our reputation is well known. Our ships and crew are reliable and law-abiding. Our schedules and routes are confidential, with extensive connections. And we have a deal

139

where we don't have to go through inspections at every port." She blinked. "Because no one has ever suspected we'd be transporting Ricytin."

He ground his teeth. How could it be that *he* was the one wanted by the law? "So stop transporting it."

Torrie stared straight ahead. "Even when we do that for this client, these guys will try to find another way to get it out there." Her face lit up suddenly, and Qaade knew she had latched on to an idea he wouldn't like. "We need to break the ring."

"Don't," he said, shaking his head.

"And there's only one way to do that. Only one way to see who we're fighting." She looked him in the eye. "We deliver their shipment."

A rumble of laughter rolled through him, slowly at first and then building to a real belly laugh. He pushed himself to his feet and gathered up his gear. "Forget it."

Torrie stood up and faced him. He could tell by her stance that he was in for a long battle.

"It's the only way to find out who the recipient is, Qaade. We deliver the shipment and follow whoever picks it up."

"No," he said, and hopped off the holo-ring.

She followed. "It'll lead us to slaves, which will put us where we can do the most good."

He swung around to face her, hot anger burning his face. "There is no *us*, Torrie. There is *me*, and there is Slipstream. You aren't a part of this."

"I'm trying to help," she snapped.

"Don't ship any more Ricytin. That'd help me a lot." He grabbed his bag and headed for the exit. Torrie ran up beside him.

"You are impossible. First, you accuse me of trafficking drugs and not caring. Then, when I offer up

140

a perfectly good plan, you turn it down. You got serious control issues, bud."

He marched down the corridor toward her quarters so he could get rid of her before she came up with any more ideas to help him. "I will not deliver Ricytin into the hands of someone who can turn around and destroy a few hundred thousand lives with it."

"It's the only way to catch them," she insisted.

"And not soil the Masters name, right?" he added. "In case you hadn't picked up on this yet, I don't give a damn about your family or its business."

"So you will let the ring continue and do nothing about it for the sake of your pride?"

He cast her a dangerous look that she ignored. "I don't think it's *my* pride we're dealing with here."

They reached her quarters, and Qaade entered the security code. Torrie glared at him as the door slid open. "So that's it? You won't even consider it?"

"The answer is no," he said, not even trying to control the bitterness.

She shook her head slowly. "Then you may as well kiss Slipstream good-bye. Because I have a feeling you haven't seen just how bad the slave traffic will get." Then she walked into her quarters, and the door closed behind her.

Chapter Thirteen

The next morning, Torrie watched the girls from Wryth play in Free Quarters with the other children, most of whom were also orphans. Even though she understood that it was their salvation, she hated this place. It smelled like tragedy and loss.

"Do you want to say good-bye to them? You might not get another chance," Brilliard said. He stood next to her.

Say good-bye? No, she couldn't handle that. Torrie glanced at him. "Will they be split up? They have only each other."

"No," he said adamantly. "We never split up a family. Ever. In fact, we try to reconnect them."

"How?"

He smiled at her. "Genetic signatures. Every slave that comes through is scanned, and their gen-sigs are added to our database for a genetic match."

Torrie thought about the astronomical odds. "How often do you make a connection?"

He shrugged. "Once in a while we get lucky. Most times, we don't know what the relationship is. Of course, if they aren't scrubbed it's much easier. But we don't receive many who aren't."

"Why scrub them?" Torrie asked.

Brilliard sighed. "Scrubbing puts them in a state of neural shock, especially in the beginning. They are very compliant and vulnerable in that stage. The slavers take advantage of that critical time to imprint them with submissiveness. And since the victims don't know any better, they accept the situation they are in."

Torrie surveyed the levels above her, all the faces staring down at them. A shudder ran through her that she could do nothing to stop. How could it be she could take on attackers left and right, and yet still not be able to control her emotions? "Where do they all come from, Brilliard?"

"Some are former Freeborns who are captured and enslaved. Some were born into slavery. Qaade picks most up en route to somewhere, but we get only a very small percentage. The vast majority never get airborne. We can't touch those."

"How many are out there?"

"Billions, probably."

Billions. "What are they used for?"

"Prostitution, hard labor, domestics, experimentation, rituals, soldiers." Brilliard stopped and looked at her, sorrow in his eyes. "Sometimes hunting. And food."

Nausea welled up in her. She turned and started walking back through the ship. She wanted to run, to get away before the horror of it swallowed her. Before anyone could see her lose her composure.

"Torrie!" Brilliard called, just before he caught up with her. "It's okay."

"It'll never be okay. How do you stand it?" She stopped and turned to him. "How do you look at those faces every day?"

He held up his hands, and then dropped them. "Because someone has to. It's not easy, I'll tell you that. There are days when I don't want to do it. But I can't stop. We are all they have."

The sincerity in his voice was so real. He did care, and in a way she never could. "Then you are a better person than I am."

Brilliard's comm chimed. He answered it calmly. "What?"

Qaade's voice: "Where are you?"

"Escorting Torrie around," he said with a concerned frown. "What's wrong?"

"We just received a distress message from Twel Station. It was cut off before they could complete it. I need you on the bridge *now*."

"On our way."

Brilliard cut his comm, then motioned for Torrie to follow him. Noting the worried look on Brilliard's face and the urgency in his step, she asked, "What would cause Twel to send a distress signal?"

He looked straight ahead. "Only one thing I can think of. It's just a matter of who found them— InterGlax or the slavers. Frankly, I'm hoping it's InterGlax."

They entered the small bridge of *Freeport* to find Qaade and three very concerned crewmen huddled around a scanner screen. He glanced up when they approached, and said, "We haven't been able to hail them since they were disconnected."

Brilliard stepped forward. "You have a message?"

"Computer, play Fren's message," Qaade said. Torrie moved closer. Atop the small holodisk on the main console, a young man appeared. He looked no more than twenty standard years and wore street clothes. He glanced over his shoulder at something out of the frame, and then looked at the holocam. "We are being attacked by a contingent of heavily armed ships and a thousand men. They got through our defenses, and are making their way through the levels." The man put his hands up powerlessly. "They are shooting everyone they see—the crew, the Free People. They won't even negotiate." He ducked his head as a loud noise reverberated nearby. Torrie listened to the sounds of laserfire and explosions.

Fren's expression turned desperate. "We need reinforcements. Please, before—" The image shifted, and then disappeared altogether.

All Torrie could hear was the pounding of her heart over the silence of the bridge. Her imagination picked up where the holorecording left off. And no matter how she played it out, the scene always ended badly.

Qaade spoke up first. "That was received fifteen minutes ago."

"We can't get this piece of junk there in less than three hours," Brilliard said.

"I don't want *Freeport* anywhere near it," Qaade said.

Brilliard blanched. "But they need help."

"I realize that," Qaade told him bluntly. Torrie could feel his tension from where she stood. "But we can't expose Slipstream any more than it has been. I'll take my ship and contact Sly to rendezvous *Exodus* near Twel."

"I'm going with you," Torrie said. Noting his frown, she added, "And don't even *try* to tell me there's another person aboard this vessel more capable than I am."

146

Brilliard gave Qaade a nervous look. "I'm not saying a word."

Qaade walked by her. "Fine. Torrie's with me."

Their ship dropped out of hyperspace with a blinding entry into star-studded blackness. In the distance, Qaade could just make out Twel Station as it orbited a small brown planetoid in the local solar system. Torrie manned scanners and weapons, and Nod was hovering over her shoulder.

"I'm not detecting any ships in the vicinity," she reported. "No unmanned drones, no surveillance equipment. It's quiet." She glanced at him. "Nothing from Twel, either. Not even a distress signal."

Qaade nodded, his worst fears confirmed. He sent a message to *Exodus* to pull up a safe distance away. He wouldn't be needing their firepower, and until he knew exactly what was happening, he didn't want them around.

He executed the commands for his ship to dock with Twel, adrenaline making his hands tremble. His anger was crippling. The image of Fren begging for help was ingrained in his memory for all time, along with the bitter taste of failure. His. He'd failed to protect Twel. They'd taken the risks for him, and paid the price. He had no doubts what he'd find here.

"Can I help?" Nod asked, which Qaade had discovered was a sort of mantra for the little lightball.

"Not right now," he answered. Torrie glanced over at him, one eyebrow arched.

"It's impossible to ignore him," Qaade said, by way of explanation. "He's damned persistent. Can't imagine where he gets that from."

She batted her eyelashes and went back to work.

"You didn't have to come along. I could have asked one of my other crewmen," he said.

"I told you I wanted to help, whether you believe me or not." She turned to him with a look of concern. "Do you think there will be anyone left to rescue?"

"If they were attacked by slavers, there won't be any survivors."

"And if it's InterGlax?"

He conceded, "They might have a chance. Inter-Glax doesn't like to slaughter innocents. Bad for their reputation."

As they drew closer, Twel's hull told the story of what had happened. Explosions and laserfire had breached and blackened the silver hull. Twisted and mangled metal protruded around all sides of the diamond-shaped station. Huge pieces of debris hung in space like tombstones. Qaade could only imagine how the inside looked.

They entered through a blown-out shuttle bay. As soon as the ship touched down, Torrie was up and heading to the rear cabin. Qaade followed her to where she was pulling on a light blue enviro-suit and magnetized boots.

"I was going to go in alone," he said, grabbing a suit for himself.

She sealed her suit and activated the force-field helmet, which cast her in a blue sheen. "You need help, Qaade."

"It won't be pretty," he warned, activating his own suit.

"I know."

Carrying a rifle, Qaade took the lead, with Torrie and Nod behind him. In his ship's spotlights, the bay looked totally gutted and cargo floated around in the weightlessness of space.

"The shuttle-bay force field is dead," he noted,

trying to keep the despair from his voice. He stopped in front of a gaping hole in the wall control panel. "So is this."

Torrie addressed Nod. "Can you tap into the computer system?"

The lightball bounced. "Yes. What would you like downloaded?"

At least Twel's computer was still up. Qaade walked toward the interior. "Let's start with a ship-wide damage report, critical systems first."

They navigated through the carnage that was once Twel as Nod lit the way and rattled off the long list of destruction. Twel's main computer was functioning but wouldn't respond to verbal commands. Every wall panel they encountered was blown out. The station had scattered power, but all other systems were down.

And then they rounded a corner and found the first body, floating in midair. The crewman's last moments of fear were frozen on his face. Torrie glanced at Qaade, overwhelming compassion in her eyes. For a woman so formidable, she was amazingly soft inside. He wouldn't have thought the combination possible.

"I warned you," he said. "You can go back if you want."

Sympathy changed to a determined glare, and she moved on. They wove through the maze of corridors where sporadic lighting cast an eerie glow over wreckage and bodies. Some crew had died from wounds, some from exposure to deep space.

They located the station's Free Quarters and looked through the hole that once had been a sealed entry. In the dim beam of emergency lights, hundreds of bodies floated frozen and blind. Entombed in terror.

"Oh, God," Torrie whispered and turned away. But Qaade couldn't. He didn't deserve to. They had died for him.

"Let's head for the bridge," he rasped. He walked through section after section, finding nothing but death. Qaade fought the hopelessness that lurked around every bend. He had to believe there was someone left alive.

"Nod, tap into the main computer. See if all the crew are onboard the ship."

"Overlaying damage report," Nod remarked, and Torrie cast Qaade an anxious look.

"Do you think the attackers took some of your crew hostage?" she asked.

He shrugged, not wanting to discuss which was better—dying aboard Twel or being held prisoner by whoever did this. "Possible."

"All one hundred fifty-two crewmen are accounted for," Nod announced, quelling any hopes Qaade had left. His heart ached. Who had done this?

When they finally reached the entry to the ship's bridge, they found it closed. Torrie examined it, and said, "Still sealed. We might get lucky. How's the air quality in there, Nod?"

"Sensors say adequate for human life," he replied.

Qaade glanced at the wreckage behind them. "We still need an air lock before entering. Is there a force field for this entry?"

Seconds later, Nod said, "Yes. Activated."

Qaade raised his rifle. "Open it," he told Nod. The door slid aside, revealing the air-lock barrier and a surprisingly intact bridge.

"It looks clear," Torrie noted with a frown. "The

obvious question would be, why? Nod, scan for any dangerous materials or explosive devices."

The lightball zipped through the barrier into the center of the semicircular room. "No such devices found."

Qaade moved in, sweeping the room with his rifle while Torrie covered him. Considering what the rest of Twel had endured, the bridge appeared eerily untouched. There were no signs of a struggle, no signs of forced entry. All the computer systems were functioning. It didn't make sense.

Qaade deactivated his suit's helmet. He looked at Torrie, who did the same. Then he heard a whimper from one corner. Torrie's gaze met his, and they moved in unison toward the sound.

Huddled on the floor was Fren, curled up in a tight ball and rocking slowly. Fearing the worst, Qaade kneeled next to Twel's ops chief. Fren's left eye was bruised, blood ran from his nose, and his mouth was swollen. But what devastated Qaade was the blank stare.

He heard Torrie gasp. "Oh, no," she said. "It can't be."

"Fren?" Qaade asked the ops chief. "Do you know where you are?"

Wide eyes focused on him, but behind them there was no light. No recognition. No memories.

Qaade swallowed both rage and pain; neither would serve him, so he let numbness consume him, shield him and block out everything else. He reached out and patted Fren's hand. "You'll be all right. We'll take care of you."

Torrie covered her face with her hands and gave a heart-wrenching sob. She lurched to her feet and wandered away. After making sure Fren understood he wasn't alone anymore, Qaade rose and followed her to where she leaned against a wall, a flood of tears streaming down her cheeks.

"Torrie," he said, as her body was racked with her uncontrollable weeping. He gently turned her around to face him and pulled her into his arms. She came willingly, clutching at him with fierce desperation. Tears burned his cheek where she buried her face next to his.

For long minutes, she sobbed inconsolably and without restraint. Qaade felt her sorrow to his bones; it melded with his own, binding them together. Her raw emotion seeped into his hands and through his body. Without warning, he felt it penetrate his heart—just a small twinge, hardly there at all. But enough to worry him. Then he shut it down, shoved it aside. A man who let pain rule him could never run Slipstream effectively. Besides, they couldn't stay here another minute. Whoever did this had meant for him to find Fren, and might still be watching.

"Why would they do that?" Torrie asked between shudders.

"I don't know," he admitted. And he didn't. Qaade glanced around the unscathed bridge. They'd murdered everyone else on board. Why would they scrub one person and leave him behind? It didn't make sense.

"They wanted us to find him alive. Maybe to make a point or send a message. . . ." Then he noted a light flashing on the central comm board. "Nod, is there a communication waiting?"

"Yes. Would you like me to have the computer play it?"

"Please."

From the comm speakers, a deep male voice emanated. "We meet at last, laghato."

Torrie's head came up, her eyes wide. Every muscle in Qaade's body froze as the message continued.

"Welcome to Twel Station. I am Chauvet. Don't bother trying to find me, you won't. But I trust you found your ops chief. As you can see, he is in no condition to tell you anything. Pity. His loyalty was commendable, but in the end, pointless."

Who the hell *was* this?

"Now that I have your attention, this is how the game works, Qaade. You have a finite amount of time to stop me from destroying the next target in your operation. I've left you and Torrie a few clues. The contest has begun. I do not wish to be disappointed."

The message ended, and the horror in Torrie's eyes mirrored Qaade's own thoughts. "He knows everything, Qaade."

Chapter Fourteen

Torrie did her best to clean up Fren as he sat on a bunk in Qaade's ship, but his vacant stare was beyond help. Guilt weighed heavily on her. Could the drug that did this have come through Masters Shipping? Could she be treating a victim of her own family's carelessness? No wonder Qaade was so angry when he found the Ricytin.

Her hands trembled as she dabbed at the lacerations on Fren's face. He hadn't gone down without a fight. Brave young man. She realized suddenly how few truly brave men she knew. Her brothers were strong and capable, always doing the right thing, but they didn't risk themselves like Qaade or his people. They didn't give their lives to save others.

Qaade was seated at the ship's controls, discussing the situation with Brilliard through the comm. He had already ordered all the stations along Slipstream evacuated immediately. In one blow,

155

Qaade's operation had been disrupted. So much work, all to be lost.

As she listened to his conversation, she wondered how he could function with such controlled emotion. He gave orders calmly, decisively. How could he act like it was just another day? Everything he'd built was crumbling around him. Even when she'd cried on his shoulder, he hadn't reacted. Maybe she was right about him from the beginning. Maybe he *didn't* have a soul. Whom had he sold it to, and what had it gotten him?

"I don't want you anywhere near the circuit, Brilliard, and that's final," he was saying.

"All we need is an escort to Keerny Point Station. You can shadow us—"

Qaade interrupted. "Not going to work, Brilliard. We don't have enough ships to defend against an all-out attack like on Twel."

"Well, I have nine hundred Free People here. What am I supposed to do with them?" Brilliard sounded frustrated.

Qaade rubbed his face with his hands. "Hold on to them until I come up with a plan."

"So, basically we are shut down indefinitely."

Qaade gave a sigh. "Yes. There's no choice. They know about Slipstream."

"That's impossible," Brilliard argued. "All our information is compartmentalized. None of the stations knows anything about the others. Fren couldn't have told them about the rest of the circuit. He didn't have that data."

Qaade stood up and glanced at Fren thoughtfully. Then he paced a tight circle in the limited space of the ship. "Maybe he didn't. But until I find out who these murderers are and what they know, *Freeport* runs silent."

"I can't believe it. After fifteen years, we're dead?"

Qaade said wryly, "Think of it as a little vacation."

"I don't need one. What does this Chauvet want? Credits? Your head? What?"

"He didn't mention any of that. He seems to think we're playing a game."

Brilliard huffed. "Some game. What are we going to do, Qaade?"

Qaade stopped pacing, and his gaze settled on Torrie with unnerving intensity. She could tell his mind was working on something, and it included her.

"Give me some time. We're leaving shortly to rendezvous with *Exodus*."

"Got it. Out."

Qaade walked over and smiled at Fren, who smiled back benignly, but lost. Sadness washed over Torrie, bringing a wave of injustice and rage. Unable to handle any more, she fled, pushing by Qaade to the ship's tiny galley. She busied herself getting Fren something to eat. Qaade came up behind her, crowding her.

"I don't want the lecture," she snapped. "I don't need to hear again how I don't care and you do. Or how greedy my family is, and you aren't. I'm in a room full of cutlery, so save it."

He chuckled softly.

She spun around to face him. "What is so damned funny? There is nothing humorous about this situation. How can you laugh?"

His silver eyes flashed in the dim light. "Because if I didn't, I wouldn't be able to function."

Anger slipped away with the realization that he was right. That's exactly what she'd done. In fact, she'd never broken down as many times as she had in the past few days, bombarded with seemingly endless tragedy, pain and hopelessness. She'd spent her life trying to attain her own freedom. Nothing had prepared her for this.

"So you laugh and it'll go away?"

His expression sobered. "It never goes away. But I can only do so much."

"It's falling apart," she said, dismally voicing the obvious.

"I need to salvage what I can."

"What about Twel?"

Torrie caught the flash of pain in Qaade's eyes. If she hadn't been watching, she would have missed it. Then his gaze met hers.

"I have to blow it up."

She gaped in utter disbelief. "Why?"

"Because I don't have a dry dock or the equipment for a full recovery operation. Even if I did, it would take too long, and the attackers could come back. It's bad enough we're here."

"So just leave it."

His expression grew tighter. "Eventually someone would find it. Someone who will want to know what happened. There's no way to guarantee something inside wouldn't lead to us."

"What about the *people* in there?"

"Bodies," he corrected, his voice emotionless and stark. "We can't do anything for them now. I'll notify the crew's families."

It was unthinkable what he was proposing. She couldn't believe that he, of all people, would do this. "How can you just forget about them like that? They gave their lives for Slipstream."

Slow anger darkened his face and lined his bitter words. "I know exactly why and how they gave their lives. If I could give mine to bring them back, I would. Trust me, they will not be forgotten."

Then she saw it, the crack in his impassive exterior. He blamed himself, completely and totally. They would never be forgotten because *he* would carry the guilt with him forever. He carried them all: every person who worked for him, every slave he saved. All those lives were on his shoulders. No wonder he hid behind a mask. No wonder he'd sold his soul. Otherwise, the burden would have killed him long ago.

She swallowed and said something she'd never thought she would. "I'll help you set the charges."

They detonated Twel Station at precisely 1804 hours. From a safe distance, Qaade watched the series of blasts rip Twel apart, disintegrating it. He said a silent prayer to any god who would listen for the 151 souls he'd just delivered.

"Qaade," he heard softly. But he couldn't face her; his shame was too great. These people had died for him and his operation. He would never forgive himself. A soft hand covered his, surprising him. He turned. Sympathetic green eyes searched his face, and for the first time in a very long time, he wanted to hold someone and be soothed. Then she smiled. "Put us in hyperspace, pirate. It's time to get some sleep."

He took one last look at where Twel used to be before doing as she said. After they'd jumped, Torrie exited her seat and went into the lav. Qaade stood up, dead tired and feeling more drained than he could ever recall. His body protested every step through the ship. He paused to check Fren, who was stretched out on one of the bunks asleep, a grim reminder of all the failures and frustrations that hounded Qaade every minute of every day.

Was Slipstream making enough of a difference? Was the cost too high? He'd lost a lot of good people on Twel, and their families had lost more.

Worse than that, his people were all in danger now, and that included Torrie. If he couldn't protect them, how would he protect her?

Despair racked his tired body, and he swayed under the crush. Without thinking, he opened a cabinet and pulled out his pik. He tossed the simple flute on a bunk and undressed, leaving himself in just shorts.

Then he eased across the bunk and brought the pik to his lips. His eyes closed of their own accord, his body giving up with a sigh. But without action and duty, he was left with only guilt and profound sadness. He pushed that through the pik. He let his fingers play a familiar melody, one played so many times it was instinct. The soothing notes whispered from a past that was gone but not forgotten. As he made his melodious way through the notes, his heart settled and calmed. He tapped into the quiet strength the song always gave him, from a time when life was simple and free.

Scraps of memories shifted through his mind. A family, a home, parents, a sister. Sweet peace. He fought to remember them, to hold on to the single reason that motivated him on the days he didn't want to continue: hope beyond hope that his life might once again be like that.

He heard a noise beside him and opened his eyes to find Torrie standing next to the bunk. She had changed into a sleep set comprised of a loose green tank and shorts that were plain and simple, not meant to be seductive. But everything looked sexy on Torrie.

Setting his pik aside, he mumbled, "Where'd you get that?"

She didn't move, a look of perplexity on her face. "From *Freeport*. Where'd you learn that song?"

He raised an eyebrow. "You don't like it?"

"No, it's beautiful. It's just . . ." She paused. "Sad." Then she frowned at the bunk that he filled. "I'm not letting you take the entire bunk this time."

Despite his exhaustion, he smiled and stretched his arms out. "It's not like I have a choice."

"I don't think you're trying real hard not to." She pursed her lips and climbed up, shoving at him while he chuckled. He rolled onto his side as she turned her back to him. Her loose hair filled the space between them and followed the long line of her body from one shoulder to the valley of her waist. He couldn't resist—he reached out and draped an arm over her. To his surprise, she didn't protest. So he moved a little closer.

"Don't get any ideas, pirate."

He grinned. He was well past the idea phase. "Just making myself comfortable."

"Is that what you call it? I thought it was following a death wish."

He settled for moving his head close enough that he could smell her heavy hair. It was fresh and inviting. He felt his body react, in spite of knowing better.

"What's going to happen to Fren?"

Her question derailed much nicer thoughts. "We'll treat him with Phellium and reorient him."

She turned around to face him, and rested her chin on her hand. "He doesn't remember anything about who he was or his past?"

Qaade left his arm around her waist, and let his

fingers strum her back. "No, but the Phellium will help him to retain new memories."

"What about his family?"

Qaade closed his eyes. "He lost his mate and two children on Twel. As far as I know, that was the only family he had. It's probably better that he doesn't remember."

He opened his eyes to find a single tear rolling down Torrie's cheek. Despair tightened her face and tugged at his heart. He felt a tiny fissure split open, exposing a place in his soul he thought he'd buried long ago.

Another silent tear followed Torrie's first, and he leaned in to kiss the wet trail away. Her soft skin seared his lips, unleashing a flood of emotions—passion, pain, fear and hope. Emotions he usually had full control over. But not tonight. Tonight, he was at the mercy of his own humanity. And Torrie's.

He kissed her again, and her hand wrapped around the back of his neck and drew him closer. A low growl signaled the end of his self-control as he took her heat and made it his own.

In an instant, their mouths melded and teeth nipped, straining to sate equal hungers. His mouth ravaged hers, and she was right there with him. He could feel it in her fierce passion—straight-on, no holds barred, Torrie-style. She was his match. That realization was enough to drive him insane and he unbridled his lust.

He gripped her hip with his hand and drew her body against his with enough force to draw a surprised gasp from her. But he wasn't worried. One thing he'd learned about Torrie: she wouldn't break. Sure enough, she locked a leg around his and rubbed against what was possibly the hardest erection he'd ever had in his life. Her consuming need flooded him and fueled his own. He filled his hands with her breasts, the soft skin pressing into his palms, hard nipples branding him.

He felt her hands explore his chest, nails scratching, fingers tracing their own path of discovery. Her moan of approval filled his ears. She wanted him; there was no doubt. He could ask her at this moment, and she would tell him so. No games, no winners or losers. Her heated scent swept over him, and he was lost in it, as mindless as Fren.

And then reality reared its ugly head.

Fren. Twel's ops chief was lying in the bunk beside them.

Damn.

Qaade broke off the siege, his body protesting loud and clear with an excruciating ache that was going to take a very long time to dissipate. Unaware, Torrie trailed kisses down his throat to his chest. Cursing his lousy luck, Qaade hooked a finger under her chin and brought her face to his. He gave her a tender kiss as consolation for what he was about to ruin. The sacrifices he made for Slipstream!

"Fren," he said against her lips.

Passion-laden eyes flickered open in confusion. Then her face flushed with realization and horror.

"Good Lord," she muttered, untangling herself from him in a flurry of hands as she pushed him away and tugged her top down to where it was supposed to be. He couldn't help but grin at her mortification. She gave him an accusing glare, and then rolled over, presenting him with her back. "I hope you found that amusing, pirate."

He slid up behind her, closing the cool gap between them. He nuzzled her ear. "Trust me. There's nothing amusing about it. If Fren weren't lying two meters from us, you'd be a happy woman by now."

She harrumphed. "Right. I bet all pirates say that."

With his fingertips, he traced circles of promise over her bare skin. He felt her tremble, and smiled at the small victory. "Maybe. But this pirate means it."

Her body was stiff, fighting him, but he knew better. He knew what Torrie Masters needed and how to make her his. Too bad he wouldn't get the chance. With every touch, he ached in want of something he had no business thinking about and would never have. That dream that had been shattered long, long ago.

Chapter Fifteen

Torrie woke with a gasp from a nightmare of ghostly bodies burning in a merciless fire. Qaade's ship's hyperdrives hummed low, marked by silently strobing lights on the panels. Slowly, Qaade's heat seeped into her, banishing the dream lingering fresh in her mind. But was the dream really just a dream if was true?

She took a shuddering breath and tried to calm her wildly thumping heart. She glanced over her shoulder at Qaade's face, close to hers, and wondered how he coped. How could he go through this day after day and not fall apart? What was his secret? Because she needed to know for her own sanity.

In the past few days, she felt like she'd been stripped, layer by layer, until her raw, vulnerable soul was bared for all to see. Every minute was a battle to hold her emotions in check, which was the hardest thing she'd ever done. She couldn't fight or shoot her way out of this. She couldn't hide from it, even in her sleep. And nothing she would ever do would make slavery or these horrors stop. It was hopeless.

She lifted her head and checked Fren, who was sleeping soundly. A pang of sorrow rolled through her at the tragedy his life had become. Would he ever laugh again? Would he understand how much he'd lost? Would he ever grieve for his family? Would anyone? All those people, gone forever.

She tried to deflect sudden, overwhelming claustrophobia. They were trapped—Qaade, Brilliard and the rest—slaves to their compassion and duty with no end in sight. Or maybe there was an end: death, like on Twel. Would that be their reward?

Carefully, Torrie extracted herself from Qaade and the bunk. For a moment, she stood in the middle of his ship looking for an outlet to vent her strained emotion. There was nowhere to go. No escape. Restless energy pulsed through her as it always did when she felt powerless.

She walked until she found herself at the bridge controls. The shadowy nothingness of hyperspace blanketed the viewport; not even stars could distract her. She slipped into the pilot's chair and idly checked the ship's stats. They looked fine. Then she noticed the comm.

For a moment, she hesitated. But with a quick look back to make sure Qaade was still sleeping, she entered a comm sequence.

A familiar voice came on. "Torrie? Is that you?"

"Greetings, Howser," she whispered back. "Keep your voice down."

He dropped his tone. "We've been searching all over for you. I was just about to call in Carmon. Where are you?"

She smiled at his frantic and familiar voice—a tenuous link back to sanity. "In hyperspace." She glanced at the current coordinates displayed on the monitors, then lied. "Not sure where."

"Who are you with? Are you safe? What happened? I swear if they did anything to you—"

"Take it easy, Howser. You'll hurt yourself," she replied with a quiet laugh. "What happened . . ." She paused, trying to figure out what to tell Howser that wouldn't kill him on the spot. "It's a long story. I'm with the pirate. And yes, I'm safe."

"That's crap. No one is safe with pirates."

A day ago, she would have agreed. She touched her lips where her memory of Qaade's passion still burned. "I'm okay, I promise. In fact, they are setting me free, but there's a problem."

"I knew it," he said. "What do they want? Ransom?"

"Actually, it's my problem, not theirs." She braced herself. "I want to stay for a while longer."

"Are you drugged?" Howser screeched, his voice reaching a fever pitch.

"No. Worse." She took a deep breath, and let go of her pride. "Two of the containers we were shipping held Phellium."

There was a potent pause. "That's impossible, Torrie. The company has a policy—"

"I saw it myself. And inside one of the containers was something else." She drew a breath. "Ricytin."

"Holy shit," Howser replied, sounding stunned. "Holy shit. Are you sure?"

She cast a quick glance at Fren. "Positive. We have to find out where it came from, and who it was going to."

"Customer 151. You know that."

"Yes, but who is that? You need to dig into our

records, find out what you can about them."

"And then what? Torrie, drug smuggling is a crime for InterGlax, not us."

She drummed her fingertips on the console. "And what do you think InterGlax will do if we tell them we have been delivering scrub drugs all over the sector? Do you have any idea what an investigation would do to our reputation if it leaked out?"

It took a moment; finally he agreed. "You're right. Carmon would go supernova. He's already calling me every day to find out why we are behind. And let me tell you, it hasn't been fun trying to cover for you, either. He thinks you live in the lav. Why can't you come back here? We'll figure this out together."

Her head was telling her Howser was right, but she couldn't do it. Part of this was her family's fault. She couldn't bring herself to simply walk away. "I need to help clean up the mess we've created."

"What mess? What are you talking about?"

She could trust Howser, she knew that. And yet, in a surge of protectiveness, she couldn't speak. This was her battle now. "Something important. I can't tell you. Have faith in me."

Howser sighed. "I don't like it, Torrie."

"I know, and I'm sorry. I'll check in tomorrow. You need to get me something by then."

"I'll do my best. Be careful, Torrie. I hope you know what you are doing."

She held on for dear life to the frayed edges of her sanity. "So do I." She cut the comm.

"Who was that?"

Torrie jumped at Qaade's voice behind her. *Oh, damn.* She wasn't up to an argument tonight. With dread, she pushed out of the seat and stood.

Qaade was leaning against the wall, watching her with a quiet intensity that brought heat to her face. Her gaze dropped to his lips of its own accord, his kiss still burning on her mouth. Pirate's lips. Pirate's hands. A pirate's rock-hard body. Obviously, she'd been dating the wrong men. It worried her only slightly what wanting a bad boy said about her.

"My first mate. Howser." She waited for a reaction, but got none. "Did you hear the whole conversation?"

"Most of it," he admitted.

She studied him. "I didn't tell him where I was. I would never do anything to jeopardize Slipstream."

"I see that. But you are still going home tomorrow. I have bigger problems to deal with now than your client."

"My client is the key to this whole thing."

He shook his head. "The man I'm after just slaughtered one hundred and fifty-one people, left one scrubbed and is gunning for the rest of my operation."

As she listened to him, a thought surfaced. "One fifty-one," she said.

"What about it?"

"That's my customer's ID number." Her eyes met Qaade's. "A connection?"

"Coincidence."

Her instincts were humming. "He certainly would have all the Ricytin he would need." She looked at Fren. "And maybe that's why one person was left alive on Twel. Because it would make one fifty-one dead."

He scowled at her. "It's just a number. It means nothing," he said. "Tomorrow you go back." He turned, and headed back to the bunk.

I don't think so, she thought. Her instincts were rarely wrong. And this time, she *knew* she was right.

A suspiciously silent Torrie sat next to him as Qaade dropped the ship out of hyperspace at the rendezvous coordinates. *Exodus* waited dead-ahead, a black knife in the star-studded fabric of space.

He'd like to think she was preoccupied by their brief, intoxicating encounter, but he doubted it. More likely, she was still working on her theory that the attack on Twel and her Ricytin were related. If they were somehow connected, then it would mean that he was dealing with someone who was sadistic beyond imagination. A man who would execute a specific number of people just to leave his signature? It was too sick to consider.

They landed in the shuttle bay, and Lapreu met them as they exited the ship. Torrie went first, followed by Nod. The old man limped over and kissed her hand. Lapreu could be a charmer when he wanted.

Torrie managed a weak smile in return. Qaade was worried about her. She was having a hard time dealing with Fren and the situation. He'd seen enough of death to insulate himself from it. She hadn't. Her heart was too big and soft. He'd chosen this road long ago, knowing how much it would cost him. She was only beginning to understand the sacrifice. Would her happiness be yet another casualty of Slipstream?

He helped a bewildered Fren from the ship and passed the man off to Lapreu, then said softly, "He needs the full treatment."

The old man took Fren's arm. He turned back to

Qaade. "Sly is waitin' for you on the bridge." Then he headed to the med center with Fren.

Qaade led Torrie through the *Exodus* toward the bridge. Torrie asked, "How long have you known Lapreu?"

Qaade pressed a hand to her back, and ushered her into a lift. "He was my first rescue."

"He was a slave?" she asked after Qaade gave the computer their destination.

"I bought his freedom from his miserable owner of fifty years."

Torrie nodded sadly. "Is that why he limps?"

"The damage is too extensive to fix. And he won't be bothered. Says it'll slow him down too long."

Torrie leaned against the wall, facing him. "Are all your crewmen former slaves?"

"Most. A few are lifelong pirates, like Urwin and Sly. In fact, Sly was one of the pirates who rescued me."

Torrie's eyes widened. "Pirates rescued you? Is that a common occurrence?"

"Believe it or not, even pirates have a code. One that in most ways is better than any legal system. When they boarded my owner's ship, they let me come with them."

"And thus began the infamous career of the Ghost Rider of the Dead Zone."

Qaade laughed. "It took a few years to get rolling, but yes. Brilliard was born into slavery, but he worked out his freedom with his owner. He sought me out, and offered to work for me."

They exited the lift toward the bridge. Sly was waiting at the main console. He gave Torrie a nod of acknowledgment, then looked at Qaade solemnly. "We were just hit again."

Qaade's heart sank. "Where?"

"Keerny Point."

"Casualties?"

Sly's solemn expression said it all. He raised his hands helplessly. "I told them to leave, just like you ordered, but they had more slaves to move. By the time we received their distress message and got a nearby friendly ship to help out, the attack was over."

"How many crew?" Torrie asked.

Sly looked at her. "The friendly reported one hundred and fifty-one dead and thirty-six scrubbed."

Qaade closed his eyes at the stab of pain. *Hell.* His worst nightmare come true. He felt Torrie brush against him and he opened his eyes. Pain, sadness and anger showed in her face as she watched him. He wasn't alone in his sorrow. He was just alone in the guilt.

"Was there a message?"

"Yeah. How did you know?" Sly asked, looking surprised.

"Do you have it?"

"Sure," the pirate said, and accessed the comm.

Chauvet's arrogant voice filled the bridge. "You were too slow to put the pieces together, laghato. Somehow, I expected more from the legendary savior of slaves. Let's see if you can do better next time. And since I've other tasks to attend to, I'll even give you a little more time. You have ten hours. Use them wisely."

The message ended, and Qaade swallowed the lump in his throat. Ten hours. What the hell could he do in ten hours?

Torrie said, "It's the same man."

Sly froze. "You know this bastard?"

Qaade rubbed his stiff neck. "His name's Chauvet. He hit Twel. He obviously knows everything about Slipstream."

Torrie added, "And Qaade."

She was right. He couldn't deny it any longer. His people's lives were at stake now, as well as Slipstream's future.

Sly asked, "What the hell is his problem?"

Qaade shook his head. "Haven't figured that out yet. I ran a full archive check on his name last night and came up with nothing. But we have only ten hours to find out where he is."

Torrie said, "You know there's only one way."

"There's no guarantee your plan will work."

"They don't know we put his clue together," Torrie argued.

Sly looked them both over as Qaade replied, "If anyone is going to move on this, it'll be me. *You* are going back where you belong."

Fire lit in her eyes. "Like hell I am. This is *my* plan, remember? Besides, how do you know where to deliver? And who do you think is going to get you a delivery pass?"

He ignored those minor details. "This might be your plan, but it's not your battle, Torrie."

She crossed her arms and arched her eyebrows. "Tracker?"

That detail wasn't so minor; even if he managed to deliver her shipment, he couldn't track it without her help. "I don't suppose you'd be willing to give me your tracking codes?"

Her silence was her answer.

"Didn't think so," he muttered.

Sly threw up his hands. "Will someone please tell me what the hell is going on?"

Qaade pursed his lips. "I'll let you know once Torrie and I hash it out. Are the rest of our stations evacuated now?"

"Every one." Sly paused. "What do you want to do about Keerny Point?"

Qaade felt his chest constrict. "Take *Exodus* there, and be sure to hide your tracks. Recover as many bodies as you can. Then destroy the station and transfer the survivors to *Freeport*. Just make sure no one is tailing you."

"Will do," Sly said solemnly. "What about you?"

"We'll switch to *Shooter* in case anyone followed us from Twel, and we'll head to *Freeport*. There's something we need to pick up." He glanced at Torrie. He tried to convince himself that he'd done everything he could to send her back to where she belonged, but somehow he didn't believe it.

"You're with me."

"And me," Nod piped up. "Can I help?"

Qaade watched the much-too-happy lightball dance with excitement. "Did you program him with your tenacity, or is he learning as he goes?"

"What can I say? He's my boy," Torrie said with a smile.

With Nod hovering over her shoulder, Torrie stared at the single bunk in this ship made for one. This was going to be interesting. *Shooter* was even smaller than *Umbra*. It was narrow, only about five meters wide and twenty meters long—most of that being engine, which wasn't a bad thing. There was practically no cargo space and a tiny forward cabin. The control panel wrapped around a single pilot's seat. Behind it sat a second seat and a small table that could be retracted when not in use. The ship's single bunk flanked one side wall, a lav and galley along the other. Space was what you'd call tight.

"Sorry about the ship," Qaade said as he squeezed by her.

Torrie eyed him. "Tell me again, why this one?"

He slid into the pilot's seat and started plugging in the lift-off sequence. "Just a precaution. I don't want anyone to follow us. This ship's fast as hell and nearly undetectable by most sensors."

"And it has nothing to do with the fact that there's only one bunk."

He glanced over his shoulder. She could see the mischief in his eyes as he looked at her. "Never crossed my mind. But now that you mention it . . ." He grinned. "Strap yourself in."

"Pirates," she muttered, and harnessed herself into the seat behind him.

"*Freeport* is going to meet us halfway, in about three hours. We won't have a lot of time."

"You're all clear," came Sly's voice over the comm. "Good luck, Qaade."

"Same to you," he replied. Then they disembarked, leaving *Exodus* behind with a quick jump to hyperspace, and Torrie got down to business.

"The way I see it, we should repack those cylinders with the original containers and drop them off at their proposed destination."

"We already used all the Phellium," Qaade reminded her over his shoulder. "We'll have a problem when they look inside."

She shrugged. "We can replace the Phellium units with a placebo, and replicate the rest of the cargo they were expecting. Then we'll follow the shipment using my tracker."

"What if it doesn't lead us to our man? It could be just some other dealer."

She drummed her fingertips on the chair arms. "Maybe Howser can help. He should have some information by now."

"Call him."

"Okay. But it's probably best if you let me do all the talking."

He smiled over his shoulder. "Why? I'm a nice guy."

"He doesn't like pirates."

"If you ask me, he needs to loosen up a little. Maybe get himself a woman."

"How do you know he doesn't have one?"

"Oh, I can tell."

Frowning, Torrie moved from her seat and leaned over Qaade to enter the comm code. The brush of his shoulder against her bare skin startled her, bringing back their killer kiss with perfect clarity. She backed away from him as he studied her, reading her mind.

And there was only one bunk between them.

"Howser here. Torrie?"

She pressed herself back into her chair as Qaade swiveled his seat around to face her. The heated look in his eyes riveted her.

She licked her dry lips. "It's me. What do you have for me on our client?"

Howser sighed. "Not much. They ship regularly and pay on time via automatic funds transfer. All cargo is dropped off at our warehouse on Dun Gali with shipping instructions, and we deliver it to warehouses across the sector. We've never had a problem or complaint. They're an ideal customer."

"Where are they based?" she asked.

"No information."

Of course not. "Can you follow the funds?"

"Already tried. They just lead to an untraceable bank box."

"Have they dropped off any more shipments?"

"Nothing in the past few days. Sorry, Torrie. It's not the easiest thing in the world to dig up info on a client when I'm trying to avoid your six brothers."

She winced. "Carmon called again?"

"What do *you* think? He wants to know where you are, and why we are now officially late with our shipment. I told him we're having engine problems, you're out getting replacement parts, and we'll be up in a day or so." He paused. "We *will* be up in a day or so, right?"

She rubbed her forehead. "Better than that. We're making the delivery tomorrow."

"We?"

She looked at Qaade, and he grinned. "Me and the pirate."

Howser huffed. "I can't believe you're cavorting with a criminal."

Qaade's eyebrows went up, and he mouthed: "Cavorting?"

She narrowed her eyes. "It's important, Howser."

He mumbled, "It better be. Don't trust him, Torrie. Don't believe anything he says. Pirates will do whatever it takes to get what they want. They are manipulative, vicious, greedy bastards. And don't go thinking he'll change, either. Once a pirate, always a pirate."

Torrie watched Qaade's smile grow. "Don't worry. I can handle him. I'll check back with you tomorrow. Keep searching, Howser."

"Okay. Take care of yourself." Then the comm went silent.

Qaade crossed his arms, looking positively pleased.

"Don't say a word," Torrie warned. "Not a word."

Chapter Sixteen

"Welcome back," Brilliard said as Qaade entered his office on *Freeport*. "Where are Torrie and Nod?"

"She's cleaning up. He's trying to figure out who, what and where he is."

Brilliard laughed. "I can't believe she drags that thing around."

Qaade dropped into a seat. "She's soft."

Brilliard cast him a pensive look. "I have to agree with you. But she's got a hell of a right hook." He leaned back, smirking, and laced his fingers together over his belly. "And I couldn't help but notice that the ships you use keep getting smaller."

Qaade smiled. If he could talk her into a true one-seater, he would.

Brilliard added, "The canisters are packed as you asked and ready to go. And since we have nothing better to do these days, I'm going to get you as close to Orland Docks as possible. We just jumped to hyperspace a few minutes ago." He raised a hand as Qaade scowled at him. "Save the argument. It's the least I can do. And this freighter will make better time than *Shooter*. We'll get you close, drop out, set you loose, and jump again. If anyone catches up with us, then we deserve it."

Brilliard was right. *Shooter* was a short-range ship at best. Still, it made him nervous to have *Freeport* so close to the action. Especially with another attack hanging over his head. "How long before we arrive?"

"Three hours. You might want to get some sleep."

He scrubbed a hand across his face. "I just spent the last two hours telling our lost crewmembers' families how they died. And I've done only a few. Sleep isn't what I need."

Brilliard nodded in solemn understanding. "I'll do the rest."

"It's my job."

"No, your job is to stop Chauvet from murdering any more of our people."

As much as Qaade wanted, he couldn't argue with that. He swallowed hard. "Tell them how sorry I am."

"They already know that. Everyone who works this operation understands the risks. We all come willingly."

Qaade felt the guilt to his bones, and for the first in a very long time, real fear. "He's going to hit us again. I don't know where or how. And I'm not sure I can stop him. It would take a small army, and we don't have one."

"We could call in some favors," Brilliard offered.

Qaade smirked. "I don't have that many. Besides, I don't need any more dead friends."

Brilliard studied him for a moment. "Qaade, I've seen you work day and night for our people. I've seen you get food, supplies, credits, whatever it took to keep this place running. I don't believe for one minute that you'll let us down."

Qaade looked at his best friend. They'd been to hell and back so many times . . . what was one more trip?

"You're right, I'll stop him. You just worry about watching your back."

Torrie jogged past the infirmary and cast a quick glance inside as she did. It was nearly empty. Even Coreana was taking a break. Speeding up, she passed the gym and the lounge, letting physical exertion work off her restless energy. She pumped her legs and sped around the exterior corridor of *Freeport*.

Her body hummed with contentment. She always felt at her best when she could move, kick, punch, sweat. When she could do something, *anything* measurable. That made her feel alive and in control of her body, the one tool she could wield with the most skill. Yes, she had her pistols and knew how to handle most other weapons; but her body was hers alone, and running was a liberation, a freedom that only she could understand and enjoy.

"Care for some company?" Qaade's voice startled her as he jogged up alongside her.

She was mildly annoyed at the intrusion. On the other hand, he was wearing only shorts and shoes. Any retort she could muster was firmly trounced by desire.

"Why not? Just thought I'd grab a run before you stuff me into another impossibly small spacecraft for six hours."

"Then you'll be happy to know we have a bit of

time here on *Freeport.* Brilliard took it upon himself to play taxi. You even have time for a nap."

"Not tired," she told him as they headed into her fourth lap. "I need to vent."

"Want to go a few rounds in the holo-ring?"

"The way I'm feeling, I'd kick your butt."

He slid her a skeptical glance. "Why don't you let me and my butt worry about that?"

His words drew a smile from her. He motioned her down a side corridor, and she followed. They ran together in silence, two bodies moving as one force. It was more erotic than it should have been. Must be his bare chest.

By the time she figured out where he was going, it was too late. Free Quarters loomed dead-ahead. She pulled up, and he jogged to a stop. "I thought you'd want to see the girls."

She did. It was the rest she wasn't up to dealing with. "Are they still here?"

"Brilliard didn't get a chance to drop them off before I shut everything down. Come on."

He reached out and took her hand. She let him lead her into the atrium, where a group of small children were playing on recreation equipment. One of them came running when he saw Qaade. The rest pursued, and Qaade met them halfway. They surrounded him, squealing with excitement as he pretended to be a raging giant. Bellowing loudly, he lurched from side to side, his arms wide. Torrie stood agape at his antics, disbelieving her eyes. Little hands, arms and bodies clung to him in a game they had obviously played many times. Finally, the giant succumbed to the tiny monsters, to their absolute delight. And as he lay on the ground vanquished, they mobbed him with glee.

Torrie didn't realize she was laughing until he

rolled up on one elbow and grinned at her. Caught off guard, she had nowhere to hide. For a split second, she knew he saw right through her. But there was no judgment in his eyes, only the crinkle of a smile. Almost like he understood.

Then he was swallowed by a wave of miniature bodies. She could hear his laughter ring out from somewhere under the pile as he struggled to stand, only to be toppled again.

A group of spectators formed around the roiling mass of giggles and screams. Among them were a young woman and two small girls. Torrie almost didn't recognize them. They were dressed in clean clothes, and their long, tangled hair was brushed and cut to manageable length. But more than that, they looked happy and unafraid.

She made her way over to them. Both girls smiled wide when they noticed her. The young woman holding their hands nodded in greeting. She had short hair and expressive blue eyes, making her look even younger than she probably was.

"You are Torrie," she said. "I heard about you. You saved these girls from Wryth."

Torrie grimaced. "Actually, that was Qaade. I was just along for the ride."

The young woman shrugged. "You still helped. I'm Clarita, their caretaker while they are aboard *Freeport*."

"Very nice to meet you," Torrie replied. She kneeled down to the girls' height. "Greetings," she said to them.

The girls didn't answer, but held tight to Clarita's legs. The young woman patted their heads. "They don't talk," she explained.

Torrie's smile faltered. "Will they ever?"

"Perhaps. They were taught not to speak. It takes

a while to get over the fear of punishment. So, until they tell us their names, we call this one Sesha"—she hugged the youngest—"and this one Reva." The girl giggled at several gentle squeezes.

Punishment for talking. Torrie swayed and rose to her feet.

Clarita frowned slightly. "Are you feeling well?"

"Fine," Torrie replied. "Thank you for taking care of them."

Clarita grinned. "I like doing it."

Torrie looked at the waif of a young woman. So much strength was in this small package. "They are lucky to have you."

Clarita's smile widened. "Thank you. But we better go. It's their naptime." She led the girls away.

Qaade came up beside Torrie. "They look good."

She nodded as the trio disappeared through a doorway, then turned to Qaade. His body was covered with scratches and marks from his recent rough-housing, but he looked as though he couldn't be happier. When their eyes met, his expression softened. Was that sympathy? Damn, it was like she'd become completely transparent. She didn't need this.

Before he could tell her something she did not want to hear, she jogged off toward the exit. He caught up, and they settled into a hard pace together through a quiet corridor toward her quarters.

"In a hurry?" he asked.

"If you can't keep up, feel free to quit."

He cast her a bemused look. "Trying to get rid of me?"

She thought about that. Maybe she was. Every time he looked at her like that, it reminded her of all the times she'd walked by someone who needed help and hadn't given any. It reminded her of how much she had and how little others possessed. It reminded her of Zoe, lost all those years ago.

And although she would probably never uncover the facts of her childhood friend's sudden disappearance, deep inside she knew what had happened. Could she have done more? Could she do more now? There had to be a better way than this—saving one life at a time and flying scared. There had to be a way to make it right for everyone.

"I guess that means yes," Qaade said. He slowed to a stop, and Torrie halted a few steps later. It took her a moment to remember what he was talking about, even after she finally focused on him. He stood there watching her, bare-chested and exquisite. His skin gleamed light gold, with muscles in all the right places. Deep pecs, broad shoulders, long, flat torso. She really had to hang around pirates more.

"I'm sorry. My mind was somewhere else," she apologized, and pulled a swath of sticky hair from her face. "Do you have anything to drink onboard this wreck?"

A slow grin crossed his face. "In my quarters." He pressed a panel behind him, and a door opened into a hallway. "After you."

She narrowed her eyes. Somehow she'd been set up, but she wasn't quite sure how. Still, a drink was what she'd asked for, so she followed him to his room. It looked much like hers, with one noticeable difference—the large bed in the center.

Her belly fluttered, which she was sure had everything to do with the half-naked man and big bed in such close proximity. Qaade opened a wall cabinet, his back to her. It was beautiful—like a work of art.

Qaade turned back with two drinks, and he

handed one to her. She took a big swallow and let it burn down her throat, banishing some of the cold that had permeated her body in the past few days.

"Strong," she managed with a cough, the drink stealing the air from her lungs.

Qaade chuckled. "I don't have another kind."

"No, it's fine," she said. "It's good."

A long pause drew out between them before he said, "The numbness will wear out after a while."

She blinked. "How did you know?"

"I see it all the time," he said over his drink. "A new crewmember starts, and they go into shock for a while. But then you get used to it. All the horror."

"I won't. Ever."

His gaze stayed on her for a long time before he set his drink down. Then he moved around behind her and placed his two large, warm hands on her shoulders. She tensed automatically, fighting the shock of intimacy, but he didn't retreat. Instead, his fingers strummed her neck, caressing and kneading.

He muttered, "You don't have a relaxed muscle in your body, woman. Are you always this tense?"

She wanted to tell him: Not tense, on guard. Protected. It was the only way to survive. But as he worked, explanations became less of a priority. She could feel the layers of stress peel away, and she let them. She wasn't in a mood to analyze why.

All too soon, Qaade stopped and turned her around to face him. He took her drink, set it aside and moved in close. Heat from his body enveloped her, penetrating straight to her soul. That's when she noticed his eyes. *Hot* didn't even begin to describe them.

"Qaade—"

He placed his palms on her shoulders and caressed them. "You need to relax."

"Relax? *Relax?*" She couldn't believe his audacity. "You stole my cargo, *purchased* me, dragged me to a ship full of slaves whose collective futures are being held hostage by a psycho who kills one hundred fifty-one people everywhere he goes. How do you expect me to relax?"

"Like this." And he kissed her.

Chapter Seventeen

She gasped, both from surprise and pleasure. But Qaade tasted so good, and she needed to feel so much, she latched on to him with shameless desperation. A red-hot rush pushed everything else away—the visual of the ship, the ghosts of death and the lunatic hunting them. She wanted this, wanted Qaade. To feel connected. To feel alive.

Qaade pulled back, eyes intense, looking surprised himself. Then his mouth possessed hers again, urgent this time. Her hands went to his chest, taking what she must to survive. She nipped his lip, ground her mouth against his and let out a shuddering moan. Fire sparked from the cold ashes of her hopelessness. It burned in her gut while Qaade's hands heated her skin, skimming her breasts and teasing her nipples. His fingers explored with skill and devastating promise.

He broke off his kiss and swore softly. She frowned at the cold vacuum he left behind. No way, he was not doing this to her again. She needed this more than he did.

"Is there a problem?" she asked, her fingers clenched around his biceps, refusing to let go.

"Yes." He led her to the lav. "I need a shower."

She did too, but she was ready to burst into flames as it was. Dousing the fire was not what she'd had in mind.

"Right now? You can't wait two minutes?"

He activated the shower and turned to her. "You could kill a man with a line like that. I can promise you, it'll take longer than two minutes." Then he stepped into the narrow stall fully clothed and tugged her in with him. She sputtered as water soaked her running clothes and shoes.

"Qaade—"

His arms locked around her and his lips claimed hers, silencing all protests. His mouth, the water washing down her and the sounds of desire flooded her senses. She hurtled toward the only thing that had the power to purge the sadness that seemed to fill her.

Save me, she thought.

As if reading her mind, he lifted her leg at the knee and removed one shoe, all the while kissing her senseless. He did the same for the other shoe. She heard it thunk to the floor of the shower, followed by his own shoes.

Qaade's lips left hers for the half second it took for him to peel her tank top off over her head. Then he bent down and tongued one of her nipples. Water misted and became rivulets that tickled down her throat and between her breasts. She lay her head back against the wall and closed her eyes. All she wanted at this moment was this one man. Nothing else mattered as he licked the water coursing across her body and his fingertips caressed the sensitive undersides of her breasts and her ribcage. Amid the overwhelming sensations of steam and touch, she felt his hands at her waist. Her shorts slid down her legs and pooled around her ankles.

She grasped Qaade's hair as his mouth descended slowly along her belly, kissing her navel and nipping at her hipbones. Then she felt his lips at her very core, answering the ache that pounded in her blood. Steam filled her lungs as she quaked at his tender ministrations. Her head rolled back and forth in mindless anticipation. Pressure began to build, from his lips through her body, until she cried out as it took hold and delivered her into rapture. Waves of ecstasy displaced all thought, and she gave voice to them with a heartfelt, "Qaade."

With aftershocks still ravaging her body, she clutched at his short hair and urged him to his feet. No doubt seeing the satisfaction lingering in her eyes, he grinned. Cocky pirate. Payback was going to be a pleasure.

He pressed into her, his mouth devouring thought. "Relaxed yet?" he murmured against her lips.

She slipped her hands inside his shorts and wrapped her fingers around his hard length. "Are you?"

He sucked in a breath and groaned his reply. She watched his head loll back, and his eyes closed as her fingers stroked the soft skin and hard length of him. She shoved his shorts down, and he leaned back against the wall, giving her free rein.

She took it—kissing him from wide shoulders to narrow hips to thick thighs. Firm buttocks and long, sinewy muscle slipped under her palms as she eased herself down him.

C. J. Barry

After thorough exploration of the rest of his body, she finally ran her tongue along his engorged length. A full-body shudder racked him. Then she proceeded with her payback, reveling in the growls that erupted deep in his chest.

That is, she proceeded until he rudely removed her. With one hand, he shut off the water while he pulled her from the shower with the other.

"You know, I wasn't finished," she said.

"Neither was I."

He turned, gripped her by the waist, and they tumbled onto the bed in a mass of slick, tangled bodies. He rolled her onto her back and settled heavily between her legs. His hands held her head still while he kissed her mouth and face. Impatiently, she arched upward, pressing his thick erection between them.

He hissed and froze. She took the opportunity to reach down and guide him into her.

"Now," she whispered. "I want you *now*."

With a guttural sound, he surged into her, stretching her tight and filling the emptiness. For a moment, neither of them moved, savoring the precious bond between them. Then Qaade withdrew and began thrusting in a perfect rhythm. She lost herself to his unrestrained force, which matched her own wild energy.

Did he feel it, too? Did he understand her desperation? Did he know how much she needed him? That thought held for a split-second, disturbed her on a dangerous level. Then, just as quickly, it was gone—smoke in the wind.

Their bodies were so in tune, she felt the change in him and opened her eyes to watch. To her surprise, he was already staring at her, his face etched with passion and pain. He clenched his teeth, picking up the pace and pounding into her with so much power that it took her breath away. In that moment, she realized he needed to escape as much as she did.

A wild inferno grew between them, flames melding and twisting, their tortured minds seeking peace. She felt a climax build, frightening in its intensity. Her nails sunk into Qaade's shoulders, but she couldn't brace herself enough for the violent wave. Just as it ripped through her, he plunged into her body one last time and let loose a primal roar of release. It reverberated through her soul, completing her.

Qaade collapsed, and she felt his heart beating wildly against hers as they both struggled for air. Residual waves of her climax skittered across her body, leaving Torrie drained. She held tight to Qaade, not wanting to lose the moment. Not wanting to go back to reality just yet.

When their breathing eased back to normal, he rolled off her onto his back and tucked her in his arm. The sweet promise of sleep whispered to her for the first time in days. Just before it took hold, she murmured, "I'm relaxed now."

He whispered. "It worked wonders for me, too."

The comm was chiming a steady beat when Qaade finally surfaced from possibly the best sleep of his life. Torrie was wedged beside him, his hand covering her breast possessively, and all was right with the world.

Except for the damn comm. He cleared his throat. "What?"

"There you are," Brilliard's voice rang out. "I've been looking all over for you. Were you sleeping?"

A smile tugged at his lips. "Yes."

"Sorry," Brilliard apologized. "I hate to interrupt a well-deserved nap, but we're dropping out of hyperspace in roughly forty minutes. You might want to gear up."

Back to the real world. "Will do."

"And I can't locate Torrie. Any idea where she is?"

Qaade turned and looked into her peaceful face. "I'll take care of her. Out."

Torrie drew in a deep breath, and burrowed into his shoulder. He'd like nothing better than to wake her slowly, watch while she blossomed in his hands and cried out his name once more. She probably didn't even remember the event, but the sound was ingrained in his mind for all time. He wanted to hear it again. Every day, if possible. Never had he made love to a woman who could match his ferocity and who wouldn't shy from his wild power. If anything, Torrie had relished it.

As he watched her sleep, he realized how damned comfortable he was, even with a full erection. As if this were something he'd like to do on a regular basis. It was more than just making love to Torrie. It was sleeping with her, waking up with her, laughing, crying, and arguing with her. That was a real life. And a family—the yearning for it made his chest ache. There was a reason why he never thought along those lines, and it was called Slipstream. He already had a family.

Still, he'd seen Torrie fight for him, seen the fierce passion in her eyes for a battle she didn't start, and didn't even fully understand. Most of his people were former slaves, and that was why they helped him. She didn't have to be here. She had a choice.

For a brief moment, he wondered what it would

feel like to have her by his side forever. He craved the passion in her heart and ambition in her soul, but even as he thought about it, he realized he could never be with her. He would never risk her. The thought of losing her or having her scrubbed like Fren was unbearable. Nothing would be worse than that. No, his life was too dangerous. He'd let her go. The sooner Slipstream swallowed him up again, the sooner he'd forget how good it felt to hold her in his arms.

He gently shook her awake. Her eyes fluttered open with marked reluctance, and she wrinkled her nose in protest. He ducked an errant elbow as she rolled over. He rolled her back.

"We have to move, Torrie."

She yawned and focused on him slowly. A few blinks later, he saw reality invade her eyes; they clouded over, eclipsing the fiery lover. He hated that. She was right; she would never get used to Slipstream. Maybe that's why she hadn't chosen the life of a warrior, despite her aptitude; she couldn't see past the struggle to the goal.

He leaned down and kissed her. Her fingers stroked his face and she rubbed her thigh against his erection.

"How much time do we have?"

He eased over her, escaping into her heat. "Enough."

Chapter Eighteen

"Coming out of hyperspace now. Get ready to launch," Brilliard said over the comm.

"We're primed," Qaade replied from *Shooter*'s pilot's seat in front of Torrie.

She closed her eyes and listened to the two men exchange departure chatter. Her body hummed along happily, relaxed at last. Maybe it was the sleep, but she doubted it. Great sex. That was better than running. Better than the holo-ring. She could still feel Qaade's hands on her body, his lips on hers.

Never before had a man made her feel like this, and she wondered why. She'd been with other men. Men who were "right" for her. Men her family approved of, who would fit into the business well. Men who weren't wanted in every quadrant of the galaxy. With more than a little fear, she realized the difference. This time, for the first time, her heart was in it. Fully, and without restraint. That was trouble. Big trouble. Because it was too late to take it back now.

She heard a chuckle, and opened her eyes to find Qaade twisted around, grinning at her. "I think I've finally found the secret to keeping you quiet."

She narrowed her eyes. "I don't see you starting any arguments."

He spun his chair to face her, and she noticed they had left *Freeport* and were in hyperspace. Qaade leaned forward and ran a thumb along her knee. The jolt raced up her leg, igniting ready passion in a flash. Damn. How did he do that?

"We'll be at Orland Docks in about an hour," he said.

Torrie licked her lips, and dragged her side-tracked brain to the present. "I should probably contact Howser before we get there."

Qaade nodded in agreement and ordered the comm up. Seconds later, Howser's voice filled the cabin. "Torrie?"

"Greetings, Howser. How's it going?"

"Going?" he grumbled. "Not good, thanks to your damned pirate."

Qaade's eyebrows rose.

"What's the problem?"

Howser gave a loud sigh. "Well, first off, our client cancelled payment because his shipment is late. You can imagine how happy Carmon is about that, and I can't even explain or say anything, because I'm not supposed to know anything. Then I find out that our ships are getting boarded left and right by pirates."

Torrie frowned. "What does that have to do with *my* pirate?"

"Because the tactic is the same—take over the

ship's controls, false core overload, cripple the computer, and board. Only this time, they aren't waiting for the crew to leave. We've had twenty-three employees murdered in the past three hours."

Torrie stared at Qaade, who remained quiet. He withdrew his hand from her knee, a deep scowl lining his face. Her heart was in her throat.

"You don't know it's them," she persisted.

"It's the same damn ship, Torrie. And they identified themselves as the Ghost Riders. They aren't making any effort to hide their identity. I warned you that pirate would never change. He gained your trust—heaven only knows how—and is now taking Masters Shipping down. And just so you know, InterGlax is crawling all over this."

Silence settled between them. Had Howser been right all along? No, she didn't believe it. She'd seen what was in Qaade's heart. Still, a niggling doubt surfaced. Had he set her up? Was he that desperate to save Slipstream?

"Hell," Qaade whispered, and reached to disengage the comm.

Torrie gaped at him as he spun his chair around to the console. "You just cut Howser off," she accused.

"Need to hail *Exodus*."

"Qaade, what is going on?" Torrie asked, her heart pounding against her chest. "Why are our ships being attacked?"

He banged on the comm. "I don't know, but *Exodus* was on a recovery mission. It's not supposed to be out raiding ships, and certainly not murdering people. Something is wrong. Where the hell is Sly?"

The comm crackled. "Greetings, laghato. We meet again. And again, you are too slow. You disappoint me. I thought you were better than this."

Torrie inhaled sharply. *Oh, no. Chauvet was on Exodus.*

Qaade stared straight ahead, the tension in his shoulders visible. "Where is my crew?"

"Ah, yes, your precious crew. I understand that some are alive and cooperating with my men. Some did not fare so well. Their loyalty to you—to the death—was truly touching."

Torrie shook her head. *Sly, Lapreu, the others. . . ?*

A muscle in Qaade's jaw twitched. "What do you want, Chauvet?"

"Want? I want to win the game, of course."

"Then you win," Qaade said. "I'll turn myself over to you if you leave my people alone."

Chauvet laughed heartily. "Much too easy. Besides, I'd still need to destroy Slipstream. I can't allow you to continue to disrupt my slave ring. Not that your little operation impacts my business. It's more of a nuisance, really. I simply can't have slaves believing in you. They need to understand."

Torrie closed her eyes. *Good Lord.*

Qaade replied, "Understand what, Chauvet?"

"That you are nothing but a lowly pirate. You make promises of freedom, but in truth everything you do is inconsequential."

"It's not inconsequential to the people I save."

"Save?" Chauvet laughed. "Lies. You feed them lies, and promises you have no right making to people foolish enough to believe. Freedom is an illusion. We are all bound to something or someone. The only way to truly be free is to be the man at the top."

"And you plan on being that man."

Chauvet's voice changed, became bitter. "I *am* that man. No thanks to you or anyone else. You don't deserve to be a legend. And when I defeat you, all false hope will die with you, as it should."

"You're insane, Chauvet," Qaade said.

The man chuckled. "Perhaps. But then again, I'm sane enough to bring you to your knees. I understand what drives you and what cripples you. Your challenge is to find out what does the same to me. It's your move, laghato. Time is running out." The comm went dead.

A sick feeling came over Torrie. "*Freeport* is next."

"I know," Qaade replied, his voice rough. "We have a leak somewhere."

"On *Exodus*?"

Qaade shook his head and, with measured effort, activated the comm once more. "I don't know. Somehow Chauvet found out a whole lot about my op. He knows our movements, who is where and when. There's only one way that's possible."

"Brilliard here."

Qaade's hands clenched into bloodless fists. "*Exodus* has been taken by Chauvet. I don't know the status of the crew, but I wouldn't count on any survivors."

"Oh, hell," Brilliard said. It was a few moments before he could speak again. "It hasn't been ten hours, Qaade. What is he doing?"

"Don't expect him to follow any rules. He's psychotic. And there's more: he admitted to running the slave ring through this sector."

"Why am I not surprised?" Brilliard muttered. "Is that why he's picking us apart?"

"Not exactly. We're more of a game to him. I don't know where this animal is getting his information from, but we can't take any chances. I want you to head out of the sector. Enter the course yourself, and don't share it with anyone onboard. Block all incoming and outgoing communications except from me. And check that ship from top to bottom for transmitters."

"Understood. What are you going to do?"

"Find him before he finds you."

"And what if the Ricytin doesn't lead you to him? You could be tailing the wrong person."

Qaade's gaze met Torrie's. Her heart ached as she noted the strain on his face. "It seems our only option. Ride low and hard, Brilliard."

"Got it. Good luck, Qaade. Out."

The silence was like heartbreak. Torrie had to believe that Sly and Lapreu were all right. That they would be found. That she and Qaade would be able to stop the madman. But first, they had to locate him. The Ricytin was their only lead. But following the shipment, even with her tracker, seemed such a longshot. They couldn't make any mistakes, or take any chances.

They needed help. Someone they could trust. Howser.

"Orland Docks will be expecting *Ventura2* to deliver that shipment," she said aloud. "Otherwise, it'll look suspicious. I think we should wait for my ship—"

Qaade shoved from his seat and walked the short distance to the lav. Torrie gaped at his abrupt departure, and followed on his heels. He was in the galley getting a drink when she came in. He tossed the glass into the receptacle and gripped the counter, his head bowed.

As she moved close, she could feel his tension—his muscles were rigid and unyielding. He wouldn't look at her, wouldn't show his weakness any more than she would show hers. Watching his silent torment, she ached for him. Who would he lean on?

Torrie ran a hand up his arm and slipped in behind him. He didn't move when her fingers gently rubbed his tight neck. He didn't move when she pressed herself to his back and continued kneading the thick, taut muscles of his shoulders. Through his clothing, she could feel the trembling heat of a man on the brink of detonation. His muscles were like steel beneath her hands, burning with aggrieved energy.

"You can't hold it in forever," she whispered.

A hard shudder shook his body as if her words gave him permission to release. He took a deep breath and held it. She waited as long seconds passed, almost afraid of what might happen when he finally let go. And then he threw his head back and roared like a wounded animal. The plaintive howl pierced her soul and brought tears to her eyes. Over and over again he roared, unleashing his anger and grief for his lost people. She wrapped her arms around his torso and held him tightly, trying to get through to the man beneath the pain. Steam rose from his skin with each tormented outburst, and her tears soaked the back of his shirt. It was like watching him be torn apart from the inside. How could she have doubted him even for a moment?

Finally he stopped, supporting his spent body against the counter. He turned around and pulled her against him in a desperate embrace, burying his face in her hair. His heart beat against hers, strong and steady, lulling Torrie into a trust she'd never felt before with any man. She didn't want to let go of him. Ever. It was the scariest, most vulnerable feeling she could imagine, but somehow she couldn't stop.

As Qaade's arms tightened around her, she felt his desperation, understood it completely. She'd do anything for him and for Slipstream. There was a madman to catch, and she wasn't going to let Qaade face him alone. If they couldn't stop him, *Freeport* would eventually be found and destroyed. And along with it, Qaade. That could never happen.

Ventura2 loomed in his viewport. She'd won. He couldn't believe he'd let himself get coerced into using her ship to deliver the Ricytin. Hell, he couldn't believe she'd talked her tight-ass second in command into going along with it either. In fact, it had been quite entertaining listening to her tell Howser what he was going to do, why he was doing it, and how he'd cooperate or else. Qaade only hoped this Howser didn't decide to take matters into his own hands. Not that it could get much worse than it was already. Guilt and grief shadowed his every move. His world was being ripped apart, one body at a time.

Nod zoomed up beside him. "Can I help?"

Qaade noted, "He's awake."

"And fully charged," Torrie replied behind him. "Do you want me to drive for a while?"

Qaade smiled at the concern in her voice. For him. Even after he'd howled in shame. It hadn't mattered to her. She'd just held on tight, refusing to leave him. He was grateful for her support and courage.

Qaade piloted the ship toward the same shuttle bay he'd used in that raid that seemed like years ago. "I've been here before, remember?"

"How can I forget? That's how this entire disaster started."

Qaade's hands froze over the controls. *How it all started.*

"He set me up," he said quietly.

"What?"

He looked over his shoulder at Torrie. "Chauvet set me up to raid the Phellium. He knew we needed it for Slipstream. And he knew I'd find the Ricytin buried inside."

"If that's true, then he set us up, too," Torrie said bitterly. "It would confirm my theory about Customer 151, but he couldn't have predicted my being here and putting the two together. So where does that lead us?"

"Back to my source."

Torrie leaned forward. "The one who told you I was carrying Phellium?"

Qaade navigated *Shooter* into *Ventura2*'s shuttle bay and cut the engines. "The same. His name's Turk. He must be working for Chauvet, or at least taking orders from him. We're going to pay him a visit." He released his harness and turned to face Torrie. "He operates out of Wryth."

She narrowed her eyes. "Isn't that the most dangerous place we can go?"

"Probably. You got a problem with that?"

A slow smile spread across her face. "Are you kidding? I haven't used my pistols in days." She stood up, but Qaade caught her by the arm. She looked at him expectantly.

"Thank you," he whispered.

Her eyes searched his. "You aren't in this alone. We'll find Chauvet together."

He understood what she was saying. She'd stay to the end. But he couldn't let her. If she stayed, she might die. Of course, if she left, he'd miss her forever. He was a loser either way. "I don't want anything to happen to you. This isn't your fight."

"It is now. He's attacking my people too, remember?" She raised her chin. "And don't you dare try to stop me. I'm not letting him get his hands on Brilliard or those two girls or anyone else aboard *Freeport*. I'll go after him myself if I have to." Then she turned to leave the ship.

He watched her go, and realized that she'd changed. She was still soft inside, but somewhere in the past few days she'd found a way to handle it. Torrie Masters was going to do what she did best: fight. It was what he'd hoped for in the beginning. Now, all he could think about was whether it would cost her everything it had cost him.

He followed her out into the shuttle bay to find her standing between him and the business end of a rifle. The rifle's owner glared at Qaade with piercing green eyes that looked suspiciously familiar. Dark hair hung over those eyes, and the man's big frame dwarfed a nervous-looking man hiding behind him who could only be Howser. Qaade moved up beside Torrie, ready for a fight, and saw the rifle barrel follow him.

"Get away from him, Torrie," the gun's owner growled.

"Macke, put that damn thing down," Torrie snapped, planting her hands on her hips. "And Howser, why didn't you tell me he was here?"

Howser shifted uncomfortably. "He threatened to call in InterGlax when he found out you were with that pirate."

"And I still plan to do just that," Macke said, his gaze pinning Qaade.

Torrie stepped up to him and pushed the tip of his rifle aside. "Don't you dare. It would ruin everything. You have no idea what's going on here."

Macke turned to her, and Qaade noted how his expression changed. He obviously knew her well.

"I know that he's the most wanted man in the sector, a pirate who's killing our people. And since Howser here didn't think it necessary, I already have a call out to Carmon."

"Cancel it," she snapped. "Howser was under my orders."

Macke pointed his rifle at Qaade. "Why are you allowing this? He's a killer."

"He's not behind this, Macke."

"Like hell he's not. I can't believe you're letting him order you around."

Torrie's eyes narrowed, and Qaade knew what was coming. He grinned. This man didn't stand a chance.

She poked him in the chest. "Are you telling me that I don't know what I'm doing? That I can't make a judgment call?"

Macke shook his head in exasperation, as if he'd done this all before. "You know that's not—"

"And you are willing to condemn him before you even hear me out," she continued. "Cancel the damned order!"

He winced and put up a hand. "Now, Torrie—"

"Don't 'now, Torrie' me. You're going to listen to what I have to say. So stow the weapon, or I will."

Macke gave Qaade a hostile glare, pursed his lips and relented, lowering his rifle. But he kept his finger on the trigger.

Torrie turned to Qaade. "Meet my brother."

For the next hour, in her office, Torrie and Qaade did their best to explain Slipstream to Howser and Macke. Howser listened with a scowl, casting Qaade an occasional dubious look. Macke appeared even less convinced. Torrie was going to have her hands full getting them to cooperate. But she would. No one was going to stand in her way. Not even her family.

"So now this Chauvet is going to capture *Freeport*?" Macke asked.

"And the thousand people aboard. It's the only piece left besides us. And I think he's saving Qaade for last."

"And you two think you can take on a guy who obviously has credits to burn and a long reach? This is a job for law enforcement. You know that."

Qaade crossed his arms. "InterGlax is worthless."

Macke fired back, "How would you know? All you do is break every law they have." He pointed to Torrie. "And you're not adding my sister to your long list of casualties, pirate."

"You're the ones who let her out into the big, bad universe," Qaade grunted. "Don't blame me for that."

Torrie put up a hand, cutting off the argument. "Excuse me, I'm right here. Can we stay focused?" She asked Howser, "Did you notify anyone that we are making this delivery?"

"Not yet. I wanted to make sure it actually got here."

"Good. If anyone asks why it's late, tell them we had engine trouble. Then we'll use my tracking system to follow the cargo to its final destination. Meanwhile, Qaade and I will take a ship and head to Wryth to find Qaade's source."

"What source?" Macke asked.

"The one who told me Torrie would be carrying Phellium," Qaade said. "He must have got his orders from Chauvet."

Macke donned a contemptuous expression. It was all Torrie could do to tell him to just deal with the situation.

"I've got a better idea," Macke said, his gaze settling on Qaade. "Chauvet has a problem with Qaade here. Why don't you let him handle it?"

"Because I don't want to," she said with fierce resolve. Macke looked at her in surprise. As much as she loved him, this battle was hers. And she didn't need her brothers, all of whom would be more than happy to step in and fight her battles for her as always. "We helped to create this mess, and our family name is on the line. Someone let that Phellium *and* the Ricytin through our doors. We are as responsible as anyone else."

"Fine. Then we'll find out who did it, and let law enforcement have them."

"That's not going to fix the damage or stop the attacks on our ships. We must find Chauvet."

Macke pointed a finger at Qaade. "And what if InterGlax catches you helping him? You are aiding a wanted man, Torrie. An outlaw. A killer. You'll end up in prison for what? Him?"

She glanced at Qaade. He watched her intently. He might be a pirate, but he was also a good man.

Macke leaned in. "You think Carmon is going to ever let you have a run again when you take pity on every pathetic outlaw in the sector?"

"You don't know Qaade," she insisted.

Macke ignored her. "And what do you think this will do to the family? If you become a criminal, you won't ever be able to see us again."

"No."

Torrie turned at Qaade's voice. "What?"

"I won't separate you from your family," he clarified. "Macke's right. You should get out now. Leave Chauvet to me."

She couldn't believe he was doing this, and in front of her brother. Her anger was so swift, she didn't have time to channel it, let alone control it. After all she'd done for him, after all she'd sacrificed to be here . . . "I'm not going to walk away from these people, Qaade. They need my help, and they're going to get it."

"Chauvet won't stop until he has me. And if you are with me, then he'll destroy you, too."

"Stop trying to protect me. I'm damned sick of it." She swung her gaze to her brother. "Same goes for you. This is my decision, whether or not you or the family approves."

Macke persisted. "You'll lose everything you've worked for. Years of training and preparing. All those arguments with Father and Carmon. I know how hard you worked to get this run. You'll never have another chance."

His words ripped at her heart, but not as much as she thought they would. There was something bigger at stake here than her old dreams: there were lives. For the first time ever, she felt like she was doing something truly important.

"I'm willing to take that risk."

Macke looked at her for a few long moments in disbelief. "Why?"

"Because I can't live with myself if I walk away."

"And what about the rest of us?"

She blinked. "What are you talking about?"

Macke stared at her. "Your family. The people who love you and actually give a damn whether you live or die. The ones you'll leave behind when Qaade here gets you killed. Don't we count more than this Slipstream?"

She didn't answer for a moment, his logic shocking her. How could he say that? Why couldn't he see how much this meant to her? That she could take care of herself—

And then she understood, because with all her heart and her soul, she was doing the same thing for Slipstream: protecting it because it was precious, and because she loved it. She simply couldn't stop herself. Her family loved her, just like that.

"You do count," she said carefully. "More than almost anything. But I have to do this, Macke. It's worth fighting for."

"Now I know who got Father's damned stubbornness," her brother grumbled, but she sensed him relent.

She glanced at Qaade, who was watching her intently but didn't say a word. He understood, too.

She turned back to Macke. "Unless you want to drag more people into Chauvet's dirty little game, you need to call Carmon and tell him you found me safe and sound. Then you and Howser follow that shipment while Qaade and I head to Wryth."

Macke glared at Qaade and said, "If anything happens to my sister, I'm coming after you myself."

Torrie speared him with a look. "And if anything happens to Qaade—like, you call in InterGlax—I'll come after *you*. Got it?"

Macke pursed his lips. "Got it."

Chapter Nineteen

"*Exodus* is ours." Chauvet's words echoed off the walls of the chamber and broke Fahlow's heart. The holo gameboard showed her owner's progress in shades of red. Slipstream's stations, and now *Exodus*. Only *Freeport* remained in blue. And the man, Iaghato.

Urwin replied, "The ship is under our control, and we are hitting as many Masters Shipping targets as possible."

"And Iaghato's crew?"

"A few still won't cooperate. I doubt we'll ever convince them to join us."

Chauvet stared into the holo, red saturating his features. "Execute them at your convenience."

Urwin stammered, "Why not just scrub them?"

"I didn't ask for your input, Urwin. You forget your place. Where is our Iaghato now?"

"Well," Urwin started slowly. "I don't know exactly."

Fahlow watched Chauvet's face freeze in its cal-

213

lous mask, and took bittersweet pleasure from his annoyance. Few had managed to escape him.

"You don't know?"

"No, sir. He hasn't tried to hail us. And our planted sensors aren't picking up any communications or coordinates from *Freeport*. It's like they stopped functioning."

"Then he's found them," Chauvet said. "He knows we want *Freeport*."

"What are your orders for *Exodus*?" Urwin asked.

Chauvet concentrated on his gameboard for a few minutes. "He will run to save his precious slaves, but he won't go too far. He'll hold out hope that Slipstream can be salvaged. Continue to hit targets and leave as many bodies behind as possible. The more that die, the more the Masters family will pressure the woman. She is the weak link, and Iaghato is keeping her around for a reason."

"Yes, sir. Out."

The chamber turned silent except for Chauvet's footsteps as he slowly circled his holo gameboard. "Such an interesting game, don't you think, Princess?"

Fahlow forced words past her heart and lips. "I do not think, my lord."

He threw his head back and laughed, mocking her. Mocking her kind. Mocking decency and justice. She closed her eyes to the world she suffered through, clinging to a whisper of hope that might get her through another day. How much longer would she last? If Iaghato failed, who would save her? Who would reunite her people? It was only for their sake that she had come this far.

Without Iaghato, how long before she deemed death favorable to this living hell?

* * *

Qaade launched Torrie's ship into hyperspace on a course for Wryth. He couldn't shake his restlessness. At least *Shooter* was his ship. In Torrie's world, he was an outsider. He didn't belong here, and he hated having to rely on Howser and Macke, and on their narrow view of right and wrong.

Torrie checked the nav next to him, and bit by bit his anger waned. He couldn't blame her. She'd fought her brother and her first mate to get this far. She was doing the best she could, more than anyone on the outside of Slipstream had ever done before. It wasn't her fault his world had gone straight to hell. But what had it cost her?

"Macke was right," he said. "I should be doing this alone."

She answered without looking up. "Don't you start with me again. I will take complete and lethal personal offense to any insinuations that I'm not capable of making my own decisions."

He grinned. "Believe me, I wouldn't cross that line fully armed. I'm just not sure I can live with myself if you get hurt."

She locked down the nav and turned to him. "I am choosing this road with eyes wide open. Just like you did. Just like Brilliard and all the others. And if anything goes wrong, I don't want you harboring guilt for my choice."

She pulled her long braid over her shoulder and started unraveling it. "I asked Macke to check in every day. Hopefully, that'll keep him happy enough not to call in any more of my brothers."

Thinking back on how protective Macke had been, Qaade wasn't sure he could deal with more than one of her brother's. "How many do you have?"

"Six."

He eyed her. "And you're the only girl?"

She laughed. "You guessed it. And I'm the youngest to boot. So you can imagine the numerous battles I've fought."

"That explains a lot," he said.

"Try it sometime."

His smile faded. A large family pestering each other all the time, squabbles, hugs—he'd love to try that sometime. Unfortunately, it wasn't looking very feasible at the moment. His whole future wasn't looking too promising. "Do you think those two will be able to track the Phellium?"

Torrie gave a small smile. "Howser may be a pain in the ass, but he's good. And Macke is even better. You worried?"

"I'm just thinking if Turk doesn't give up Chauvet, then we won't have many options left. If the trail doesn't pan out . . ."

"Then, what?" she said, deftly untwisting long strands of hair between her fingers.

"Then he wins."

Torrie's hands stilled. "Just like that, you're going to give up?"

The full weight of despair settled over him from every direction. The chances were so slim. For the first time he could remember, he felt hopelessness prevail. "If we can't locate Chauvet, sooner or later he'll find us. He'll find *Freeport*. And I don't care about myself, but I don't want the others to be killed. I'll decommission *Freeport* before I let that happen. There will be nothing left of Slipstream."

For a while, Torrie didn't respond. Then she leaned closer, her loose hair cascading over her shoulder. "Why did you start Slipstream?"

He closed his eyes wearily. "It won't work, Torrie."

"Tell me *why*."

When this woman made up her mind . . . "To save slaves."

"Why do you save them?"

"Because no one else will."

"Why, Qaade?" she fairly yelled.

"Because no one should have to live the way I did," he snapped. His words echoed through the cabin. Memories overwhelmed him; memories of his past. He pushed from his seat and tried to escape, but there was nowhere to go except four more chairs and a drop-down bunk. He stood in the middle of the ship, fists clenched against a demon he'd never be able to escape.

He felt a warm hand caress his shoulder, defusing his aggravation. "Talk to me, pirate."

He wasn't in any mood to dredge up the past. On the other hand, he wasn't in any mood to spar with her. And unfortunately, that's exactly what Torrie Masters would do to get what she wanted.

She moved around in front of him, green eyes searching his before she softly kissed his lips. Tension poured from his body, seeking an outlet, and Torrie was it.

He seized her, pulling her hard against his chest while his mouth took possession of hers. Her arms wrapped tightly around his neck. As their mouths joined, all his restlessness channeled into wild passion.

Torrie's hips pressed into his, drawing a hiss from his lips. He dropped into a nearby seat and took her with him. She straddled his thighs with her strong legs, and he filled his hands with her. Tight nipples pushed through her tank, front and center. He slipped the shoulder straps down, revealing ivory breasts and dusty rose areolas. Torrie threw her head back and moaned when he bent his head and claimed one hard nipple. He drew the tip into his mouth, rolling it gently with his tongue. He nuzzled the soft skin between her breasts, savored their weight and warmth.

He felt her plucking at his shirt, and helped her pull it off him. Once it was discarded, her fingers spread across his chest, exploring and caressing. She pushed him back against the seat and pressed her breasts to his bare chest. She kissed him hard, grinding her hips into him and whittling away at his limited patience.

And he would have done much better if she hadn't reached down and stroked him through his pants. His lips froze over hers as she ran her fingers up his length, stealing what little of his self-control remained. He growled in approval when she unfastened his pants and freed his burning erection.

Laying his head back against the chair, he let her caress every centimeter with maddening skill until at last he could take no more. Tossing patience aside, he lifted Torrie up and tugged her pants off. She kicked them aside, discarded her tank top and settled over him, her eyes locked on his. They were heavy, laden slits of passion. Passion for him. She wanted him and only him. He bared his teeth, surrendering to a primal swell of possession, and bound them together in a ritual older than time.

He gripped the thick muscles of her thighs as she lowered herself slowly onto him, until at last she accepted him completely. His hips flexed, driving deeper still and earning a gasp from her. He lifted her up, then pulled her down again as he drove into her. She took over, meeting him with a frantic rhythm that wiped everything else from his mind. Nothing else mattered—not time, not space, not any previous failure. Just this woman, whom he needed more than air.

She threw her head back, her long hair swaying behind her, lips parted, eyes closed. Then her pace slowed, her breathing deepened and she tightened around him. His own orgasm threatened, but he held on, knowing that she was close. He could almost taste her climax. Seconds ticked by like eternity. Then her cry of release echoed in his ears, moments before his own.

It took a long time for Qaade to surface. His restless energy had ebbed, and he wanted nothing more than to remain like this forever with Torrie wrapped around him. If he could stop time, he'd do it right now. Her head rested on his shoulder as she settled comfortably in his arms, with only bare skin and steamy heat between them.

She sighed softly, and he smiled at his woman. *His woman.* If he said that out loud, she'd probably shoot him. But he couldn't help it, not after she'd given up so much for him and for Slipstream.

All her dreams, all her hard work . . . no wonder she'd followed him earlier. Her cargo was everything to her. He was humbled by her recent sacrifice. It was more than he could ask, especially considering her family. He knew what it was like to lose one's family. He couldn't imagine giving them up voluntarily. Or maybe she didn't realize what she was doing yet. Even if Chauvet was eliminated, Qaade had every intention of starting Slipstream back up and pirating to fund it. He'd be an outlaw, and if she stayed with him, she would be too. The sweet moment turned bitter, and he knew that there was going to be a very difficult good-bye in his future.

She played with the hair on the nape of his neck. "How did you come to be a slave?"

He caressed her long bare back, surprised that he actually wanted to share his past with her. "I was eight when they attacked our rural village. There were only about a thousand of us, and everyone knew each other. Slavers came in the middle of the night with laser cannons and shackles. They burned people out of their houses, slaughtering anyone who wouldn't surrender to them. My father died trying to protect us. They took me, my mother and my sister to a slave hauler, along with the other survivors. I was sent to male quarters, my mother and sister sent to the women's. I never saw them again, but I know they are still alive."

Torrie hugged him, giving him her strength. "I'm so sorry, Qaade. I can't even imagine." Then she pulled back and looked at him with a frown. "You remember them? You weren't scrubbed?"

"They tried. But it didn't work on me like it did on all the others. I'm not sure why. Perhaps a natural immunity. But I knew enough to not say anything at the time, or they probably would have tried again. So yes, I remember."

She searched his face with empathy. "I'm glad."

He brought her hand to his lips and kissed it.

"Then I was sold to a real bastard who enjoyed beating me on a daily basis. When InterGlax wouldn't help me, I figured I'd end up dying a slave. But then a band of pirates raided our ship. They found out I'd been a slave, and they took me in." He grinned at the memory. "Taught me everything they knew."

"Mmm, and you learned well," Torrie noted.

He slipped his fingers through her heavy hair. "I

tried. We were successful enough. Once I saved enough credits, I left and bought *Exodus*, then *Freeport*. Established Slipstream. Recruited a bunch of ex-slaves and old hands to help me."

She smiled, soft and sexy. "They love you, pirate."

His hand paused in her hair when she said the word *love*. Their eyes locked, and Qaade felt the tug of a longing he couldn't hide. Torrie's eyes widened marginally, and he knew he'd given away too much.

She cleared her throat. "So, did you start Slipstream to find your family?"

"I did it to find them all."

She studied him for a moment. "And did you?"

He couldn't believe it. How had he been tricked into talking so much about his past? "There's no way I'll ever save them all, Torrie, no matter how long I keep Slipstream running."

"There's always hope. Sometimes, you just have to remind yourself."

Maybe she was right. He'd spent his life beating the odds, believing in himself—something his parents had always taught. Perhaps he'd retained his memories for a reason. But as he gazed into her compassionate eyes, he realized that sometimes memories were a curse.

Chapter Twenty

Torrie smoothed the skin-tight dress against her body and looked at herself in the mirror. She'd left her hair down and loose. A touch of makeup on her lips, eyes and cheeks added to the sultry look she was going for. But it would be the dress, or lack thereof, that won Turk's attention. Thin shoulder straps nearly disappeared into her skin, the color almost identical, making her look nude at first glance. The plunging neckline revealed deep cleavage, adding to the illusion. Slippery fabric hugged every curve of her torso and hips before flaring at midthigh.

She looked striking and definitely on the prowl. No one would recognize her.

"Can I help?" Nod said, taking his one hundredth lap around the tiny lav.

"I don't think so, Nod, but thanks anyway. I need to do this one solo."

She lifted her skirt and slipped a small pistol into an inner thigh holster. That would be her only protection. That and her transmitter to communicate with Qaade. She was traveling light on this outing.

She took a deep breath, feeling practically naked without her long pistols. But Wryth awaited, along with the hopes of a lot of good people.

Torrie stepped out of the lav, followed by Nod. The lightball zoomed to where Qaade stood facing her, near the ship's pilot's seats. Behind him was the drab green of the private shuttle bay they'd landed in an hour ago.

Qaade glanced up from his datapad. Instant heat registered in his eyes. He tossed the datapad aside, giving her his full, undivided and smoldering attention.

Torrie narrowed her eyes. "Before you get too excited, this isn't for you."

"Like hell it isn't," he said with a devious grin. "How would you like to get boarded by a pirate?"

A smile played at her lips. "Maybe later."

He looked like he was doing his best to see through the dress. "What do you have on under that?"

She crossed her arms. "A loaded pistol, so behave yourself."

He frowned as it finally dawned on him what she was up to. "You aren't wearing that for Turk."

His words irked her. "How else do you think we can get him alone? We discussed this. We agreed that *I* would find Turk and make him an offer he can't refuse."

"I didn't mean *that* kind of offer."

"What kind of offer did you expect? He won't do business with me if he doesn't know me, and if he sees you, this little exercise will be over. You want him to tip Chauvet off?"

"He dealt mostly with Sly. He might not even remember me."

"Are you willing to risk it?"

He looked ready to argue, but he knew she was right. Finally he said, "No. But I'm still going to cover you. If he does anything stupid, I'm stepping in."

It was her turn to scowl. "You step in *when I tell you to*." She patted the comm under the dress. "That's what this is for."

"Dammit, Torrie—"

"Don't, Qaade. Don't treat me like a child."

He looked at her with thoughtful concern, and she was almost afraid he was going to fight her, make her prove once again that she could be trusted to do something this important. But he didn't. "At least take Nod with you."

"I'd rather not. No offense, Nod, but I don't think too many street molls have their own lightballs."

"Fine," Qaade said grimly. Then he scanned her slip of a dress. "What are you armed with?"

She lifted the skirt to her waist, exposing the thigh strap and flat pistol pressed against bare skin. Qaade's silver eyes intensified and unleashed desire deep in her belly. He raised his gaze to hers, full of respect and desire. "You are one dangerous woman."

She smiled and dropped the skirt. "You're just saying that to get me back into bed."

"No, if I wanted to get you into bed, I'd say something like, 'You are the most passionate, sexiest woman I've ever met in my life.'"

Every muscle in her body froze. "Am I?"

His eyebrow rose. "You don't believe me?"

"I prefer to think of myself as . . . capable."

He moved closer, his eyes riveted on her as he

did. His fingertips brushed a stray hair from her face. His hot fingers grazed her cheek, and she inhaled at the rush that triggered.

He traced her jaw line with one finger and lifted her chin. She drew in his scent as he leaned in and kissed her. She sighed.

"Sexy," he whispered. Then he slanted his lips across hers to kiss her again. "Passionate." Once more, his mouth caressed hers. "Beautiful."

Torrie absorbed his words, amazed at the genuine sincerity in his voice and touch. Did he really think she was all those things? No one had ever described her in those terms before. Most of the relationships in her life had been short-lived, with men who fit into her schedule and often wanted a piece of the Masters empire. A few had tried to tie her down, but she knew that there wasn't a man alive who would understand how much she needed her freedom. They'd all been busy trying to keep her safe. Until now.

A pang of yearning pierced her heart. She hadn't thought about what would happen *after* Chauvet was defeated. Would she ever be able to go home? Would she want to? Could she live in Qaade's world? Would she die without her family? Between Slipstream and Masters Shipping, where could she be happy?

Qaade pulled back. He saw her ache before she could mask it with something else. With the warm pad of his thumb, he caressed her cheek. "I know you don't believe me, but that's what I see. You're sexy, passionate and beautiful."

She shuddered. He did see those things, and he wasn't afraid to tell her. She swallowed and said, "I better go."

Qaade released her slowly. "If Turk touches you, kill him."

She blinked at the casual order. "And what about Chauvet?"

"I said, kill him."

Prepared for battle, a masked Qaade slipped behind Torrie as she sashayed into a nameless saloon. Once inside, he found a dark corner where he could watch the action. Under his long coat, he fingered the trigger of his laser rifle. He'd promised to let her handle things, and he told himself he would. But he knew Turk and, more importantly, Turk's many friends. Drawing the man from his crowd wasn't going to be easy.

Even though Qaade couldn't actually see Turk, the informant's usual table was surrounded by obsequious minions who vied for his attention. But all action stopped when Torrie shimmied up to the bar. The sea of unsavories parted in male respect and awe. She leaned over the bar to order a drink from the barkeep, giving every male a mouthwatering view. Damn. That woman had no idea how stunning she was. Even with the shameless dress, she was higher-class than this place had ever seen.

Every eye was on her as she draped herself against the bar and swung a long, shapely leg from side to side. Qaade had to control himself before the possessive, primal urge to protect what was his consumed him and ruined everything. He hated this, hated her playing bait for him. This would be the last time.

A gentle thump against his thigh was following by muffled words. Nod wanted out, but this wasn't the place or time. The man beside Qaade glanced at the bouncing bulge in the front of Qaade's coat.

"Later, my pet," Qaade said, loud enough for all to hear, and put his hand over the impatient lightball. The man's eyes widened and he tripped over his feet to get away.

Qaade chuckled and focused his attention on Turk's table. It took exactly fifteen seconds before one of the man's friends scurried over and invited Torrie to join them. Qaade hardly recognized her slow waltz and the sexy roll of her hips. Gone seemed the woman who could take out the occupants of this room without breaking a sweat. He had to admit, as good as she looked, he preferred her normal appearance.

She approached Turk's table, and Qaade got his first glimpse of the man who'd betrayed him—the pinch-faced, squinty-eyed bastard. He gave Torrie a long once-over that was enough to send Qaade into a rage. She shook her red hair and leaned forward, no doubt giving Turk an eyeful. Whatever she said had the immediate effect of bringing a deep, lusty smile to the man's skinny lips. Then she tossed a marker on the table containing directions to a predetermined rendezvous place.

At last, Torrie straightened and turned for the door, glancing at Turk one more time before leaving. The crowd closed around the table once more. Qaade breathed a sigh of relief. The worst was over and Torrie was still safe. She'd head back to the rented room as they'd planned and wait. Qaade would make sure Turk followed alone.

An hour passed before Turk extracted himself from his friends, but to Qaade's dismay he headed toward the back of the saloon instead of the front. Qaade hadn't expected that. He didn't want to follow and draw attention to himself. Cursing his lousy luck, Qaade exited out the front door and fought through the pedestrian traffic toward the room where Torrie waited.

He tapped his comm. "Turk is on his way. I lost him, and I think he's ahead of me."

Torrie's voice returned. "I'm ready for him."

Qaade clenched his jaw, fighting panic. He'd screwed up, left her unprotected with the traitor. And dammit, he thought as he skirted yet another cart, these people wouldn't get the hell out of his way.

Torrie studied the datapad beside her on the bed. Despite Qaade's wishes, she'd removed and deactivated her comm in case Turk carried a scanner, or worse, Qaade tried to contact her. It was just too risky. Besides, it wasn't like she was unarmed. Her hands rested on her thighs, her pistol centimeters from her fingers. Through the datapad, the hidden holocam she'd planted outside confirmed Turk's lone entrance into the complex of the rental unit. Qaade was nowhere to be seen.

As she slipped the datapad under the bed and adjusted her dress, she told herself she was cool and relaxed. All she had to do was hire Turk to deliver one of her custom containers to Chauvet so they could track it. That was a simple mission, but her belly was flip-flopping like crazy. She'd never tried to play seductress before. Would Turk see through her act?

The door chimed and she walked over to open it. Turk's scrawny body materialized in the doorway, clothed in nondescript layers. He consisted of black eyes, thinning hair, and a gaunt face that broke into a toothy smile when he saw her. His gaze dove to her cleavage. A creepy shiver ran down her spine.

"Hey, baby," he said as he stepped into the room and pressed the panel to securely lock the door behind him. That would be a problem. Qaade was outside, ready if she needed him. He wasn't going to be happy about being locked out, especially since she'd shut off her comm. But she couldn't very well unlock it without raising suspicion.

Turk didn't waste any time, reaching for her like a prize. She sidestepped him and said, "Your boss sent me."

He stopped dead, a look of shock morphing his lust into disbelief. She waited. If Qaade was wrong, then this conversation would go nowhere fast.

"Who?"

She raised her chin. "Have you forgotten who pays your bills?"

Turk crossed his arms, still looking skeptical. "He usually contacts me via comm."

"He wanted me to meet you . . . personally."

"Really?" Turk asked, his beady eyes nearly disappearing in a squint. "And what was my last job?"

A test, she realized. "Does a certain load of Phellium sound familiar to you?"

The man's face brightened. "It does," he said.

Yes, we have contact.

Then Turk scrutinized her from head to toe. "What exactly do you do for Currier?"

Turk knew Chauvet as Currier? Torrie smiled. She supposed that made sense. "You have to ask?" She strolled around Turk. "He has another job for you."

There was a noise on the other side of the door, and Torrie stiffened. *Qaade.*

Turk frowned. "What was that?"

She shrugged. "Here? Could be anything. So, are you interested in hearing the job?"

There came another bang, and Turk turned his gaze from the door to her. He reached into his jacket and pulled out a pistol. "What *is* this?"

She resisted the urge to draw her own. *Stick to the plan, Torrie,* she told herself. "The job, Turk?"

The door slid open and Qaade burst through with Nod. Turk lifted his weapon, but Qaade was already on him, propelling them both onto the bed. Torrie growled and hit the door panel to close it before anyone else arrived and really screwed things up.

She pulled her pistol and aimed it at the two men wrestling on the bed. "Drop it, Turk," she said. Both men froze and turned to her. She held the pistol aimed at Turk's crotch. "Now."

The man tossed his pistol aside, and Qaade checked him over for more weapons. After relieving Turk of his entire small arsenal, Qaade walked over to her. She glared at him. "I'm not sure who I should shoot—him or you. What the hell do you think you are doing?"

Qaade's silver eyes narrowed under the black mask he wore. "I thought you needed help."

Turk's eyes widened in recognition of Qaade's voice. *Oh, great.*

"Did I ask for help? Did I contact you?" she snapped.

"Your comm wasn't on. I didn't know what was happening in here," he replied, having the nerve to sound offended.

"So, naturally you assumed that I was in trouble and needed rescuing."

He had the grace to grimace.

C. J. Barry

She added, "For your information, things were going perfectly. Now, they aren't."

"What is this?" Turk asked, and looked at Qaade. "And what are *you* doing here?"

"Expect me to be dead by now?" Qaade asked, his rifle trained on Turk.

The man blinked furiously. "What are you talking about?"

Qaade said, "You fed me bad info."

Turk looked from Torrie to Qaade. He stabbed a finger in the air. "My info is always right."

Torrie asked, "And you get a lot of it from Currier?" She gave Qaade a warning look regarding the alias.

Turk shook his head. "Well, no. He contacted me one-way, gave me some intelligence and dumped a shitload of credits in my account. Look, I just passed it along."

"He paid *you* to give me information?" Qaade asked.

Turk shrugged. "Hey, I'm not gonna complain."

Qaade's tone turned serious. "A lot of people died because of you."

Turk ran his hands through his sparse hair. "I don't know anything about that."

Qaade cast Torrie a quick glance, and she could see the concern in his eyes. Maybe Turk didn't know anything.

"New transmission received," Nod announced.

Torrie turned to her lightball, who was hovering just behind them. "What transmission?"

"Authorization to play?"

"No, wait—," Torrie said. But Nod had already begun.

"Hey there, Qaade. This is Brilliard. We're in *Free-*

232

port waiting for you just off Wryth. Why don't you join us?"

Torrie sucked in a quick breath. "Nod, cut comm now!"

She looked at Turk, knowing it was too late. Judging by the look in the informant's eyes, he'd heard enough.

"Damn," she muttered. "Now what?"

"Let him go," Qaade said.

Torrie turned to him. "Are you insane?" she mouthed.

"He doesn't know anything," Qaade said. His silver eyes shone in his black mask. "Trust me."

Chapter Twenty-one

Qaade punched the controls and the ship disembarked Wryth. It was bad enough he'd had to let Turk go without getting the information he wanted, but to have Brilliard screw up like that . . .

Torrie checked the scanners. "*Freeport* is ten minutes away. And quit banging on my console. Take your frustrations out on your own ship."

He ignored her comment. "Right out in the middle of the shipping lane. What the hell is Brilliard doing? It's not like him to be so sloppy."

"I don't know," she said, shaking her head. "But I'm sure he has a good reason."

He gave her a hard look. "I can't think of one, can you?"

"He would never do anything to jeopardize Slipstream."

"Well, he has now," Qaade snapped. "How long do you think it'll take Chauvet to notice *Freeport* sitting here for the picking?"

Torrie crossed her arms. "Do you trust anyone to do anything besides you?"

"I don't know what you're talking about," he said, even though he did.

"I'm talking about Brilliard. I'm talking about what happened back there. You blew our op."

He looked at her then, and grimaced at the fierce anger in her face and the fire in her eyes. "I just wanted to back you up."

"We had a plan. I don't recall your storming in to rescue me being part of it."

"I thought you were in trouble," he said. "We were supposed to be partners. I was just covering for you."

"I told you I could handle it. Why didn't you believe me? What do I have to do, Qaade? Tell me, and I'll do it." She gave him a look of hurt and frustration. It occurred to him that Torrie had spent a lot of time trying to prove herself, and all he'd done was deny her his trust.

He shook his head. "It's an old habit I'm finding very hard to break."

Her eyes remained hot. "You're lucky I didn't shoot you when you came through that door. You could have been anyone."

She was right. "I appreciate your not shooting me."

"For now. I make no future promises," she said with little emotion in her voice. She added, "Of course, I also don't understand why you just let Turk go. He knows about *Freeport*. He knows who you are. He'll call Chauvet."

"Exactly."

The look on her face was priceless. "Have you lost your mind?"

"I slipped a tag on him when I let him go. I knew

he wouldn't have given us anything voluntarily, and something tells me Chauvet wouldn't divulge his location to an idiot like Turk anyway. He didn't give him his real name."

Torrie's expression changed to one of admiration. She smiled wickedly. "You have a positively devious mind."

He eyed her. "Tell me you like that."

"You have no idea." She wet her lips, distracting him completely. "What about *Freeport*?"

That one word reminded him of his duty. "As soon as we dock there, we'll jump *Freeport* to hyperspace. Hopefully, Chauvet won't have time to catch us."

"Transmission," Nod chimed.

Qaade turned to him. "Turk?"

"Yes."

"Excellent. Run the trace, Nod."

The transmission came through Nod, and Turk's misery was unmistakable. "He just left with that bitch after he got a call from some guy called Brilliard. He said *Freeport* was sitting just outside Wryth waiting for them. What's *Freeport*?"

"I'm paying you for information, not questions, Turk."

Qaade's blood turned cold at the sound of Chauvet's voice. His ruse had worked.

Turk replied, "Well, I expect compensation for this, because they weren't too damned polite. I'm lucky to be alive. I thought you were going to take care of them."

"Do not make the mistake of thinking me a fool, Turk. I will dispose of them in due time."

The comm went dead.

"Bastard," Torrie summarized eloquently. "Nod, did you get a fix?"

237

The lightball bobbed slowly. "A partial trace was completed."

"Where did the trace end, Nod?"

"Sector 28-A443."

"It's better than nothing," she noted, but Qaade shared her obvious disappointment. Without a complete lock, they couldn't even tell if Chauvet was working from a planet or a space cruiser. He could be anywhere.

Torrie asked, "Should we go back for Turk, since he obviously had a memory revival in our absence?"

Qaade put the ship into high gear. "No. He doesn't know where Chauvet is either. Besides, right now I have an ops chief to chew out."

Chauvet was closing in on laghato, and Fahlow could feel the light in her soul fading. Every day, her cage robbed her of the tactile world she once knew. Grass, trees, the creatures of her world—all were just the remnants of a former life. Her fingers clutched at the hard metal bars. Her feet padded over unforgiving stone. Her skin felt only cold.

There had been no way to escape from the insidious technology she couldn't comprehend. Her peaceful people and their simple way of life had not prepared her. She closed her eyes and remembered sun and warmth, the lushness of a living world and nature's harmony. But she couldn't hide in her good memories forever. They weren't enough to sustain her if laghato failed. Already, Chauvet had ordered his spies to track the final pieces. Once he had them, he would win.

"So, laghato surfaces," Chauvet said aloud, banishing for good her sweet memories. She opened her eyes to see him strolling around the holo image.

He stopped, and addressed the computer. "Move

the Qaade and Torrie pieces to *Freeport* just off Wryth Station." The pieces shifted as ordered, and Chauvet looked on, supremely happy. He laced his fingers behind his back. "The end is at hand, Princess. What do you think would be an appropriate end for laghato?"

Fahlow forced the words past her breaking heart. "I do not think."

He smirked at her response. "No? Not even a good-bye for the great legend?"

She swayed under the weight of her hopelessness. She would never see her world again. After thousands of years, her people would die off, destroyed and enslaved. All because of this man who considered life and death a game.

Chauvet paced. "Do not fear, Princess. I have the perfect end." He stopped before his gameboard, a grin blossoming on his face. Fahlow waited for the blow that would sink her into darkness forever.

"Computer, move the *Exodus* piece to take *Freeport.*"

Torrie's ship had barely touched down before Qaade was out of his seat and heading for the exit with enough controlled anger to keep even her out of his way. She followed in his wake. Nod brought up the rear. "Now, Qaade, give Brilliard a chance to explain," she called.

"I'll give him exactly three seconds before I kill him," Qaade replied. He jumped from the hatch.

Brilliard was waiting for them, grinning like a lunatic, and Torrie's jaw dropped at his obliviousness. *Run, Brilliard, run for your life.*

Qaade got into his ops chief's face with all his fury. "Explain."

Brilliard leaned around him and said, "Hey, Torrie. Nice to see you again."

Hesitant, she waved back. "You too, Brilliard. Whatcha been up to?"

He shrugged. "You know, same old stuff. Hey, Nod."

The lightball danced to his side. "Greetings."

"Brilliard," Qaade ground out in warning. "I want a goddamned explanation as to why you are parked in full view of Wryth and every goddamned ship that passes through here."

A wide smile spread across Brilliard's face. "How else are we going to get Chauvet's attention?"

Torrie watched the muscles in Qaade's back tighten. He was on the verge of an explosion.

"What?" he hissed.

"I said, how else—"

Qaade cut Brilliard off. "I heard you. I gave you direct orders to leave the sector. What the hell are you doing?"

Brilliard only grinned. Then he turned and headed out of the bay with Nod in tow. Qaade stormed after him. Torrie threw up her hands and ran after them all. This made no sense.

She reached the center atrium of the ship and stopped dead beside Qaade. Before her stood a sea of burly men, all armed to the teeth. A chorus of whistles went up when they spotted her and her barely there dress, but she hardly heard them; she was too busy gawking at the arsenal displayed by a thousand men who looked like they knew how to fight.

One of the men stepped forward with a broad grin. His hair was white and pulled back into a long, thin braid. Blue eyes set off a ruddy complexion and rough stubble. He spoke with a thick, rich accent.

"We hear you're in need of a few good pirates."

A beaming Brilliard settled into a chair across from Qaade, Torrie and Zergot in his office. Qaade realized he'd never hear the end of this little coup. Still, it was good to see his old captain again, even under the circumstances. Qaade noted that Zergot looked older now, but the man's brash smile hadn't faded, and neither had his passion for beautiful women. However, Torrie was taking the man's overt charm in stride. In fact, Qaade noted with some consternation, she seemed to enjoy having her hand kissed twenty times.

Qaade cleared his throat. "Brilliard. Explanation."

His ops chief broke into a wide grin. "Don't worry, the slaves are safe. Zergot here found them good temporary homes until we can regroup."

Qaade looked at Zergot, who only had eyes for Torrie. "Thank you for taking care of my people," he said. He jerked his head toward the door. "Where'd you find all those men?"

Zergot's eyes gleamed. "Have you ever known a pirate to give up the chance to attend a party?"

"Especially if there's women involved," Qaade noted, looking at Torrie and Zergot.

Qaade's old captain's deep rumble of a laugh filled the room, and Zergot gave Torrie's hand a final kiss. Then he turned his chair around to face Qaade. The corners of his eyes crinkled as he said, "They're friends of mine. Friends of yours. Even a few enemies. You know how we all feel about the slave trade. Most of these boys were slaves themselves at one time." He shrugged. "All I did was put out the call after Brilliard contacted me. They came running. Got twenty ships in the wings. All of them itchin' for a good fight."

"Another two hundred are slaves we've rescued over the years," Brilliard added. "They found out about Slipstream shutting down through its conductors. I guess they figure this is their way of repaying you."

Qaade swallowed hard at the lump stuck in his throat. They'd all come to his rescue. It was more than he'd ever expected. "I appreciate it." Then he glared at Brilliard. "Of course, it'd be nice if I'd known."

The guilty party raised his hands. "Before you have me shot, let me explain. You said yourself that Chauvet wants *Freeport*, right?"

"So you just figured you'd give it to him. We already discussed this. Chauvet has his own private army. If we don't have enough men or ships, he'll wipe us out. I don't want any more needless deaths in my name."

Brilliard grinned at Zergot. "Deaths? He'll have to get past us first."

"You're setting him up?" Torrie asked.

Brilliard shrugged. "Of course. He's done it to us enough."

"You should have talked to me first," Qaade complained.

"Right," Brilliard huffed. "I can tell you how the conversation would have gone. I'd say 'Let's do it,' and you'd say 'No,' and that would be the end of the discussion. You're a good man, but you hate to share the risk."

Qaade scowled. "Slipstream is—"

"Ours," Brilliard finished with rare tenacity. "All

of ours. Slipstream belongs to the freed slaves and the people who run it. It's a team effort. It has to be. Because if it's otherwise, if you suddenly disappear from the picture, then Slipstream collapses and Chauvet wins more than just this battle. So that means you get this help whether you want it or not."

Qaade pursed his lips. Damn. He hated Brilliard's words because he knew they were true. The last thing he wanted was for Slipstream to die. It was more important than him. He had to think about tomorrow, next month, next year. Slipstream needed to live on, even if its operators changed.

The three of them watched him: Zergot his past, Brilliard his present and Torrie . . . his future? His future. Their eyes locked, and Qaade saw the graveness in her face. Even she saw what he'd been doing and what he should do. But she wouldn't tell him what path to take, any more than she would want him to tell her. So here they all were, waiting for him to come to his senses. A team effort it was. He'd agree for the sake of Slipstream, but it was hell admitting it was bigger than him.

Then, in that moment, hope rose from the ashes. He breathed deeply as if a great weight had been lifted from his heart, a weight now shared by these people who cared about Slipstream and about him. His family was gathered around him. He vowed he wouldn't let them down. Not this time.

Qaade tapped his fingers on the tabletop. "It was a good idea, Brilliard."

Relief crossed Torrie's face, and she gave him a small smile. For some reason, making her happy helped allay Qaade's worried heart. Just one smile, that's all it took. He committed it to memory for all time, surprised how it warmed his soul.

Brilliard slapped his hands on the table. "So, now we just wait for Chauvet to make a move."

Qaade nodded. "Turk heard your message on Wryth and contacted Chauvet directly. We won't have to wait long for him to find us."

Zergot leaned back in his chair and smiled. "Good. Can't wait to meet the bastard."

Chapter Twenty-two

While Qaade reacquainted himself with a thousand of his closest and dearest pirate friends, Torrie returned to her ship to change into something more substantial. The thin fabric of her dress had made her feel vulnerable, even with the comforting feel of her pistol against her thigh. She couldn't pinpoint why the outfit bothered her so much. Maybe it was because she liked how the fabric wrapped around her legs when she walked, and the way Qaade's eyes narrowed with longing whenever he looked at her. It made her think about staying, about tomorrow. And she wasn't ready to do that just yet.

She closed the hatch behind her, and was surprised to see that Nod had tagged along.

"Can I help?"

She tapped him lightly. "We need to get you a job, Nod."

"I have a job," he responded.

She tilted her head and looked at him. "What is that?"

"Watching you for my report."

Report? She didn't like the sound of that. "Who asked you to watch me?"

"Macke. He requested that I track your location and activities so that I could update him on a regular basis. He said you wouldn't mind."

She growled. *Brothers.* "I'm overriding those orders as of now. No more updates to Macke."

"Overridden."

Torrie pulled her street clothes out of a cabinet and started changing. "Computer, comm on. Hail Howser." Seconds later, Howser answered. "Greetings, Torrie."

"Same to you, Howser. Where's Macke?"

"On the bridge. I'll get him online."

"Do that. What's the latest?"

"We dropped the cargo and tracked it to a small moon in the Altae solar system. We're hanging back far enough to slip any sensors. The cargo hasn't moved in over twelve hours, so I have to believe this is the final destination."

"Computer, bring up Altae solar system," Torrie ordered as she tugged on a top and moved to the front of her ship.

The holodeck sprang to life and displayed a minor moon revolving around a giant planet. Torrie slipped into a seat while a list of stats scrolled by.

"This is Sector 29?"

"Correct. Problem?"

She pursed her lips. "Chauvet's not there. We were only able to get a partial trace on his last transmission, but it was in the opposite direction. So much for following the shipment."

"Maybe he's not here, but something strange is

going on. We're only detecting a few large facilities on one region of the moon. The rest of the bodies in the solar system are uninhabited."

"So?"

"So, there's a whole lot of traffic to and from this moon. Big freighters and haulers, most of which don't look like they'd pass a sub-class inspection. I'd sure like to know what they are all doing down there."

Torrie frowned. "Drug traffic?"

"If they were running drugs, they'd have nicer ships and that Ricytin would have moved by now."

Torrie stared into the holo image and uttered the only thing that made sense. "They're using it. This must be where they process the slaves."

"You really think so?"

"It fits."

Howser sighed. "Great. How soon can you be here?"

She glanced toward the exit. "Not soon enough. We can't go anywhere until Chauvet finds us. We're playing bait."

"Bait? Macke will love that. So what do he and I do? Sit here and watch?"

Torrie rubbed her forehead. Every ship that pulled into that processing plant might be delivering innocent people to memoryless lives of servitude. She couldn't let that happen. Still, Qaade had all he could handle with Chauvet.

She made the only decision she could. But the betrayal tasted bitter as she said, "Call InterGlax, Howser."

"Finally," he said in obvious approval. "It's about time. I'll contact the local—"

"No, not local," she interrupted. "Contact General Lundon directly. No one else, Howser, you understand? Tell him that I am requesting a full investigation be launched on a suspected slave processing plant using Ricytin."

"Why Lundon?"

"Because I know he can be trusted. He was the man who cleared Zain."

"And how do I explain how I uncovered this? I can't exactly tell him I tracked the highly illegal drug shipment of a Masters client."

She swallowed. "You tracked Qaade's ship after it hit one of ours."

"No kidding? What's Qaade think of this?"

Her heart ached. "He doesn't know. This is my call. Not a word about this to him, Howser. Not a word."

"Understood." Howser hesitated. "And what if Lundon doesn't believe me?"

"Then tell him Masters Shipping is requesting the investigation. Tell him the truth."

"Oh, no, you don't," Macke said over the comm. "You aren't bringing the family into this."

Torrie leaned back and crossed her arms. "So nice of you to join us, Macke. Next time you want to keep tabs on me, you can call me yourself. My lightball is busy."

She heard him grumble. Then he said, "I'm sorry. I didn't think you'd bother to keep in touch."

"I said I would. I'm an adult, Macke. This is how adults treat each other."

"Maybe so, but you can't use the Masters name to bring in InterGlax, Torrie. Not without Carmon knowing. He would never approve."

Macke didn't understand. How could she make him feel the desperation and determination she did? She took a breath. "Macke, do you remember Zoe?"

"Who?"

"She was a playmate of mine when I was seven. Short brown hair, sad eyes, a slip of a girl. Part of the family who lived next to us for a short time."

Macke didn't say anything at first. Then, "I remember her. She was a servant."

Torrie corrected him. "She was a *slave*. She told me her family was free once, taken from their homes and sold into slavery."

"That's illegal, Torrie."

"How would anyone know? Owning servants on our planet is perfectly legal."

"We never owned any," Macke said.

Torrie pursed her lips. "Do you know what happened to Zoe?"

"No, I don't."

"She disappeared one day," Torrie said. "Just vanished. When I asked Mother, she told me Zoe died. She didn't know how. I did."

Macke sounded exasperated. "Torrie, that was twenty years ago. Those things happen."

"I didn't tell anyone about the bruises on Zoe's back and arms. I didn't try to help her when she told me what her owner was doing to her."

"Hell, Torrie," Macke said. "It's not your fault. You were just a little girl yourself."

"No, that wasn't it. I knew what was going on, but she begged me not to interfere. She told me they would punish her more. So I didn't say a word, not even after she died. I was too ashamed." She clenched her fist. "But I'm not doing that this time. I'm not turning my back on someone who needs me."

"It won't bring Zoe back."

"No, but maybe it'll save other children. And there are others, Macke. I've seen them. I've held them. I've touched their scars. I can't quit now. If you won't help me, I'll find a way to do it alone."

"Damn." Macke gave a sigh. After a few minutes, he came back on the line. "You aren't alone, Torrie. You win. Again. If you weren't my sister, I'm not sure my ego could handle it."

She smiled wearily. "You have to find a way to stop that traffic."

"Don't worry. I've got my orders, boss. I'll keep you updated."

"And, Macke . . . ?"

"Yeah?"

"Thanks."

"No problem. What's a brother for, if not to share a prison sentence with his only sister?"

She'd changed clothes. As she strolled toward him on *Freeport*'s bridge in tank top and pants, with twin pistols strapped to each thigh, part of Qaade was relieved. Probably the part that had been keeping an eye on a thousand devious pirates who'd taken an instant liking to her and her dress.

However, the part of him that wanted to get her alone, to peel that dress off one centimeter at a time and worship every strip of exposed skin, was sorely disappointed. Of course, he could do the same thing with what she was wearing now. That thought sidelined him for a few satisfying moments. The woman beneath the clothing was still the same.

Nod zipped over to his side. "Can I help?"

"Not right now."

It wasn't until Torrie stood beside him that he noticed the shadows in her eyes. She looked drained. "Are you all right?"

She glanced around the bridge at the skeleton crew. "I'm fine. Any sign of Chauvet yet?"

Qaade checked the scanners and smiled. "Nothing yet. Don't be surprised if he doesn't let us know he's coming, though. I moved us out of the shipping lanes so we don't draw a lot of attention when he finally does show himself."

"You think he'll come himself?"

"I don't know. It would make things easier . . . but I doubt he'll get his hands dirty."

She leaned against the console and rubbed her arms. "What are you going to do when they show up?"

"Hope they don't blow us to hell before our plan works."

Torrie cocked an eyebrow. "Our plan?"

He grinned. "If they want me, they'll have to come and get me. We'll give a little fight and then surrender. Once they link up, we'll be able to board their ship."

Torrie looked skeptical. "The pirates?"

"Yes. Trust me, they are more capable than they look."

"That's not the problem. You can't just jam them through a link-up. All they'd have to do is shut the doors. We'll need to be a little more subtle."

"I've been thinking about that." Qaade braced himself against the console. "We can lure some of them out of their ship, then cut them off and attack."

"It won't be all of them. Some will stay behind," Torrie noted.

Qaade replied, "Exactly. What we need is to get someone aboard their ship to give us access to it. That way, we can control their comm, doors, and weapons. It has to be someone they wouldn't notice or view as an immediate threat." He looked at the lightball bobbing over Torrie's shoulder.

Torrie grinned when she realized what he was thinking, and she said, "He'll be *so* happy."

"I didn't want to risk him without asking you. You think he can handle it?"

"I'll explain it all to him. No one would pay any attention to him if he slipped aboard during their raid. If he can gain access to the systems, we'll have a good chance. Then what?"

Qaade replied, "If Chauvet's onboard, we'll deal with him then. If not, the ship's records or crew should know where to find him. We'll force his people to notify Chauvet that they've captured both *Freeport* and Iaghato. He'll want to get his hands on me immediately."

Torrie grimaced.

Qaade continued, "Once we arrive, it'll be an all-out battle. And before you say anything, Chauvet is going to die—by my hand if necessary."

She blinked. "I'd rather see him pay for what he's done."

Qaade shook his head. "Forget it. I'm not handing him over to InterGlax. He'll buy his way out. I want him dead and gone forever."

He could see the disapproval in her face, but he wouldn't change his mind. Not for her, not for anyone. Too many of his people had died because of this man.

"And what if there's someone else to step in for him? Or two more? There will always be someone to replace Chauvet. Are you going to kill them all?"

"If I have to," he said harshly.

"Then you'll turn yourself into a butcher just like Chauvet."

His teeth clenched in fury. She didn't understand. "I have my way. You have yours. When you get back to your own ship, you can make the decisions."

Torrie's eyes narrowed—in disappointment, no doubt. Or had the words *your own ship* affected her as it had him?

The sensors came alive, and the air was filled with chatter.

"Sir, we have incoming," the navigation officer shouted. "A single vessel has just dropped out of hyperspace, and it's heading straight for us."

Qaade scanned the approaching ship for weapons and capabilities, but grimly he realized that he already knew them. A mix of anticipation and dread filled him.

Torrie moved close. "What is it?"

He closed his eyes. "He sent *Exodus*."

Chapter Twenty-three

Exodus fired first, and *Freeport* absorbed the plasma blasts with a dimming of the bridge lights.

"Nice guys," Brilliard muttered, taking a seat at one of the weapons stations. "No 'Great to see you again'? No 'Surrender or else'? Not very sporting, are they? Maybe they don't want you alive, after all."

Torrie and Qaade exchanged a glance, knowing better. Chauvet hadn't come this far just to blow them to bits. He wanted to watch them suffer.

As *Freeport*'s bridge became a war room around them, Torrie gave Nod instructions and the list of possible access codes Qaade had relayed to her. Hopefully, one of them would work so they could regain control of *Exodus*.

"Shields holding," yelled one of Qaade's crewmen.

Another blast, and *Freeport* lurched to one side. Torrie grabbed on to the console. "Are we going to fire back?"

Qaade focused on the virtual holodeck image of

the battle, where *Exodus* was circling *Freeport* in real time. "Brilliard, hit them with something that appears to be retaliatory but won't damage *Exodus* too badly."

"Got it," the ops chief replied, and Torrie watched laser torpedoes hit *Exodus* broadside, causing little effect. However, the shots unleashed a heated exchange of fire that had the *Freeport* bridge crew scrambling. Damage reports began coming in.

"Outer shields at twenty percent," Brilliard said.

Qaade contacted Zergot below, via the comm. "Ready your men. We're surrendering as soon as we lose shields."

"About damned time," the old pirate responded. "My men are about ready to burst."

Torrie turned to Qaade. "I'm going too. I'll need to move Nod into position."

His silver eyes locked on hers. "I know you won't like this, but I'd rather you didn't. It's going to get nasty down there."

Normally, she'd be angry. Normally, she'd tell him to stop treating her like a child. But the fear in his eyes drew a reaction from her that she hadn't expected. She inhaled at the sharp spike to her heart. He was afraid of losing her, just like her brothers. And she felt the same way about him. No matter how good he was, or how much she believed in him, if she lost him—

She stepped up, wrapped her arms around his neck and kissed him with the depth of her very essence. He gripped her with equal desperation. Then she whispered against his lips, "I'll be careful, I swear. Promise me you will too."

The lights on the bridge browned out, and she could just make out the torment in his face.

"I promise," he whispered back. "I need you."

His words lingered between them, binding them together. If it weren't for the fact that they were about to go to war, she'd never release him. He needed her. She doubted he'd ever said that to anyone in his life.

Freeport buckled under another salvo, and Torrie extracted herself to do what she must to save the man she loved and his world. She took one last look at him amid the mayhem, and ran for the link-up.

"This is Qaade Deter, captain of *Freeport*. Stop your attack. We are surrendering," Qaade said after he'd hailed *Exodus*.

A few seconds later, a familiar voice responded. "If it isn't Cap himself."

Brilliard unleashed a slew of curses.

"Urwin. What a surprise," Qaade said. "Didn't we pay you enough?"

"Not even close. I'm surprised no one sold you out long before now."

"Unlike you, they have honor."

Urwin laughed. "You wouldn't say that if you saw how eager they were to switch sides. In fact, I've got Sly here manning the nav systems. He's been real cooperative."

Brilliard raised an eyebrow, and Qaade smiled. Sly wouldn't switch sides unless he'd been scrubbed, but if he were scrubbed, he wouldn't know how to operate navigation.

Qaade replied, "I'm sorry to hear that. I could use his help right about now."

"You'll have plenty of time to catch up with your old friends. My orders are to bring you in alive. Of course, that part's up to you. Don't matter to me how I drag your ass back to Chauvet."

Qaade opened up the comm channel so Zergot and his men could hear the proceedings. "I'll turn myself over to you without a fight if you let *Freeport* go."

There was a long pause before Urwin responded. "Deal. I'm sending a shuttle over to pick you up."

Not in *my* plan, Qaade thought. "And as soon as you pick me up, you'll obliterate *Freeport* and everyone aboard. I don't think so."

"Then take a shuttle over here," Urwin snapped.

"Can't do that either. You damaged our bays. If you want me, you'll have to link up. Then I don't have to worry about you destroying *Freeport* without destroying yourself in the process."

Urwin sounded frustrated. "Fine. Ready for linkup. I'll expect you waiting on the other side. Out."

Qaade cut the comm. "Chauvet's not aboard. He'd be at the comm if he were. Zergot, get into position."

"We're ready below."

Qaade checked the live cam displaying the airlock entrance. It looked empty, but behind every container and column lurked a pirate.

"And Torrie?" Qaade asked.

"Right here. What a lovely sight she is too."

"Hands off, you old thief."

Zergot gave a booming laugh. "Alas, she only has eyes for you, boy."

Qaade felt warm to his very soul. "Watch her back for me."

"Don't you worry. She'll be safe enough."

Exodus moved in to connect. Qaade gave his men orders for when the ships' systems registered that the air lock had sealed between them. Doors at both ends opened, and Qaade watched six of Urwin's men move slowly into *Freeport*. A flash of light zipped through the air lock into *Exodus*: Nod.

Urwin's men looked around, visibly baffled. Seconds later, Urwin came over the comm. "What are you pulling, Qaade? You were supposed to be waiting."

Qaade watched the comm for Nod's signal that he'd established access to *Exodus*'s systems. Nothing. He stalled for more time. "I'm running a little late. Give me a minute to say good-bye to my crew."

"Get down there," Urwin demanded.

Nod's voice overrode Urwin's orders. "Access granted. Transferring control to main console."

Freeport's console lit up, and Qaade locked down the comm to keep *Exodus* from sending any messages to Chauvet. Meanwhile, Brilliard started commandeering *Exodus*'s engines, weapons systems, and internal controls.

"What the—" Urwin started when he noticed the systems failures. "It's an ambush. Disengage!"

The order came too late for Urwin's men already on *Freeport,* as pirates stormed them. Qaade worked to shut down *Exodus*'s final systems, all the while trying to see Torrie in the live cam. Zergot's pirates made quick work of Urwin's team, then rushed aboard the craft. Qaade caught a glimpse of Torrie's swinging braid, and that was all.

The comm was still open to *Exodus*'s bridge where Urwin could be heard barking orders that wouldn't be carried out. Qaade realized *Exodus*'s systems were turning over on their own. *Sly.* He grinned. A few more commands, and *Exodus* would be entirely his. Now it was up to Zergot and his men to subdue the enemy. It wasn't over with yet. Capturing a ship the size of *Exodus* would be tricky. And he didn't know how many of his people had truly turned against him.

"Nod, do you see Torrie?" Qaade asked, unable to control his concern.

"Negative."

Brilliard looked up. "Go, Qaade. Find her. I've got everything under control here."

Qaade hesitated, torn between wanting to let her fight her own battles and making sure she didn't get killed fighting his.

Brilliard added knowingly, "The rest of them could probably use your help, too."

Qaade gave his ops chief a grateful smile, turned, and headed below at a full sprint.

Torrie moved out in front with Zergot shadowing her. They'd teamed up almost immediately. He reminded her of Howser, only without the whining. And she'd learned he could kick ass with the best of them. They'd taken out most of the crew they'd run into with little difficulty so far, and with only a few nicks and bruises to show for it. But up ahead, three of Urwin's men held a long corridor, taking turns firing around the corner. Torrie heard Zergot's men clearing the ship, but this was the only way to the bridge.

"This could take all day," Torrie muttered.

"You're right about that. We need a diversion," Zergot said between laser blasts.

Torrie smiled. "I have just the thing." She activated her comm. "Nod, where are you?"

"I am located three meters from the bridge entrance."

Behind the men. Perfect. Torrie asked, "How are you at simulating the sound of a team of attackers with a couple of standard pistols?"

"I can do that."

"On my mark, start your noise and move toward the main corridor nice and slow. Watch out for weapons-fire."

"Ready," Nod replied cheerfully.

Torrie gripped her pistols and eyed the next doorway. "Now."

She heard the ruckus echo through the corridor even before she jumped from cover and fired a round down the hallway. Laserfire lit up the end of the corridor as the men realized they had incoming. She ducked into the open doorway and peered out. No return fire, so she hitched her head at Zergot. He moved ahead while she protected him, and Nod's phantom army got closer and louder. Then all gunfire stopped. Silence. Torrie glanced at Zergot in concern. Where was Nod?

She sprinted the last few meters to find the three men holding up their hands in surrender. On the other side stood Sly, with a big grin and a long rifle. Beside him, Nod bounced.

Sly said, "It's about damned time you got here."

Chapter Twenty-four

As the last blue object in the holo game turned red, Chauvet gloated. Darkness seeped into Fahlow's bones, chilling her blood and stealing the last vestiges of light from her soul. The game was nearly over.

"We have *Freeport* and Qaade," Urwin reported.

"How long before you arrive?"

"Two days."

"Excellent," Chauvet replied, savoring the word. "I'm looking forward to meeting laghato. *Alive.* If he is to die, it will be by my hand, Urwin."

"Yes, sir."

"And the woman?"

"She is here also."

"I want her alive as well. Out."

Fahlow closed her eyes and suffered—for her own life and for the lives of her people. There would not be another man with laghato's strength and courage. It was his courage that kept hope alive in the hearts of so many. Without him, no one would challenge Chauvet. No crusader would come to their rescue.

"It was a good game, don't you think, Princess?" Chauvet finally asked.

Silence was her answer. Let him humiliate her. Let him beat her. All he would batter was an empty shell.

"What's the matter? Didn't you enjoy it?"

He was directly in front of her now, but she knew exactly the look on his face without looking. He'd tried to break her using his degradation and his hand. With hope in her heart, she had survived. But now that was gone and, with it, her will to live.

She opened her eyes to stare at him, hate and anger filling the void in her soul. "I did *not* enjoy it."

He gave a cruel, twisted smile of victory. He'd finally defeated her, and she'd accepted her fate. She didn't even brace herself for the blow.

"Well done, Urwin," Qaade said after the comm was cut. "I appreciate your cooperation."

Bound in restraints with Sly's rifle shoved in his back, the traitor sneered. "You'll never win, Qaade. Chauvet is a tactical genius."

Qaade replied, "Chauvet is a killer. Nothing more. Just like you."

"And you aren't?" Urwin sneered. "I've seen you kill, too. You seem to have found a way to live with yourself."

Qaade clenched his jaw. "You executed four of my crewmen. People you'd worked with for the past year. *Friends.*"

Urwin gave a short laugh. "They would have died eventually."

Qaade resisted the urge to strangle the traitor

where he stood. Unfortunately, he might still need the little bastard. Instead he told Sly, "Lock him up with the others until I figure out what to do with them."

Sly stabbed the rifle into Urwin's back. "Move, scum."

Qaade watched them go. Yes, he'd found a way to live with himself. It was called Slipstream. And he was taking it back with a little help from his friends.

He turned to Zergot. "I'm sorry about the men you lost today."

Zergot glanced up from the main console and shrugged. "Happens to the best of us."

"If anyone wants out before the final battle, there'll be no shame."

The old pirate raised a white eyebrow. "You forget who you're dealing with, boy. No one is leaving. The men are split between these two ships. The rest of the fleet awaits your orders."

Qaade smiled. This man had saved him more than once. It was good to have him at his back. "I owe you."

Zergot replied with a gruff, "Don't work that way. Now, what'll it be?"

"Now that we have Chauvet's coordinates, we can move. *Freeport* and *Exodus* will arrive together first. Shortly after that, the fleet should drop out of hyperspace around the target but far enough away to avoid short-range sensors."

"That's going to have to be pretty far," Zergot noted.

"We'll have to make do." Qaade turned to his nav officer. "Transfer the destination coordinates to *Freeport* and the rest of the fleet so we can synchronize a hyperspace jump. Set it for as soon as we disconnect the link-up."

"You got it, Cap," the navigator replied with a grin.

Qaade looked out of the viewport of his flagship. His ship. His world. Plus, he had *Exodus* back and most of his crew. Chauvet was going to pay for the lives he'd taken.

"Disengaged and ready to jump, Cap," the nav officer called out moments later.

"You ready, *Freeport*?" Qaade called aloud.

Brilliard's voice came back. "Good here."

"Let's give Chauvet the surprise of his life."

The ship shifted into hyperspace, and they stormed toward the killer's lair. If Chauvet wanted a game, he was going to get one. But now it would be on Qaade's terms.

Lapreu hobbled up to him. "Feel good to be back on the bridge, sir?"

"Yes, it does." Qaade noticed the battered right side of Lapreu's face. "And you need to learn to play along."

The old man grunted. "That'll be the day. I kowtow to no one. Sly said you wanted to see me."

Qaade showed him Chauvet's location on the holodeck. "We already determined there are no planets in the vicinity, which means he's working out of a spacecraft. Since he thinks *Exodus* is his now, see if you can use that trust to pull information about his base of operations through our computers. Floor plans, systems analysis, access codes, whatever you can get without raising suspicions on the other end."

Lapreu replied, "Will do. Anything else?"

Qaade glanced around. "Have you seen Torrie?"

"She mentioned taking Nod back to your quarters," Lapreu said. "He passed out from all the action."

Zergot said, "Me and Lapreu here have the bridge. And you have two days with nothing to do."

Qaade looked at the pair, and realized they were trying to help him again. "Is that right?"

Zergot grinned. "I know what I'd be doing."

Torrie felt the hyperdrives kick in just before she stepped into Qaade's lav and activated her comm. Time to check in with the real world again. The sweet victory of *Exodus*'s return was lost under an unshakable blanket of guilt. She hated sneaking around, hated lying to Qaade. But she knew there would always be another Chauvet—even if Qaade didn't want to face that fact—and the only way to stop this madness was to shut down such operations for good. For that, she needed the authorities.

Howser finally answered, and Torrie got down to business before Qaade could return to his quarters.

"What's your status?"

"Nice to talk to you, too," Howser said.

She winced. "I'm in a hurry. Sorry."

"You are always in a hurry, girl. You need to slow down."

Torrie clenched the comm hard enough to break it. "Look, it's been a long, hard day of fighting bad guys, and I could use some good news."

"Oh, hell, are you okay? What happened?"

Torrie hung her head and tried to figure out how to explain her day in twenty words or less. "I'm fine. We recaptured *Exodus* and are heading toward Chauvet's location now. We'll be there in two days. Happy? Now cough up some news, or I'm going to flush you."

"You really think you can take this guy down with two ships?"

"We have help."

"What kind of help?"

Torrie laid her head in her hand and stared curiously at a four-meter-wide circle in the floor in front of her. "The kind you wouldn't approve of, so don't ask. What did Lundon say?"

"It's pirates, isn't it?" he pressed her.

"Howser, I'm not saying another word until you hand over the info."

"Okay, fine. Yes, Macke talked to Lundon—"

She stilled. "Macke talked to him?" Why did that scare her?

"Yes, and he did a damned impressive job of convincing Lundon that slave traffic was coming through here. He's sending out a man named Major Wyatt."

"I know him. Good man. When will he be there?"

"Tomorrow. In the meantime, we are monitoring all activity. When Wyatt arrives, he'll launch an official investigation."

"Sounds good." And legal, she added silently. "Just don't mention the pirates, okay?"

"As if I'd include them in casual conversation. Don't worry, I won't give up Qaade."

"Thank you. And thank Macke for us." She winced as she realized she'd said *us*.

"Well, like you said, I suppose it's the right thing to do—even if it isn't the smartest."

"Don't I know it." She studied the wall panel beside her, then pressed a codebox. The circle on the floor slid away to reveal a large hole with a clear blue, undulating bottom. Steam and water began to fill it. A plasma jet tub. She nearly groaned with pleasure in Howser's ear.

"I'll contact you when I have more information," he said, intruding on her delight and jolting her back to the present.

"No," she said, louder than she meant, and glanced at the closed lav door. "I'll contact you tomorrow."

"Take care of yourself, Torrie."

"You too," she said. "Out."

Torrie tossed the comm aside and slid her tired body to the floor. The jet tub was nearly filled with blissful promise. She tested the temperature of the water with her fingertips. Perfect.

Her clothes were stripped off and in a pile in less than a minute. She unbraided her hair and slipped into the water. Light suction pulled her down as the plasma bottom rose to mold to her body and hold her head just above the waterline. She relaxed, letting the tub support her as it was designed. Her hair floated around her before succumbing to the depths.

The rhythmic rumble of the jets numbed both her mind and the thoughts that crowded her peace. She tried to convince herself that everything would be all right, that she was doing the right thing for the right reasons. But was she? Was she just keeping Qaade safe for herself? After all, everything she'd done up to this point in her life was for her own benefit, and for her own dreams. Would she even realize if she was just being selfish again?

Zoe's face flashed in her mind, and the guilt that came with the memory. Then the two girls and the other nameless faces of the slaves she'd seen on *Freeport* crowded Torrie's thoughts. No, she wasn't doing this all for herself. She wasn't even doing it just for Qaade. She was doing it for the slaves. With resignation and fervor, she vowed she'd sacrifice whatever she had to in order to break Chauvet's ring. There was no turning back, no matter what happened. Her personal goals paled in the face of others' plight. And, she realized with great sadness, her sacrifice might very well include whatever relationship she had with Qaade. If it came down to him or them . . .

She pushed such painful thoughts aside, unwilling to consider it unless she had to. Instead, she rolled over on her belly. The plasma support adjusted.

Escaping into wondrous sensations, she cushioned her head on her arms over the rim. Jets of water kneaded her muscle and bones, while the plasma membrane gently massaged her skin and took her far away from killers and slaves. She had nearly dozed off when she heard, "I see you've discovered the benefits of the captain's quarters."

Torrie turned her head and gave Qaade a lazy look over her shoulder. He would have stood there a lot longer, admiring her long back, narrow waist, and the dangerous curves of her bottom partly submerged in the water, but no man possessed that much willpower. He started undressing at the door. His shirt came off first, and Torrie's eyebrow rose in marked interest. He grinned and kicked off one shoe. Then waited.

She narrowed her eyes. "More, pirate."

He kicked off the other one.

Torrie made a growling sound and rolled over, giving him a hell of a view. Exquisite breasts peaked above the bubbling water as she draped her arms behind her along the bath's rim. Her green eyes regarded him with hot desire.

He reached down and popped the first fastener

on his pants. Torrie didn't move, her gaze never wavering from his. He could see her hunger, almost taste it on his lips. The next fastener unsnapped. Torrie's fingertips made mindless circles as she waited. Qaade's pants' last fastener released with a distinct click. She smiled.

Qaade shoved his pants down and stepped out of them. His erection drew her gaze. Both her eyebrows rose, and she said, "Are you going to stand there all day, or would you like some help with that?"

He broke into a wide grin, took one step and landed in the middle of the tub. Torrie screamed with laughter, water splashing up on her face and flooding the lav. The bath's plasma bottom went crazy, trying to factor in another body, and Qaade had to fight to get to her. He grabbed Torrie's leg and pulled her toward him. She slid underwater. His mouth was over her lips before she surfaced. Her hands already gripped his slick skin, and she pressed his erection between them. He loved Torrie when she was like this, shameless in her lust. He knew she wanted him—no games, no hiding and no lies between them.

The plasma accommodated them as Qaade stood and laid her back. Her hair fanned out around her. The plasma bottom rose to support her horizontally for his viewing pleasure. Water lapped over her, wetting skin that slid smooth beneath his hands. He caressed her neck and shoulders with long, slow strokes, watching Torrie watch him. Rosy nipples beckoned, and he was happy to oblige, leaning down to inhale one between his lips. She arched into his mouth, a low growl in her throat.

His hands explored her body with all its wonder, valleys and curves so unlike his own. He sipped water from between her breasts, and grazed her soft skin with his lips so that he could feel the silkiness. She clutched at his hair and tried to pull him to her, but he wasn't about to be rushed. They had time and, for once, he was going to take it. Slipstream would still be around tomorrow.

He heard her gasp as his fingers reached between her legs. Her smoldering green eyes told him what she wanted. He slipped a finger between her soft folds, seeking the sweet spot. When he'd found it, he kissed her, invading her mouth. His tongue mimicked the slow movements of his fingers. With every flick, every rub, she reacted, growing more restless.

When she was on the brink, he moved between her thighs and positioned himself at her center. She groaned in protest, and the desperation in her face said it all. Delicate muscles closed around him with the promise of ecstasy. He gripped her thighs and slid her across the plasma, impaling her on his aching erection. A long moan escaped her, and she latched on to his forearms for support. He pushed her back up the plasma and then slowly over him again. They both moaned. He repeated the agonizingly slow maneuver until the sound of the tub's jets faded, leaving only water and woman in endless, seamless oblivion.

Rising from his own pleasure, he felt her tighten around him. Her nails sank into his forearms as she climaxed in rolling waves. He didn't move, didn't want to break her moment. She let out an audible, "Oh, Qaade," that went straight to his heart.

His chest filled with raw emotion he couldn't contain any longer. All his humanity, all his love poured through him, overflowing every cell of his being. His own release welled up within him like a powerful wave suspended in time. When it finally crashed, he buried himself deep within her and joined himself with the woman for whom he'd give up his soul.

Chapter Twenty-five

Torrie woke alone for the first time in thirty-six hours. She yawned and stretched across Qaade's bed, feeling better than any woman had the right. That man could make love. His lips, his hands, his touch, his eyes . . . all just for her. He'd worshipped her like a goddess, and for the first time in her life, she felt sexy beyond words. Loved, not like a sister or a daughter, but like a woman. He'd whispered words of lust and desire and tenderness. He was hers and hers alone; she knew that with all her heart.

She glanced at the side table and smiled at the drink he'd left for her. As she sipped on the cool beverage, she sighed. If only it were this simple. Drink when she was thirsty, eat when hungry, make love for hours on end. No worries, no bad guys, no lies. No guilt to cloud every bright moment.

Just one man—that's all she needed to make her happy. Torrie chuckled, not believing she'd just thought that. So much for conquering the universe, and all those big plans for the future she'd had; she was down to one pirate who held her heart in his hands.

She set her glass aside and stood up in the middle of his private quarters, surrounded by his world. A few precious mementos were displayed atop shelves. Torrie picked up what looked like a child's sculpture—a hunk of hardened clay crafted by little fingers. No doubt, it was a gift of a child to his savior. Qaade probably had a roomful of such gifts, and he'd kept them all. Those children were his family.

She'd grown up with a strict father, but there was always plenty of love to be found. She couldn't imagine life without her family. But soon she would experience it firsthand. Macke was right. Even if this mission went exactly as planned, she couldn't go home. Her family wouldn't understand why she would put herself into this position freely. But she couldn't leave now. A lifetime of regret would be worse.

She set the statue down and touched the slender pik she'd heard Qaade play onboard *Umbra*. His song had been so poignant and heartrending, like it was born from his pain. She wondered where he had learned it. The notes had touched her on a level she didn't recognize, kind of like Qaade did.

The thought of him drew a smile; then she noticed her comm lying next to the pik. She swallowed.

Yes, he was hers—right up until he found out that she'd called in InterGlax. But if all went well, he would never need to know.

Wrapping a blanket around herself, she sat back on the bed and activated the comm. Howser's voice came through. "Torrie?"

"Greetings, Howser. Did Wyatt show?"

"He's here. We've been monitoring the space traffic for a few hours. He's as convinced as we are that something illegal is going on."

"Good. He didn't contact the local authorities, did he?"

"No. He doesn't want to tip anyone off."

She exhaled in relief. She had no doubt local law enforcement would contact Chauvet as soon as they suspected anything.

Howser echoed her thoughts. "Wyatt isn't too happy. There are no reports of this activity by the InterGlax units in this region. Totally missing."

"They're corrupt, that's why," Torrie said.

"Exactly. You were right."

"Actually, Qaade was right."

Howser let out a long sigh. "Yeah. I guess there's more to your pirate than I originally thought. I understand why he did what he did. It's hard to work within a system when that system fails."

Finally, she thought. "What's Wyatt going to do about the facility?"

"He's planning a raid as we speak."

She gripped the comm as panic overtook her. "When?"

"Soon. Is that a problem?"

"A big problem. Chauvet thinks this ship is under his crew's control with Qaade and I as prisoners. If you raid that facility before we get to him, you will tip our hand. He'll know his operation has been breached, and he'll raise his defenses. It'll destroy our element of surprise."

Howser replied, "*You* wanted to call InterGlax in."

"I didn't expect them to move so fast. It took them three damned months to clear Zain. Why would I

277

think they'd be any different with this?" She rubbed her forehead. "Howser, you have to stall them."

"Right. And how do I do that? There's nothing I can say without giving up you or Qaade or Chauvet."

"Hell," she muttered. "Then I'll have to push the attack on Chauvet from here."

"Look, just tell Qaade what's going on. He'll understand."

"No, he won't. InterGlax already failed him too many times. He hates them with a passion second to none."

There was a long pause. "In other words, if he finds out you got InterGlax involved, he'll never forgive you."

She closed her eyes. "Exactly." *I'll lose him*, she thought.

"Your personal life is none of my business—"

"It's not? You could have fooled me."

Howser gave a chuckle. "Fine, it is. I know you feel compelled to help these people, but I also know it's more than that."

"It is," she agreed solemnly, gazing around Qaade's cabin. "Much more."

"You're playing a risky game, Torrie."

Emotion thickened her voice as her heart squeezed in her chest. "The most dangerous kind. So we must not fail."

"You have a plan for taking Chauvet down?"

She bit her lip. "Sort of. Qaade wants to kill him. I'd rather see him brought to trial and his entire network exposed. But we don't know how extensive it is. He could have slave traffic running in every quadrant of the galaxy."

"Well, if you want justice, then you'll need Inter-Glax there," Howser said, voicing a thought she couldn't bring herself to say.

She pulled her knees to her chest and wrapped her arms around them. "Call InterGlax in at this location, too? I just can't do it, Howser."

"What if InterGlax finds something here that leads them there?"

She laid her head on her knees. Oh, damn. That's all she'd need. InterGlax here with Qaade and his crew, his ship and a band of pirates.

"Then we'll have major problems. But Chauvet wouldn't be that stupid."

"He might not. His people might."

She lifted her head to face the truth of that statement. "If InterGlax makes the connection, let me know. I'll have to get all the pirates out."

Howser didn't reply for a minute. "Torrie, what will you do if this blows up in your face? Whose side are you going to be on?"

She was going to be a loser either way. "I don't know, Howser. I don't know."

Zergot, Lapreu and Sly were crowded around the holo table with Brilliard on the visual comm when Qaade walked onto the bridge.

"Greetings," he said.

"You look well rested," Sly commented, not even attempting to hide his smile.

Qaade grinned and bellied up to the holo table. *Well rested* barely covered it. He'd never felt better. It was only because Lapreu had information that Qaade had left Torrie's warm body. And as soon as he was done here, he was going back.

A spaceport floated in the holodeck, intricately detailed and spectacular against the black backdrop of space: two massive plates of golden triangles fused together at their pinnacles, their tops and bottoms forming flat plateaus. Each half spun independently on a delicate apex, while colossal etchings on its surfaces gleamed with interior lights. It was nothing less than an architectural masterpiece moving through space, and not at all what Qaade expected from a man like Chauvet.

"It's called *Abaccus*," Lapreu said. "It was originally commissioned by a businessman by the name of InSereay as luxury accommodations for the wealthy who were passin' through. He died a few years ago. The accommodations were closed, and ownership transferred to an unidentified entity."

Qaade looked at Lapreu. "Chauvet?"

The old man shrugged. "Must be. The information trail dead-ends."

"That's a big place for one man," Brilliard noted, also watching the holo image.

"You can bet he's not alone," Qaade muttered.

"Quite right," Lapreu said. "A spaceport this size would take about a thousand support people. That not be includin' housekeeping staff. Add another hundred. And, of course, security forces."

Over a thousand people to get through, Qaade guessed grimly. He studied the holo image. "Do we have the schematics for this thing?"

"Sure do. The original construction specs were archived with the structural authorities for approval," Lapreu said, and he brought up a rendering of the spaceport's innards. The skin of the spaceport dissolved, leaving six levels of white mesh like structural elements.

"Perimeter defenses?"

Lapreu entered a few commands, and the weapons systems leapt forward in red, followed by two rows of shuttle bays large enough for a fleet of fighter ships. Finally, an enormous, oblong mesh bubble appeared and wrapped around the entire spaceport.

Zergot whistled, giving expression to all their thoughts. "That's some serious shielding. Why do I get the feeling this was more than just a place for rich people to sleep?"

"Maybe it was rich people who'd made a few enemies along the way," Brilliard said.

"Makes sense to me." Sly crossed his arms. "Nice station. I almost hate to plunder it."

Qaade agreed silently, but this wasn't about preserving architectural art. "I'm open to ideas."

The four men gaped at his agreeability, and he smiled. "You wanted teamwork. Here's your chance."

"Chance for what?" a new voice said.

Qaade's body reacted instantly. When Torrie moved next to him, he had to make a conscious effort to control himself, even after nearly two days of their making love more times than he could remember. Instead of satisfying him, all it had done was make him want her more. She gave him a slow, wise smile that convinced him that there was too much physical space between them. He moved closer to her.

"We need a strategy to infiltrate, and to take over Chauvet's spaceport."

She frowned at the holo image for a long moment. "Attacking a spaceport isn't going to be easy. There's no cover, nowhere to hide, and forget about sneaking up on them undetected."

"And check out the defense systems," Sly muttered. "Maybe what we need here is simple brute force. What if we just ram the thing at the apex here?" He pointed to the slender section in the center. "We could empty *Freeport* and send her through. At full tilt she might be able to penetrate the force field and slam into the structure. Once it's split, it'll break the defenses and we should be able to destroy it."

"Along with everyone aboard the station," Torrie noted. "Including any possible slaves Chauvet has."

Qaade eyed Torrie, surprised by her insight. She turned to him. "And what about the innocent people who work for him, who don't know what he is? Should they have to die, too?"

Dammit, she was asking him, and he had no choice but to answer. "No, they shouldn't."

"It's always the hard way," Sly grumbled.

Zergot clapped his hands with enthusiasm. "I love the hard way."

Qaade motioned to the landing pads at the top and bottom of the space station. "If we dock the ships at each end—*Exodus* up top and *Freeport* below—we can split the interior attack and come from two directions."

Zergot nodded. "Too bad the rest of the fleet will have to lay back until after you bring down the shielding."

"Actually, I can use them up front. If they attack the spaceport, it will create a nice diversion."

The old pirate shrugged. "Sure, but we won't be hurting them from the outside until you drop those shields."

Qaade said, "Maybe we can take a few of you with us. Do you have any ships small enough to fit inside our shuttle bays?"

"Now there's a hell of an idea," Zergot said with a growing grin. "That would get us in. Don't know if small ships would have enough firepower to do much damage to this monster, but it's worth a shot."

Qaade said, "Once we land, we'll use Urwin and his crew's passes to gain access to the spaceport. From there, Brilliard will lead the lower attack first. Can you handle that, Brilliard?"

Brilliard smiled in the holo. "You bet."

"I'll lead the top assault," Qaade continued. "We'll take over the interior systems, including the lifts and door access. We also need to shut down all escape routes. I don't want Chauvet getting away. Then it's a level-by-level assault until we locate him."

"Where do you think he is?" Sly asked.

Qaade studied the massive structure. "Lapreu, what's the nicest room in the place?"

The old man pointed a bony finger toward the center, and the hologram zoomed in to the middle of Level Zero—the pivotal point of the structure. "No doubt about it. Right here."

The level consisted of two separate suites on either side of an octagonal room, connected by a pair of slender walkways. The center room was small, more like a viewing area. The two suites were larger, with all necessary facilities for a control center on one side, and premium living quarters on the other.

Sly shook his head. "In the heart of the beast."

Qaade noted the escape pods. *No.* They weren't going to get this close and let him get away. Anger burned in Qaade's belly for all the people he'd lost, and all the people ever enslaved. "Whoever gets to Chauvet first has orders to kill him. Understood?"

The bridge grew quiet as the men nodded. Only Torrie's gaze flickered with uncertainty. Qaade knew she didn't approve, but it wouldn't matter. He had every intention of getting to Chauvet first.

"How long before we arrive?" she asked.

Qaade checked the time. "We drop out of hyperspace in six hours."

"I'll let the boys know," Zergot said, and gave Torrie a wink before leaving.

Qaade glanced at her. She was staring into the holodeck, looking concerned. Did she have doubts about taking on Chauvet? She should. Any normal person would. He wanted more than anything to keep her safe and as far away from Chauvet as possible. But if he tried to do that, she'd see it as yet another attempt to control her.

So he went for subtle. "I could use someone to stay aboard *Exodus* to keep an eye on the overall attack."

Her green eyes turned slowly to regard him. "Are you talking to me?"

He pursed his lips, resigning himself to the fact that trying to keep Torrie safe was a losing battle. "No."

"Good," she said with a nod. "Because bloodshed on the bridge is so hard to clean up." She rubbed her belly with a frown. "I'm starving."

"No wonder, I've held you hostage for the past two days," he said low enough that no one else could hear.

Her eyes narrowed. "And here I thought I was the one holding you hostage."

"I'll survive. You can have your way with me anytime. Let's get some food."

He ushered her off the bridge, and they headed through the ship back to his quarters. Even though she was next to him, she seemed far away.

Something was bothering her enough to keep her quiet. He hadn't known such a force existed.

"Have you heard from Howser or Macke?"

She swung her head around to stare at him, and her eyes widened slightly. "They're still tracking the cargo."

He shrugged. "It's not necessary anymore. You tell them thanks for me. We'll take it from here."

"What about the rest of the network?" she asked.

"It will fall apart without Chauvet."

"How can you be sure? How do you know he doesn't have networks all over? Or someone ready to step in for him?"

Besides being damned persistent, she had a point. "Once we take over *Abaccus*, we should be able to see just how big his network is. We'll see his records. We can decide what to do from there. I want to get Slipstream back up and running as soon as possible."

They entered his room, and Qaade ordered up two meals from his private galley. While he waited, he leaned back against the wall. Torrie sat in a chair across from him.

He asked a question that had been haunting him for days. "So, this time tomorrow, what are your plans?"

"If I'm still alive?" she replied with a wry smile.

"Is that why you've been so quiet?"

She laid her head back, and watched him. "No, that's from pure sexual exhaustion."

He smiled at her obvious attempt to divert his thoughts. She didn't want to deal with his question yet. But he wanted an answer. *Stay here with me,* he wanted to say. As if it would be that easy. He could simply take her away from her world and family, ask her to give up everything for him, become a wanted woman and lead a pirate's life. If he asked her, she would probably say yes. For Slipstream's sake. And he was tempted. Just once, he had a treasure he wanted to keep for himself.

If she offered, he wouldn't be able to refuse her. But he wouldn't ask her.

He turned to check on their meals. Then he felt Torrie behind him, and glanced at her. Her eyes were luminous and soft. She stared at him for a long moment with such a look of longing and love that his heart filled to bursting. Then she closed the space between them and slid into his waiting arms. She reached out and traced his lips with a feather-light touch.

"On the other hand," she said, "there's something to be said for pure sexual exhaustion."

Her soft lips replaced her fingertips, and she kissed him with poignant tenderness. He returned the gift, his kisses as deep and gentle as hers. His hands slid across her skin, absorbing her into his senses. And before he was completely overwhelmed, he thought again, *Stay with me.*

Chapter Twenty-six

Mercerr entered Chauvet's inner sanctum silently, as if disturbing a giant. He glanced at Fahlow with his customary sympathy, then executed a salute at Chauvet's back.

"Both ships have docked, sir."

"Excellent," Chauvet replied, strolling around his gameboard before stopping in front of the man. "Escort the legendary laghato and the Masters woman in here."

"What about the others? The captured crew."

"Execute them at your leisure."

Mercerr blinked several times, and swallowed. "Yes, sir." He exited the room in a hurry, leaving Fahlow alone with the beast. Pain radiated from her right eye and pierced her skull. Her lip was swollen and bruised; her body ached in its entirety. She closed her eyes and prayed for death. And not the slow, agonizing, fear-filled one Chauvet would give her, but a swift, merciful end. Because there was nothing left to live for.

"So, you will get to meet the great man who would save all slaves," Chauvet said. He was close, probably watching her. But she didn't care. She didn't bother to give him the respect he awaited. Perhaps if she ignored him long enough, he would reward her with the death she craved. Perhaps if he beat her again, that would be enough.

"Princess, you are looking a bit tired today."

She held her ground, counting down the seconds.

"Look at me," he hissed.

Fahlow opened her eyes, not in humility, but in hate. A flash of surprise showed in Chauvet's face. Then he smiled as he raised his hand. She knew her doom was sealed.

The comm chimed, and Chauvet's hand froze. "What?"

"Sir, we have a problem," Mercerr's voice called. "The spaceport is being attacked by a small band of merchant ships. They came out of nowhere."

Annoyed, Chauvet turned from Fahlow, and said, "Computer, display the spaceport in the holodeck. Open the viewports."

A long expanse of windows appeared, framing deep space. Fahlow watched a ship soar into view, its laserfire bouncing harmlessly off the spaceport's shielding.

In the holodeck before her, the image of the spaceport revolved. On each end, she could just make out Iaghato's vessels. Around the belly of the spaceport, tiny ships darted. She wondered whose they were, and why they had come to face such a powerful man. Did they know whom they were fighting?

"Send out the ships to engage and destroy them," Chauvet ordered.

"Ships launched," Mercerr replied seconds later.

Fahlow caught a glimpse of a smile from Chauvet. He would enjoy watching each enemy die, one by one.

His sleek silver fighters filled the viewport, but the attackers didn't flee, and deep in Fahlow's heart a tiny glimmer of hope cried out: *Please fight. Don't leave us.* As if they heard her, the strange ships engaged in silent battle.

"They stand and fight. How refreshing," Chauvet noted. But Fahlow barely heard him, immersed in the action playing out on the holodeck. Suddenly, more ships streamed from both ends of the spaceport, and she realized they were coming from Iaghato's ships. Her heart beat louder, awoken from the dead just as one of Chauvet's fighters exploded. Then another, and a third.

Chauvet frowned, rage rolling up his face. "Mercerr, what is the problem with our shields?"

"I'm not sure," the man responded. "We seem to be having system malfunctions." In the background of the spaceport's control center, Fahlow could hear chaos.

Chauvet stared straight ahead. "Where is Iaghato?"

Fahlow's heart leapt. Could it be? Optimism soared through her veins like cool water to a parched woman.

"I don't know. I can't raise the post guard."

Chauvet hissed, "Send out the guards, Mercerr. We have infiltrators!"

A laser sizzled past Qaade's ear as he sprinted through the corridors with Nod and Torrie by his side. They'd made it well into the landing bay and out through the main passage before Chauvet's men realized they were about to have a very bad day. Unfortunately, they were well trained, and taking the spaceport was a lot harder than Qaade had hoped. Alarms blared and warning lights flashed, adding to the general pandemonium.

Nod had managed to establish system access, and had turned most over to their control. Escape routes and shuttle bays were locked out, surveillance cams had been deactivated, and all internal communications were jammed. The boys outside had been keeping things lively since the shields came down. Sounds of destruction filled the spaceport as it shuddered under the siege.

All in all, things were looking good. He and Torrie were on point, taking one level at a time—the hard way. No lifts; just stairs. Safer, but slow. Behind them, Zergot and crew were cleaning up the chaos they left in their wake. Surprisingly, most of the housekeeping personnel and many of Chauvet's men had surrendered without firing a shot. But not all were so cooperative, and the closer Qaade and Torrie got to Chauvet's location on Level Zero, the more resistance they encountered. Obviously, Chauvet paid his personal guards better.

Halfway down the passageway on Level One North, Qaade ducked into a shallow doorway. Torrie and Nod took cover in another, directly across from him. Laserfire streaked between them.

Qaade hit his comm. "Zergot, where are you?"

"About one hundred meters behind you. Hold on until we catch up. Got a stubborn element between you and us to deal with first."

Qaade peeked around the corner up ahead. A group of Chauvet's men were holed up in doorways similar to theirs about fifty meters down, but they were slowly moving forward. If Zergot didn't hurry, there'd be a messy situation.

"We need to figure out how to get rid of these guys," Torrie said, and she took a turn at sweeping the passageway with laserfire.

"I can help," Nod said.

Qaade raised an eyebrow at an equally surprised Torrie.

"That's a first," she confirmed. "What's your idea, Nod?"

"Watch." He zoomed around in a tight circle, and then flung himself into the passageway emitting an ear-splitting, mind-numbing shriek. He zipped down the center of the hall.

"Nod, no!" Torrie yelled and ran after him.

Qaade swore and followed. Around him, laserfire washed the walls. Shocked, most of Chauvet's guards retreated deeper into the spaceport, and many fell to their knees, covering their ears with their hands. When Qaade reached them, Nod was dive-bombing their heads with an occasional thump of contact.

"Nod, that's enough," he yelled. "And stop that damned noise." The shrill halted, leaving Qaade with ringing ears and a major headache.

A pale Torrie scolded, "Don't ever do that again, Nod. You could have been killed."

He took a low dip and said quietly, "I *can* help."

Qaade proceeded to restrain the captives. "That's not quite what I had in mind, Nod. Is there anyone located on Level Zero?"

"Ship's sensors are not working on that level."

"Great. A blind spot," Torrie grunted. "Chauvet has to be there."

Qaade agreed. "Nod, lock down all doors on Level Zero."

C. J. Barry

"I cannot gain access to that level."

"They must have isolated those systems," Qaade said. "Nod, keep working on access."

They continued toward the nearest flight of steps, which would take them down to Chauvet, but holed up behind cover in sight of the stairs were more guards. Trying to take it, Qaade would lose a lot of good people. So would Chauvet, although Qaade doubted Chauvet would care. His guards were probably used to dying and . . .

A thought occurred to him, and he turned to the lightball. "Nod, can you simulate any human voice?"

"Of course. *'Don't ever do that again, Nod. You could have been killed,'*" he replied, mimicking Torrie's voice exactly. Qaade chuckled, despite the circumstances.

"Very funny, you two," Torrie grumbled.

Qaade said, "Nod, broadcast a command in Chauvet's voice for all personnel to report to Level Two North immediately."

"You really think they'll fall for that?" Torrie asked, looking skeptical.

"If Chauvet runs this place like I think he does, then they'll do whatever he tells them." Qaade hit his comm. "Zergot, tell your men to expect company in Level Two."

Zergot replied, "About time we saw some *real* action. We're ready. Out."

Moments later, Qaade watched a group of guards head up the stairs. A few less to deal with, but he still didn't know how many were waiting below. He tapped the comm. "Brilliard, how are you doing?"

In the background they could hear laserfire and men shouting. "I'm on Level Two South, heading for One."

Qaade replied, "Keep the pressure on. Clean up as you go."

"I don't suppose you'll wait until we get there to move in?"

Qaade mentally calculated the time it would take Brilliard to clear the lower levels. Too long. "I'll think about it."

Brilliard huffed. "Right. Be careful."

"Anything yet, Nod?"

"Negative."

Torrie whispered, "Their systems must be shielded. We might have better luck with our sensors once we move down there."

Qaade scanned her face, fraught with concentration. "We're going to have to go in blind. You want to wait for reinforcements?"

She slid him a quick glance. "We've already wasted enough time. Chauvet could already be gone." She jerked her head. "Brilliard has South covered, Zergot is securing North. I vote we go in while the troops are mixing it up."

Qaade felt his chest squeeze. She'd always be his partner, would be there for him no matter what. She was the one person he could trust with his most guarded possession—his heart. In fact, he'd given it to her without even realizing it. He knew she'd take good care of it.

"Whatever happens, I am grateful to have you with me, Torrie," he said.

Genuine appreciation shone in her eyes, filling him with satisfaction. Then she scowled at him. "You make it sound as if we will fail. You have me, remember?"

He grinned. "How can I forget? You won't go away."

"Damned straight," she said. "I didn't come this far to lose hope now. We are finally in control of the game."

She was right. It was time. Qaade raised his weapon, turning to the grim task at hand. "Let's get this over with."

Chapter Twenty-seven

"Sir, we are surrounded above and below. All systems on those levels are under enemy control, and many of our men listened to that fake broadcast before I could stop them," Mercerr reported. Bitter lines etched Chauvet's face as he frowned at his suddenly losing game.

Fahlow could barely contain herself. Laghato was here, in the spaceport, a touch away. Her excitement soared, giving her a reason to breathe.

Mercerr continued, "Two escape pods in the adjacent bay are still operational. Once jettisoned, our fighters can provide cover for your escape."

Chauvet speared him with a glare. "I will not run now, and neither will you. Where is he?"

"On Level One, but this level is locked down. No one will get through. However, I cannot guarantee your safety—"

"Let them in," Chauvet interrupted. "And when they enter, seal the doors behind them."

Mercerr blinked and stammered, "Here? But, sir—"

Chauvet cut him off. "It's called an ambush, Mercerr. Maybe you've heard of it."

The young man stiffened. "I know—"

Chauvet continued, "Let them think we've evacuated the level. Be ready to move when they enter, but do not shoot. I want them alive."

"I understand, sir." Mercerr spun on his heel and exited the chambers. Chauvet paced before Fahlow, his eyes glued to the holo gameboard. His entire manner had changed. His eyes were wild with volatile excitement . . . and insanity.

Part of Fahlow wanted nothing more than for laghato to come through those doors. But part of her feared for him, for his safety and his legend. For the fate of them all.

Torrie peered around the corner of the stairwell into the Level Zero entry, a cavernous room decorated elaborately like a grand hall. She stepped out and swept the room with her pistols while Qaade covered her. Empty. No movement.

"It's quiet. I don't like it," she whispered to Qaade, who moved up behind her. Nod swung back and forth in her peripheral vision. "Nod, are you picking up any personnel?"

"My scanners do not detect any comm units or lifeforms."

"Hell," Qaade muttered. "He's gone."

Torrie grimaced. If they lost him now, she doubted they'd ever find him again. Perhaps there was some useful information he'd left behind.

She asked, "Nod, any luck tapping into the systems?"

"Not yet. Working."

Qaade slid past her, toward the passageway to the center room. "I'll go in and check it out."

She replied, "And I'll be right behind you."

"How did I know you were going to say that?" he asked, shaking his head.

"You need me, remember?"

He glanced over his shoulder, silver eyes penetrating to her heart. *And I need you,* she thought. She loved him to her core, and if they won, she would give up everything for him. No one would ever get this close to her heart again, and she didn't want anyone else to. This was too perfect to ever repeat. There would be only one man. Ever.

She should tell him about InterGlax. Get it over with, and accept her fate before it got worse. But she couldn't do it. Not to him, and not to her.

Suddenly, the room came alive. Doors in the walls all slid open in unison, and armed men rushed forward. Torrie spun around to find eight armed guards surrounding her, blocking any escape.

"I am detecting personnel," Nod said.

Torrie's breath caught, and a few of the guards looked at the lightball hovering over her shoulder.

"Nod, go! Get out of here!" Torrie yelled.

Nod whizzed toward the last exit. Several guards took shots at him, but they missed. Then Nod disappeared up the steps with two guards in hot pursuit.

Torrie backed into Qaade, and they both pointed their weapons at the guards, but it was hopeless. Her mind scrambled for a strategy, but she couldn't come up with one. All she knew was that it was not going to end this way. It *couldn't.*

A man with blond hair and blue eyes stepped forward. He addressed her directly. "I'm Mercerr. We don't want to hurt you, but if you fire, we'll be forced to kill you."

Torrie's finger tightened on her triggers, adrenaline flooding her muscles. She'd rather die quickly than succumb to whatever Chauvet had planned.

"Don't shoot, Torrie," Qaade whispered.

"I won't become Chauvet's prisoner," she hissed. "Or his shield."

The guards moved closer, and her heartbeat drummed in her ears. She pressed against Qaade and prepared to shoot her way out.

"Trust me, Torrie. It's our only chance," he murmured low. Then he threw his weapon on the floor, and said the words she dreaded more than death itself.

"We surrender."

Fahlow watched Iaghato enter Chauvet's chambers. He looked as she thought he would: tall and strong, with determination in his face and fire in his soul. He scanned the room, and his gaze rested on her for a moment. Compassion flickered in those silver depths as he noted her battered face. Then he turned to face Chauvet. Surely it was Torrie Masters beside him, who gave Fahlow a nod of acknowledgment. Dark red hair framed a serious face and sharp, fiery green eyes. This was Iaghato's mate.

The guards exited, leaving Mercerr covering the prisoners with his rifle. Chauvet took his time circling them, obviously enjoying the success of his ambush.

"We finally meet, Iaghato. As you can see"—he motioned toward his gameboard— "you were a formidable opponent."

Laghato ignored the hologram. "It's not over with. My men are filling your spaceport as we speak."

Chauvet laughed, and leaned forward. "They

won't be after I tell them to surrender or you will die."

"You are wrong, Chauvet. They don't need me. They are perfectly capable of running Slipstream without me. There will always be someone to take my place."

"You think so?" Chauvet replied with another laugh. "Not after I've shown them what happens to men who make promises they can't keep."

Laghato narrowed his eyes. "Who are you?"

Chauvet's expression turned to ruthless amusement, and a chill ran through Fahlow. He raised his hands. "Don't you recognize me? I'm one of you. I was a slave." He waved at his surroundings. "Of the man who built this lovely facility. Look around you. How do you think this spaceport was built? With slave blood."

"InSereay was a slaver?"

Chauvet grinned. "Of course. And he used hundreds of them to work his hotel. A very few he relied on to be his personal servants. Fewer still he entrusted with his life."

"And that would be you," laghato said.

"Precisely." Chauvet moved around his gameboard, his hands behind his back. He ignored Fahlow as he walked by, lost in his victory. Hatred burned deep in her bones.

"It took only a few years to gain his absolute confidence. After all, scrubbed slaves are obedient and compliant, practically incapable of independent thought and unable to capture memory long enough to form strategy. They are worthless human machines whose sole function is to serve the needs of others." Chauvet stopped in front of his prisoners. "Except for me."

"You murdered him," Torrie said.

Chauvet turned to her. "What else could I do? *Laghato* didn't come." He spun on his heel and snarled, his madness getting the better of him. "I waited. I *hoped*," he said as he paced in short, angry steps. He stopped a hair's-breath away from Iaghato's face. "You never saved me," he whispered. "So I had to save myself."

A long silence held the room before Iaghato replied, "I tried to save as many—"

"You didn't. You are a lie that fools believe in. They lie awake thinking about you, night after night."

Above them rose a loud rumble. *Rescuers*, Fahlow prayed.

Chauvet also heard. "Tell them to surrender, Qaade."

Laghato shook his head slowly and smiled. "Never."

Rage filled Chauvet's face, and he grabbed Mercerr's rifle. Fahlow's breath froze as he pointed it at Iaghato. "Tell them."

"Even if you shoot us, they will never stop chasing you. You will be hunted for the rest of your life, Chauvet," he responded.

Chauvet scowled. "Not if I'm already dead." He swung the gun around and shot Mercerr in the chest. His lieutenant crumpled to the floor as Fahlow watched in horror. *No.* She moved without realizing it, sliding behind Chauvet and to her knees beside Mercerr. She could see the man struggle to breathe. When he realized she was there, he opened his eyes. He fumbled with his uniform, shoving something into her hand. He gave her one last, painful smile before he succumbed.

* * *

Qaade watched Chauvet's man die in the ghostly glow of the holo-game, while the battered waif of a woman wept over him in grief. He must have been a good man. Only a pawn. Nothing more than a gamepiece, just like the rest of them.

Chauvet's demented eyes stared at him, inhuman in their cruelty. The youthful face was lost through years of hatred. This was a man who thrived on death, delivering it with guiltless pleasure. He had to die.

Chauvet grinned. "That solves that problem. Your men will find his body—that of the powerful Chauvet—along with yours. I will go down in history as the man who executed laghato. And won't they be surprised when I reappear to destroy your precious Slipstream once and for all?"

Torrie growled and took a step forward, but Qaade blocked her. She wouldn't die. This battle was between him and Chauvet. Regardless of how far she'd come with him, or how much she'd given up. He would stop Chauvet from destroying everything and everyone he loved.

"Slipstream is yours," Qaade whispered to her. "Keep it alive." Then he coiled himself to launch, to stop the man who intended to destroy them all.

Suddenly, the entire room was plunged into blackness as everything powered down. It took a second for Qaade to realize what had happened. *Nod.*

"No!" Chauvet roared. Qaade pushed Torrie to the side as a stream of laserfire spit from Chauvet's rifle, illuminating everything. Qaade scrambled behind a column, and turned to see Torrie do the same. Chauvet stood in the center of the room, spraying lasers indiscriminately, his face a twisted mask of insanity.

Qaade assessed the situation: they were unarmed with nowhere to run, and with a madman bent on murder.

Then the laserfire stopped. Qaade waited for his eyes to adjust to the pitch-blackness, broken only by the viewport's blanket of stars. Outside the chamber doors, Qaade heard explosions and the shouts of his men. But would they arrive soon enough?

"Come out, laghato, and finish the game." The bitter words filled the darkness. Qaade watched Chauvet's silhouette move across the starry background toward Torrie's position, and panic seized him.

He shouted, "Not much of a game if we don't have weapons, too. Why don't you toss one over, and *then* we can finish the game?"

The killer's shadow halted, and his head turned. Qaade sprinted to another column. Laserfire burst and trailed in his wake. He hit cover with ammo bouncing off the walls behind him.

"You're nothing but a gutless coward, Chauvet," Torrie yelled.

Dammit, that woman was relentless. He was trying to save *her*. Qaade peered around to see Chauvet changing direction, his rifle discharging and pinning Torrie down.

Now was his chance, with Chauvet distracted. He slipped from the safety of cover. His eyes saw Chauvet turning at the sound of his footsteps, and the stream of laserfire veered toward him.

A sudden arc of light sliced through the darkness behind Chauvet, followed by a gasp. The madman stopped dead, his face frozen in shock though his rifle continued to fire. His eyes widened, horror creeping into them. Qaade slowed, trying to make sense of the unexpected turn. Then Chauvet fell forward, landing on the floor with a dull thud.

The chamber doors burst open and Zergot and

several pirates entered. Light flooded the black chamber, to reveal the woman—the slave—spattered in blood. She held a plasma blade in her hand.

Chapter Twenty-eight

Whoops of victory surrounded Torrie as the lights came back on. Everything seemed so surreal with the hologame in the center of the chamber and the pirates celebrating around it. Chauvet lay dead on the floor along with his lieutenant. Qaade was being mobbed by his crew.

Relief eased into her—slowly at first, and then gaining momentum. They'd done what they'd come here to do. She was almost free and clear. They'd leave the spaceport, InterGlax could take over, and she could stay with Qaade. Slipstream and the people who ran it would be safe. Her future lay bright before her.

The slave woman stood still amid the excitement, staring down at Chauvet. Blood dripped from her blade onto her gossamer gown. Torrie made her way over, but as she approached, the woman's large, crystal blue eyes fixed on her. The delicate face had been recently bruised, but even beneath that Torrie could see regal strength. This was no ordinary slave.

"Are you all right?" Torrie asked.

The woman answered calmly, as if drawing from a deep reserve. "Yes. I feel no remorse for this man."

Torrie nodded in understanding. "I don't doubt that."

The slave dropped the plasma knife onto Chauvet's body and smoothed her dress. "I am Fahlow, Princess of the Ell Gree people of the planet Ikora," she said, her voice like a song. "You saved me."

Torrie's gaze flicked to Chauvet, and she raised an eyebrow. "I think you saved yourself."

Fahlow smiled tentatively, as if unaccustomed to the expression. "Yes. It would seem so, but I would not have had the opportunity if not for you."

Qaade appeared beside Torrie, and Fahlow's face lit up. "Laghato," she breathed reverently. "I knew you would not let us down."

He gave her a warm smile, and Torrie could see the satisfaction glow in his eyes. "I do my best."

While Fahlow introduced herself to Qaade, Torrie glanced around for Nod. She spotted him hovering outside the chamber doors as if he were afraid to come in.

"Excuse me," she murmured and, after receiving a full-body hug from Zergot and a kiss on the cheek from Brilliard, she stepped into the empty entry.

"Is something wrong, Nod?"

The lightball dipped. "Howser wants you to contact him immediately."

"Did he say why?"

"No."

Her heart sank. It couldn't be good. She glanced behind her to the revelry in progress, and activated her comm in a secluded alcove.

Howser's voice came over, sounding frantic. "Torrie, thank the stars. Where are you?"

"Inside Chauvet's spaceport. What's happening?"

"Damn, you have to get out of there right now. InterGlax raided the slave-processing facility. They have a lead to Chauvet. His entire network is about to be taken down, and they are moving at light-speed for fear he might run."

Every muscle in her body froze, including her heart, all suspended in shock. *No. Not now.* "How long do we have?"

"Hours, maybe minutes. I tried, but I couldn't stall them without drawing suspicion." He paused. "But Torrie, think about it. This works out perfectly. Let *them* deal with Chauvet."

"Too late. He's already dead," she whispered. "The spaceport is ours. Everyone is celebrating." She leaned back against the wall and rubbed her head. *Why now?*

"I'm sorry, but you have to get them out, or it'll get bloody."

She said, "I will. I'm transmitting our coordinates. Come and pick us up as soon as you can."

There was a pause. "Aren't you going to leave with Qaade?"

Hot tears burned her face as if leached from her very core.

"I need to stay behind and clean up. Out." She closed the comm, and tried to breathe, but she couldn't feel the air in her lungs. She tried to think of a way out, but there was none. Her body ached with what she must do next. *Minutes*, Howser had said. She glanced toward the inner chamber, and the good men there. She couldn't delay the inevitable, no matter how painful.

Nod hovered beside her. "Can I help?"

She smiled and brushed useless tears aside. "You already did, little man. You are a true hero."

His inner light glowed a little brighter. "I am?"

She tapped his smooth exterior lovingly, and gave him a sad smile. "You belong with them, doing better things than I ever could."

Then she took a deep breath and walked into Chauvet's chambers.

Qaade gazed into the holo gameboard at Slipstream as Brilliard told him their status. "We have all the guards restrained in a lockup on the second level. Most of the housekeeping staff are slaves who've been scrubbed. They are pretty much lost. We'll take them with us when we leave."

Beside him, Zergot added, "And my men have wiped out any of Chauvet's fighters that did not voluntarily return to the spaceport. The upper levels are secure as well."

"Good job," he said to them both, and slapped Zergot on the shoulder. "Tell your boys I appreciate their help on this one."

The old pirate waved him off, his blue eyes sparkling. "Nothing to it."

Gratitude and pure ecstasy flooded Qaade's weary body, giving him much needed strength. They'd done it, defeated the man who'd tried and failed to destroy Slipstream. He'd told Chauvet the truth—Slipstream could live on without him. It *would*. As long as enough people cared, it would go on forever. The realization lightened his load, giving him hope for a family he could call his own some-day. A family with Torrie.

He glanced over to find her standing beside him. Her face was pale and drained. Alarmed, he ran his hands over her shoulders. "Are you hurt?"

She took a step back, out of his reach. "I'm not injured." But pain marred her face and beset her body. She looked like hell. What could be wrong? They had everything they needed now.

She licked her lips and then lifted her chin. "You have to leave."

"We'll leave in a few hours," he told her.

"Now."

He blinked, confused by her unexpected declaration and the defeat in her eyes. "Torrie, what are you talking about? We just took the spaceport. Chauvet is dead—"

"InterGlax is coming," she interrupted in a raw voice. "They will be here any moment."

The chamber suddenly turned silent and cold. Qaade's stomach twisted, a feeling of doom settling over him. "And how would you know this?"

"Because I called them."

A low groan filled the room at her admission. In the pit of his soul, Qaade felt the heart he'd left vulnerable crack. Torrie stared at him as if her words meant nothing. As if she didn't know what she'd just done to Slipstream, to him or to their future together. It was all he could do to utter a single word. *What?*

"Howser followed the Ricytin to one of Chauvet's slave-processing centers." She raised her hands and then dropped them. "It's a huge operation. Massive. Heavy traffic. He couldn't stop it alone."

Bitterness seeped into his voice. "So you took it

309

upon yourself to call in InterGlax after I told you they were corrupt?"

She focused on him in stubborn defiance. "And I told you that I knew a man we could trust. You didn't want to listen. For your information, they raided the site and are now on Chauvet's trail. Here."

Percolating anger surfaced with full ferocity. He'd trusted her above all else, above his own people, giving her his heart and soul. And she'd repaid him with betrayal that could ruin him and Slipstream. "You had no right to call them in. You knew I was taking Chauvet out. *I* was going to shut down his operation."

Her face set. "And you have no right to do that. It's not your place, Qaade. You can't take the law into your own hands, deliver justice the way you see fit."

He felt like he'd been slapped. "I do what I have to because the system has failed us. Do you really believe that InterGlax gives a damn about any of this?"

Long seconds ticked by before she answered. "Yes. They care as much as I do."

Her words drove a spike into his heart. She would never change, never accept him. He'd thought she had; but he'd been wrong. His love wasn't enough to hold her here. She'd chosen her world over his. He forced his emotions aside so that he could focus on the danger she'd brought to them all, concentrate on saving what was left.

"Brilliard, take Chauvet's slaves to *Freeport*. Leave the captured guards here along with Urwin and his men. You need to be out of here in ten minutes."

Brilliard hesitated, looking from Qaade to Torrie in uncertainty, then left.

Zergot was squinting at her while Qaade addressed him. "Tell your fighters to clear the area, and get *Exodus* ready to move. We're leaving now."

Zergot frowned, and walked away without a word. The room was cleared by the time Qaade turned around to face Torrie again. To his surprise, Fahlow stood beside her.

"We'll take you to *Freeport* now," he said to her.

Fahlow tilted her head. "I am one of the few aboard who can explain the situation accurately to the authorities. And I need their resources to gather my people back together. I will stay."

"As you wish," he said. Then he looked at Torrie. For a moment, a rush of anger and betrayal choked him. "I'm sure InterGlax will be very interested in your account as well."

"I won't tell them about Slipstream," she said, her voice wooden.

He smirked. "Are you giving me your word? Because if you are, then it doesn't mean much."

Hurt flashed in her eyes, but he didn't flinch, didn't fold. Whatever pain she felt couldn't match his. He would never recover.

"Then I won't give it," she said.

The pirates disappeared one by one into hyperspace, leaving Torrie with only the stars to keep her company. She closed her eyes to the pain that squeezed her chest, and the dreams that lay there, crushing them beyond recognition. Qaade's bitter words, the anguished look on his face that he tried to hide, the anger in his heart—those were her final memories of him, and she deserved them. If she could rip out her heart and give it to him, it wouldn't hurt more. Maybe she had.

Tears spilled down her face unchecked. There

were times when all a woman could do was cry. When no other solution could be found and no words could be said. There was no one to hold her or tell her everything would be okay. She'd pushed them all away.

He was gone, and he would never be back. Once Qaade turned his back on something, he didn't return. It was what had protected him all these years. He'd buried his heart deep in Slipstream where he wouldn't have to think about it, where it would be safe from pain and loss. But despite losing his family and his horrible past, he'd taken a chance, unmasked his love and given it to her. And she'd destroyed it with a lie.

"Are you all right?"

The soft voice pried her from her self-induced misery, and Torrie pulled herself together to face Fahlow. The woman watched her intently, as if seeing far more than she would ever acknowledge.

"I'm fine," Torrie replied with a deep breath. She noted Fahlow's bloody clothes, and the other incriminating evidence left behind for InterGlax. There was a lot of work to be done before they arrived. The risk was too great that they'd be able to track something to Qaade or Slipstream.

After she dumped the bloody plasma knife in a nearby trash incinerator, Torrie paced the rest of the inner and outer chambers on Level Zero, picking up any other evidence and disposing of it. Then she examined the contusions on Fahlow's face. "Have you had medical attention yet?"

"No."

Torrie clenched her teeth in anger. "Where is the infirmary?"

"Follow me," Fahlow said.

They walked into the lift, and punched their destination into the console. En route, Torrie said, "We have to come up with a viable story for what happened here—before InterGlax arrives."

"Of course."

"The guards could be a problem," Torrie reminded her.

"They won't protect Chauvet. Most despised him."

"Big surprise there," Torrie muttered. Then she studied Fahlow for a moment, incredulous. "Your memory is intact."

"Yes," she said with a nod. "Chauvet would never let me forget where I came from. It was one of the ways he could torment me."

"I'm sorry," Torrie said. "How long have you been here?"

The princess's big eyes closed for a moment. "Three years ago, his men raided our village. Some of us escaped into the safety of the forest, but not many. I was considered a prize. One Chauvet couldn't pass up."

"You endured a lot."

"I fear my people have endured worse."

Torrie asked, "So what will you do now?"

"Return to my planet to locate any survivors. Then I will find and gather the rest."

"Do you have ships?"

"No. Nothing like yours."

Torrie pursed her lips, not wanting to voice the obvious. Fahlow wasn't going anywhere without wings, and even then, the odds of ever tracking her people were slim.

"Maybe you should have gone with Qaade. He maintains a database of all the slaves they rescue. He might have been able to help you. Much more than I can."

"Perhaps. However, Chauvet did considerable

damage. At the moment, Iaghato has more pressing concerns than me."

Torrie supposed that was true, but it also left Fahlow with few options. So who *would* help her? Where would she go until such time as a rescue party could be formed to take her home?

After a few seconds of silence, the princess turned to Torrie. "You care a great deal for Iaghato."

Torrie blinked at the sudden change in subject, and her body staggered a little. She ran a shaky hand through her thick hair. "I do." Then she corrected herself. "I did."

"You do," Fahlow insisted, her voice clear. "And he cares for you. So, why didn't *you* leave with him?"

Torrie leaned wearily back against the wall. She'd never felt so exhausted in her life. "It's a little more complicated out here."

"Is it? He needs you."

"He needs only Slipstream."

The lift opened, but Fahlow didn't move. She looked directly at Torrie. "He needs love, like everyone else. Needs and deserves it. And so do you."

Then the princess exited the lift, her words lingering in Torrie's mind. They were wise words she couldn't deny. Too bad she couldn't use them. Even if she could find Qaade and try to make him understand, he would never trust her again. He couldn't. Protecting Slipstream was too much a part of him. And she'd managed to do the one thing that could never be undone—jeopardize it.

Chapter Twenty-nine

Brilliard entered Qaade's office on *Exodus* and took a seat at the table across from him. Qaade glanced up from damage reports, noted the man's stubbornly set chin, and turned back to his work. "Do *not* talk to me about her."

Unperturbed, Brilliard braced his hands behind his head. "I was just thinking how nice it is that we don't have to chase down all of Chauvet's network. I, for one, am grateful."

Qaade growled. "You won't be so grateful when she tells InterGlax about us."

"Oh, hell, she won't do that and you know it. The woman has enough integrity to put *you* to shame."

That did it. Qaade scowled. "Integrity? She called in InterGlax when I specifically forbade it."

Brilliard leaned forward. "And where would we be if I listened to everything you've told me to do or not do? Dead in space, that's where. So don't go crucifying Torrie because she has a brain and isn't

315

afraid to use it. You want us all to be like scrubbed slaves?"

The observation stunned him, but Qaade couldn't disagree. If Brilliard hadn't shown up with *Freeport* and the pirates, they never would have defeated Chauvet.

"No, I don't want that," he conceded. "And in case I haven't said it, thanks for coming back for me."

Brilliard chuckled. "See? That didn't kill you."

Qaade managed a smile through his heartache. A cold, black hole in his chest consumed him. The initial anger had passed with his return to duty. Slipstream was in shambles and needed to be rebuilt. *Freeport* was out of commission until they could repair the damage from the battle at the spaceport. And there was still the recovery effort at Keerny Point to coordinate. He had plenty to keep him occupied. Unfortunately, it wasn't enough to stop Torrie from haunting his every waking moment.

He rubbed his chest where it hurt. "I just wish she'd told me."

"She didn't because she knew how you'd react. Even though bringing InterGlax in was the right thing to do."

Qaade frowned at Brilliard. "The right thing to do? How do you figure that?"

The man looked smug. "I'm not in the assassination business. InterGlax can have all those slavers for all I care. And you want to know another thing?"

Qaade rubbed his face in frustration. "Not really."

"Even Fahlow understood where she belonged."

"Brilliard, she has nothing to do with this."

The ops chief continued, "She chose them over us, Qaade, even though she worships you. Why do you think that is?"

"I don't know. So what do you want to do, join InterGlax?" Qaade asked sharply.

Brilliard shrugged. "Hey, I'm just thinking how many more people we could help if we didn't spend half our time hiding in the shadows. I don't know about you, but I wouldn't mind sleeping easy for the rest of my life. It beats sleeping alone." He eyed Qaade.

"Real subtle, Brilliard. I don't need any reminders, thank you."

Still, he couldn't shake his friend's point. Chauvet's angry words replayed in his mind. *I waited. I hoped. You never saved me. So I had to save myself.* He'd failed Chauvet, and how many others? If Slipstream were legal, could they really save more lives? Could they have prevented Chauvet from perpetuating slavery, from creating a game of vengeance that killed so many? Had Qaade inadvertently made slavery worse by creating a legend he could never live up to?

The office door slid open, and Zergot entered with a grin. Qaade groaned. He was now officially outnumbered. The pirate sat next to Brilliard.

"I don't want to talk about her," he warned.

"I'm not here to talk about Torrie," Zergot sniffed. "Found a stowaway onboard." He reached into his pocket, and let Nod go free. Nod zoomed around the cabin with glee. "I can help. I can help."

Qaade felt a pang at the connection to Torrie. "Nod, where did you come from?"

The lightball zipped in front of Qaade, then stopped. "Torrie told me I belonged with you."

The lightball must have run low on memory again. "Why would she say that?"

Nod's voice morphed into Torrie's: " 'You are a true

hero. You belong with them, doing better things than I ever could.'"

The room became very quiet. Pain radiated across Qaade's chest with her heartfelt words, bringing with it all the love, the passion and the courage that were hers.

Brilliard shifted in his seat. "Funny, I don't feel particularly heroic right now."

Qaade swallowed the lump in his throat. He didn't either. Torrie was the hero, and she would never know, because he'd been too caught up in protecting his pride to tell her.

Zergot spoke up. "I think she gave up a hell of a lot more than we did. She did what she thought was right, despite what it cost her. She even got us all out of there in plenty of time. Gotta respect a woman who doesn't take the easy way out."

Qaade looked him in the eye. "Aren't you worried about InterGlax?"

Zergot shrugged. "They could track us down anyway. It's business as usual."

With dismay, Qaade realized his friends were absolutely right. Nothing had changed except they no longer had a madman to worry about, and Torrie was gone. She'd fought beside him, cried in his arms, and vowed to help him. She'd even followed him when he'd crazily told her to surrender to Chauvet. But all he could see was the lie, the betrayal—of him, his love and his trust. She knew what his reaction would be, had understood the risk. But she'd done it anyway . . . to do what was right.

"Damn," he groaned. She'd learned that from him. He'd asked her to choose between him and helping people, and she had. She'd put the slaves first, just like he'd wanted, and just like he'd been doing for the past fifteen years. And for that, he'd thrown her out.

His heart ached in his chest, burning with a fire for one woman and one woman alone. He wanted her more than anything at this moment, to hold her and feel her strength, her passion. And he'd do just about anything to get it. That included getting down on his knees and telling his pride to go to hell.

He glanced up at Brilliard and Zergot watching him, and thought about all the other people who'd helped him. Slipstream was in good hands, but those hands didn't have to be his. Maybe neither he nor Torrie had to choose. Maybe they *could* have both. He simply had to find a way.

He eyed Nod, who was floating around the room, and said aloud, "We should probably return Nod to his owner."

Brilliard's eyebrows rose and a big smile crossed the man's face. "Would be the right thing to do."

Torrie walked through the corridors of *Ventura2*, a ship that suddenly felt claustrophobic—as if it were no longer a vessel of freedom, but a cage to be escaped. After a full day of explaining what happened on Chauvet's spaceport to Wyatt and his men, she was too tired to fly.

It hadn't been easy fabricating a story that would fit the scene left behind on the spaceport, but it had helped that Fahlow confirmed her version. Simple: Chauvet's slaves finally rebelled, locking up the guards, killing Chauvet, and then escaping in the missing ships. It was close enough to the truth to fit. After taking one look at Wyatt's troubled face, Torrie knew he wouldn't hunt down a bunch of destitute slaves. He'd seen the slave processing center. The numbness from that would take a while to wear off.

Urwin, of course, had his own version, which included all the details of Slipstream. But Torrie had convinced Wyatt that Urwin and his crew had been partly scrubbed and didn't know what they were talking about. Torrie hadn't offered any more information, and Wyatt hadn't asked. The bottom line was that Chauvet was dead. That should keep InterGlax happy enough. And bringing his slave ring down was the shining triumph they needed to help boost their tarnished image. They wouldn't jeopardize that opportunity by finding whoever had *really* executed the ringleader. And they could take credit for all she cared. She just hoped Qaade was wise enough that no one would be able to validate Urwin's claims.

She'd also convinced Fahlow to come with her. InterGlax was too busy to be bothered with a former slave who needed to find her people. So when Torrie returned home, she was going to make sure Fahlow got her wings.

The office door opened, and Torrie took a seat beside the comm.

"Hail Carmon," she told the computer.

She leaned back and waited for her oldest brother's face to appear on the holo. When it did, his image surprised her. Carmon had aged. And with his strong, broad face, piercing blue eyes and thick head of hair, he was a dead ringer for her father.

"It's about damn time you called," he said, looking quite unhappy.

She folded her arms. "I've been busy."

"So I hear. Macke filled me in." He shook his head

slowly. "What were you thinking? Chasing pirates for a shipment? And then to get involved in drug smuggling!"

She raised a hand. "I know. It was a mistake. And against company policy."

He zeroed in on her with an incredulous look. "Screw company policy. You could have been killed, Torrie. We can replace cargo. Don't you get it? There's only one you. If anything ever happened to you . . ." He stopped and ran a hand through his hair. "Don't do it again."

She raised an eyebrow. "You're not grounding me?"

He gave a short laugh. "As if I could. No. I'm not going to stand between you and your one true passion."

Her one true passion? Right. Once, maybe.

"InterGlax has contacted you?" she asked.

"Yes, and I'm glad. I want to find out everyone who's been using us to traffic drugs."

"It might hurt business to dig."

"Running drugs would hurt us more, to say nothing of the ethical issues. I'm glad you exposed it, even if your methodology was questionable." He looked at her. "Father would have been proud. Of course, he also would have gone on a tirade for ten minutes before saying so."

She smiled. "I appreciate your restraint."

He chuckled. "How long before you arrive?"

"About two hours."

He checked something offscreen. "I'll be in meetings when you get here, but I'll catch up with you after that."

"Sounds good."

He paused. "Mother has missed you. You might want to see her."

"I will. Thanks, Carmon."

Before his image disappeared, he gave a mischievous grin that took her back years.

Silence descended. She would have the chance to run freight forever. She'd gotten exactly what she always wanted. So why did it seem so . . . insignificant? There was an emptiness in her soul, and it was more than just a broken heart.

The office door opened, and Howser, Macke and Fahlow walked in. They took seats around the table.

"You need some sleep," Macke noted with a frown.

"I'm too wound up. Did you find Nod?"

Howser replied, "He's not on the ship. I'm going to start deep-space scans, but frankly the odds of finding him are slim."

Torrie shuddered at the thought of her little guy all alone in the big universe. "I can't believe I lost him. I don't know what could have happened. Maybe he fell asleep somewhere on the spaceport."

Fahlow said, "I'm sure he will be found."

"I hope so," Torrie said, but her heart sank. If Nod had fallen asleep, he'd be up by now. "Any word from Wyatt on the cleanup?"

Howser nodded. "The information they recovered from the spaceport's computers laid out the rest of the slave network. He's ordered all facilities to be raided. There's also a lengthy list of slavers and slave ships to be tracked down."

"I hope Turk is on that list."

"He was. I just worry he'll give up Qaade in the process," Howser noted with a frown.

Torrie smiled at him, and at his genuine concern for Qaade and Slipstream. How far they'd come.

"I don't think Turk's word will carry much weight with InterGlax. He'll be lucky to save his own hide, let alone implicate anyone else," she said. "Besides, he doesn't know what the man behind the mask looks like."

They all nodded in silent agreement, and in an unspoken vow to protect Qaade.

The comm chimed, and Macke looked at the display. He glanced at Torrie. "It's Wyatt for you."

"Put him through," she said. The lawman's face appeared on the holo—a long visage with sharp eyes and no smile.

Torrie spoke first. "Greetings from *Ventura2*. What can we do for you?"

"I'm hoping you can help me." He looked positively exhausted and frustrated.

"How?"

"Since your people were the ones who discovered this ring to begin with, I thought you might . . ." He raised his hands helplessly. "I don't know, be closer to the situation than I am. Maybe suggest possible solutions to this mess."

She was intrigued. "Perhaps. Go on."

"The raids are progressing very well, but we underestimated the scope of Chauvet's operation. After capturing just two of the sixteen facilities, I now have over ten thousand slaves in need of medical attention. More are being pulled off the slave ships en route. Our medical units are not prepared for this influx, nor do they know how to treat scrubbed slaves."

Torrie crossed her arms. "And let me guess, you don't have the network to reunite them with their families or move them back into society."

Wyatt sighed. "Exactly. I want to do what's best for these people. I know you were closer to this than you want to tell me, and I understand your position. But I'm desperate. Do you have any ideas?"

Macke and Howser grinned at her, looking ready

to burst, while Fahlow's wise eyes watched her intently. Torrie's mind raced at the challenge laid at her feet. A plan began to take shape quickly, as if it were already there for the taking. It would require the cooperation of some obstinate parties, but she could handle that. In fact, she suddenly felt like she could handle anything. Energy flooded her body, revitalizing hope for the future. She had a mission. A purpose. Whether or not Qaade liked it, he was going to listen.

"I think I might have the perfect solution," she said.

Wyatt squinted skeptically. "I need it soon."

"Give me a day. I have to track down a few people first. And Wyatt, there will be some serious compromises on InterGlax's end. Will you be able to push those through?"

"I will do whatever I have to to help these slaves. We've ignored them long enough."

Torrie smiled. "I'll contact you when I have the details worked out."

"Thank you. Out."

"Yes!" Howser said after the comm went silent. His face was flushed with excitement. "Whatever your plan is, I want in."

"So do I," Macke added.

She eyed her brother. "You coming over to the dark side?"

He looked at her solemnly, then at Fahlow. "I saw those slaves, remember? It's important." Torrie noted the way his eyes held the princess's, and the way Fahlow smiled back. *Well, well.*

"Then it's settled." She glanced around the room. "Anyone know how to track down a stubborn pirate in under two hours?"

Chapter Thirty

"Any luck finding Qaade?" Macke walked up behind Torrie and leaned against the balcony railing.

She stared out over the Masters estate. "Not yet. It's kind of hard to find a man whose entire life revolves around stealth."

"You could always load up a ship full of Phellium and wait," Macke said, amused.

She smiled. "Not a bad idea, but I'm afraid that would take too long. We need a solution now."

"Can you get by without him?"

She felt the tug of her heart. "No. I can't."

"Then keep trying, Torrie. I'll back you every step."

"I appreciate it."

He grinned, looking happier than she could ever remember. "I couldn't help but notice that you've been spending a lot of time with Fahlow," she said.

"She's an amazing woman." Torrie could hear the sincerity and respect in his voice. He shuffled a little. "I'm going to take her back to her home planet."

Torrie's eyebrows rose. "Really?"

Macke held up his hands. "It's not what you think. I'm just giving her a lift."

Torrie wanted to laugh, because she could tell by the look in his eyes that he was already gone. She was going to enjoy watching him twist in the fickle winds of love.

Another set of footsteps got her attention, and she turned as her mother approached. Macke greeted her with a kiss on each cheek, winked at Torrie, and left them alone.

Her mother reached out and brushed Torrie's long hair from her face. Nevica Masters's green eyes shone with years of living and wisdom. Soft lines on her face held countless smiles and tears, and streaks of glorious red peeked through now mostly white hair.

"It's so nice to have you back, dear," she said wistfully. "I don't suppose you'd like to stay."

Torrie smiled at the irony. "Actually, I'd love to stay. But it looks like the universe has other plans for me."

Her mother appeared surprised. "And what plans are those?"

Torrie cast a pensive look to the west. "Do you remember Zoe? She lived next door when I was a child. Sweet little girl."

Nevica nodded. "I do. Poor thing died so young."

"She was an abused slave, who probably died at the hands of her owner. No one cared about her. No one tried to save her."

"The investigation deemed her death accidental," her mother said.

Torrie smirked. "The authorities were probably paid off. I know what really happened. And I was the only one who did."

Her mother took Torrie's hand between hers, and

squeezed it. "Don't do that to yourself. You were a child. You can mourn for your friend, but you can't live your life with the guilt."

"It's not just guilt," Torrie said. She tapped her chest. "It's in here. This is the place I need to fill. I've spent my life trying to prove myself to all of you. I wasted so much time looking inside that I never noticed all the people outside who need my help."

Her mother studied her. "And that is why you have returned?"

Torrie took a breath. "I'm here to convince Carmon to part with a significant amount of credits and ships."

"How significant?"

"Very. We are partly responsible for the slave situation in this sector. It's only right we should help fix it."

Her mother said, "And you have a plan?"

"Yes. InterGlax is already onboard. All I need to do is convince Qaade—" She stumbled over his name. "A man I know, to cooperate."

"The pirate, yes. He must have a good heart for you to risk so much."

Torrie dipped her head. "He does."

Nevica linked her arm with her daughter's. "Did I ever tell you how hard it is to find a truly good man?"

"No, you didn't. But you showed me. Father was one."

Nevica smiled, a flash of melancholy in her eyes. "He was. He was also demanding, stubborn and tenacious. And he loved you more than life itself, even if he didn't say it often. He was so focused on taking care of us, sometimes love seemed to be forgotten. But it was there all the time."

Torrie blew out a breath. She understood exactly what her mother was saying. "So, how do you deal with a man like that?"

Her mother chuckled. "Eventually, they come around."

"I was afraid you'd say that. I'm not sure it'll happen in my lifetime. It didn't happen with Father. He never approved of my having my own run."

"He didn't know how to handle your ambition. I think it frightened him. You have so much passion, you tend to overwhelm any mission you tackle," Nevica said with a wink. "That's not a bad thing, but sometimes you have to slow down long enough to clue everyone else in to what you are trying to accomplish."

Torrie frowned. "Are you calling me high maintenance?"

Her mother gave a hearty laugh. "No, dear. You are perfect. You just have to find a man who can keep up with you."

"I found one," Torrie admitted sadly. She flinched under a crush of emotion. "And I betrayed his trust."

"Did you do it for a good reason?"

"Yes. The best reason."

"And now you require his assistance with your mission?"

"Exactly." Torrie pursed her lips. "Didn't plan that very well, did I?"

Nevica gave her a fond look. "You'll have your credits and ships. The rest is up to you."

Torrie blinked in disbelief. "What about Carmon?"

Mischief showed on her mother's face. "Regardless of what Carmon thinks, *I* run the family business. Who do you think has been keeping him from chasing after you?" She patted Torrie's arm. "Go find your pirate. I'll talk to your brother."

Torrie hugged her mother. "Thank you."

"I'm so proud of the woman you have become, my dear."

Torrie held her tightly, relishing the feeling of being accepted and loved. But part of her ached for Qaade, that he might never know how it felt. She wanted more than anything to give him back his family, and she would try her damnedest, with or without his permission.

"Excuse me."

Torrie separated from her mother to find an embarrassed Howser beside them. He greeted Nevica, then looked at Torrie. "I have a message from Nod."

"Where is he?"

"Apparently, he went with Qaade."

Hope surfaced. "Tell me we have rendezvous coordinates."

Howser grinned. "But of course."

They dropped out of hyperspace directly in front of *Exodus*. Just the sight of it was enough to send Torrie's pulse racing. She took a deep breath, then let it out slowly, trying to regain control over her body. Lately, that simple task was becoming more and more difficult. But this wasn't about her heart, or her hopes. It was bigger than that, and that's what she needed to concentrate on.

"Hail *Exodus*, and tell Qaade to shuttle over here with Nod. I'll be waiting in my office," she said, and pushed from her seat.

"Will do," Howser said. "Good luck, Torrie."

"Thanks, Howser." She paused long enough to kiss him on the cheek, and then headed for the back.

Regardless of Howser's concern, she wasn't about to fail. Qaade would have to listen for once. No matter what had happened between them, the slaves were going to win. She'd use whatever tools necessary to gain his cooperation. He could stand to be around her for that long.

After the initial setup, he would only have to see her when their paths accidentally crossed, she reasoned, ignoring the pained nagging of her heart. The only way to see this project get off the ground was to shut down her emotions. If she had to sell her soul to accomplish it, she would.

She entered her office and took a seat at the table. As she activated the comm, she fought back a yawn. She felt tired, as if she were carrying around extra weight. Yet sleep seemed like a waste of time under the circumstances. There was so much to be done.

After she completed the secured comm link, Wyatt's face appeared in the holodeck. Torrie said, "Greetings, Wyatt."

"Is he there yet?"

She checked the shuttle bay cam. His ship was docked already, but there was no sign of Qaade or Nod. "They just landed."

The door to the office slid open, and Nod flew in. Torrie burst out laughing as he zipped around her head ten times before stopping in front of her with a triumphant, "I'm a hero!"

"Yes, you are," she said with a smile, rubbing his smooth belly. "I missed you, little man."

"I missed you too," he said, shining extra bright for her. "Need to see Howser now." He zoomed out of the office, past the shadow that stood in her doorway.

She steeled herself as the door slid shut behind the lightball. Silver eyes captured hers. Her heart leapt, joyous in her chest, even as she tried to tamp down her excitement. Qaade studied her for a long moment, and in that moment, she relived all the reasons why she loved him—and the heartache she'd never shake.

His gaze flicked to Wyatt's image in the holodeck, reminding her that she was on a mission, and that it was time Qaade found out what it was.

"This is Major Wyatt"—she took a breath—"of InterGlax. He is in charge of dismantling Chauvet's slave ring."

Qaade stopped a few feet away, and narrowed his eyes at the image of Wyatt looking at them. She half expected him to turn and walk out.

"Don't worry," Torrie added. "He can't see you. It's a one-way."

"Greetings," Wyatt said with a slight frown. "I'd call you by your name, but apparently it's supposed to remain a mystery, as is your appearance. I don't generally work this way."

Qaade gave her a curious look, but took a seat beside her. "Just call me Cap. Mind telling me what this is about?"

"Your guess is as good as mine. This is Torrie's meeting. All I know is that I've got a problem, and I'm told you are the best man to help me with it."

"Is that right?" Qaade said, watching Torrie. His eyes were intent, but to her surprise they held no anger. Instead, she swore there was a sensual undertow pulling her toward him. Great. Just what she needed—a little sexual distraction to *really* mess with her.

"I explained to Wyatt that you work in the private sector, and specialize in treating scrubbed slaves."

"And I've got about fifteen thousand of them right now with more coming," Wyatt interrupted.

331

"We don't have the expertise or the facilities to treat them. They are scattered around medical centers now, wherever we can find room, but that's not the place for them." The lawman paused, looking thoroughly discouraged. "I've never seen anything like this. These people are lost. They're like walking shells."

"And you want to help them?" Qaade asked.

Wyatt's eyebrows rose. "Yes, I want to help them. Why wouldn't I?"

"InterGlax didn't seem to care about them over the past fifteen years."

Wyatt shook his head. "It's not that easy when slavery is legal in half the sector. We don't make the laws, and we don't have the manpower to check every slave's background. Granted, it doesn't help when we have corrupt people looking the other way." Then his eyes narrowed and anger laced his words. "But this scrubbing is going to stop. I had no idea how bad it was until we came in."

Torrie watched Qaade's stoic expression as Wyatt spoke, looking for a glimmer of hope. For the sake of the slaves, she had to make him understand that this could work. And for the sake of her heart, she had to make him safe. "I have a plan that I think will solve InterGlax's problem."

Qaade focused on her, and she shook off his cool stare. "This is what I'm proposing. Since Chauvet's spaceport is now unoccupied, I'd like to convert it into a permanent shelter for treating and relocating slaves. It would require renovations, but we could move people in immediately if we complete one level at a time."

"That's an excellent idea, Torrie," Wyatt said with real sincerity. "But I'm not sure I can get you the necessary funds in such a short amount of time."

"Masters Shipping will pay for the work. All I need from you is the title to the spaceport. I want sole ownership."

Qaade showed marked surprise—a good sign. After a few thoughtful moments, he gave a single nod of approval, for which she was relieved. But this was only the beginning. He hadn't seen anything yet.

"I think I can get that approved," Wyatt conceded. "I assume Cap comes in at this point."

"Correct," she said. Qaade's steady gaze was on her. "Cap and all his staff move in. That includes trained medical personnel. You can start bringing the slaves in as soon as everyone is settled."

Wyatt responded, "That works. InterGlax would handle operating expenses—"

"Masters Shipping and private donations will cover expenses," Torrie interjected. "This won't be an InterGlax facility."

She detected a slight twitch of Qaade's mouth. Then he gave her another nod. So far, so good. "The spaceport would accept slaves from InterGlax raids, or any other source. Masters Shipping has agreed to provide any ships necessary for transportation of slaves to their new homes." She took a breath. "Also, Cap will need unlimited access to your personal identification databases."

Wyatt blustered at that. "Why?"

"Scrubbed slaves don't have memories. How else do you plan to reunite them with their families? Fathers. Mothers. Sisters," she said with emphasis. Qaade's expression sobered in the silence that followed.

After a few moments, Wyatt said, "Agreed."

"And one more thing. No questions asked about Cap or his staff. No background checks, no digging into their pasts. They need complete immunity. Most of them are former slaves who have done what they had to in order to survive the worst circumstances. I won't have them persecuted for that."

Wyatt scowled. "Now I see why you don't want this to be an InterGlax op."

"Take it or leave it," Torrie said.

Wyatt scratched his head. "Since I don't have a better solution, I'll take it."

Torrie inhaled a breath. "And what about you, Cap?"

Qaade tilted his head at her, as if wondering whether he could trust her. The rhythmic pounding of her heart ticked off each second. With every tick, Torrie realized just how important this was to her. She loved him so much. She would do anything to keep him safe. Anything. Plead, steal, kill. Whatever it took to make sure he'd be here tomorrow and all the days after that.

She begged him with her eyes. *Please, Qaade. For your people. For the slaves. For me.*

Then his gaze switched to Wyatt's image in the holodeck. "It's a big move for my people," he finally said. "I need to discuss it with them first."

Torrie let out the breath she didn't realize she was holding.

Wyatt nodded. "I understand, Cap. But I'd really like to move on this as soon as possible. You could have the spaceport today, and I can work on the other requirements immediately."

Torrie said, "I'll contact you later with his answer."

"I'll be waiting. Thank you both. Out."

She stared at the holodeck long after Wyatt's image faded, and prepared to face Qaade alone. It might as well start now: the daily heartbreak of working with him and not being able to touch or hold him. But she would do it for *them,* the multitudes who needed her help. Let the suffering begin.

Very slowly, she turned her gaze to find him grinning.

Chapter Thirty-one

Torrie's green eyes narrowed. How he loved those eyes. Loved her smile, her skin, her laugh, her scent, her soul.

"Do you think this is a joke, pirate?"

And her fight. How had he ever thought he could live another day without her?

"Not at all. I just find it interesting that you used slave guilt on Wyatt."

She eyed him skeptically. "It worked, didn't it? Now all I have to worry about is you. Look, I know you hate InterGlax, but this isn't about you. It's about Slipstream. It's about freed slaves. So I expect you to give this plan serious consideration."

He crossed his arms, enjoying the way her passion flared before his eyes. He'd missed it more than he realized. "Have you forgotten that I have a lot of enemies?"

She shrugged. "You'll have an official pardon from InterGlax. For the others, you'll create a new identity. No one will recognize you, except maybe

Urwin. But he'll never see the light of day again anyway. He's imprisoned."

Qaade studied her. "An expert in the private sector, you called me? You're turning me into a legitimate businessman?"

She raised her chin. "Think of all the good you can do. All the slaves you can save. No more pirating. No more masks."

"True. But like I said, I have to talk to my people."

"You never did that before," she noted.

"Yeah, well, they are kind of demanding equal rights these days."

"Really? Huh," she said, sounding stunned. "Will they go for it?"

"I think so." He looked at her. "It's a good plan."

Surprise and a little bit of apprehension crossed her face. He hid a smile and stood up to stretch. "In fact, it's damned brilliant. You thought of the slaves, my people, even my family. I couldn't have done any better."

Torrie got to her feet and moved in front of him. It was all he could do not to grab her right then and there. But he held back. He wanted to do this right.

"Even *with* InterGlax?"

He shrugged. "I can see where an alliance with them could be advantageous."

She put a hand to her forehead. "I think I may faint."

He said pointedly, "Where do you fit into this plan?"

Her gaze fixed on him. "The spaceport would be *ours* to run as we see fit. The family has agreed to that. I will act as the liaison between InterGlax and Masters Shipping. So whether you like it or not, we will be partners. Don't even *try* to push me out. The slaves, the crew, the girls mean as much to me as they do to you, and I'm not letting them down. This is where I belong."

She finished with a stubborn scowl, making it clear that no amount of arguing was going to stop her. Her spirit was strong and vibrant. Harnessed, it would carry the weight of everyone she touched. All he had to do was let it. But after the way he'd treated her, the hard part was convincing her that he would.

"Sounds fair enough. Except for one item."

Torrie's eyes narrowed dangerously, and he stifled a grin.

"I would like to be the InterGlax liaison."

Her eyes widened. "Are you serious?"

"Wyatt seems honest enough, but I want to make sure they stay that way. I also think it's high time the laws were changed and slavery was abolished across the sector. I plan to find a way to do that, legally. I'm thinking of going into politics."

Her jaw dropped, and for a whole three seconds she was speechless. "I don't believe it. I *am* going to faint."

"Unless you'd prefer that I do it the pirate way?"

She held up a hand. "Forget I said anything. You can have InterGlax and politics. On one condition." She licked her lips. "If we can't locate the girls' mother, I want to raise them myself."

It was his turn to be surprised. "That's a pretty serious commitment to make alone."

"I know," she said with a firm nod. "I've been thinking about it for days. They need a stable home, with people they trust to take care of them and keep them safe. I believe I can give them that. My family would adore them, and my mother will be in heaven." She smiled. "Instant grandchildren."

Children. He hadn't even gotten that far, but the

more he thought about it, the more he wanted them. With Torrie. The realization nearly choked him. He wanted it so much, he was almost afraid to ask. Hope whispered, sustaining him as it always did. "And what about us?"

Her gaze shifted to him, and regret flashed for a split-second. "I know you have a hard time understanding why I called InterGlax, but I did what I had to. I'm not going to apologize for that. I don't expect you to forgive me, although it would be nice," she added in a mutter. "Regardless, we both know that Slipstream is what's important."

"Not more important than love. Nothing is."

She frowned. "Love? I love the girls."

"I'm not talking about the girls." He took a step, bringing them closer. His heart pounded in his chest with anticipation and desire as he lifted her chin, then traced her perfect lips with his thumb. Then he leaned down and kissed her. She didn't respond for a second, and he worried she wouldn't, that he'd hurt her beyond repair.

Suddenly her hands gripped his shoulders hard enough to make him flinch. Her mouth took possession of his, feeding his empty heart with more wonder and dreams than he'd thought possible. He reveled in their passion, and in a love strong enough to ease the past and build the future. It burned between them in a flame that would never die.

He murmured against her lips, "Forgive me, Torrie. I'm sorry. You did exactly what I would have done. The problem was, I didn't do it. And I should have."

"Forgiven." Then she grabbed his face and kissed him again, hard, sealing her absolution. All the love she'd locked away burst through in a deluge of hope and dreams. She had her pirate back, the man who made her whole.

He broke off the kiss and pressed his forehead to hers. His words were soft and sure. "I love you. I want to raise the girls together, and have our own. My life begins and ends with you. Be my family."

She pulled in a shuddering breath, and tears rolled down her cheeks for a few moments before she answered. "I'm yours forever. I hope you can handle it. This is your one and only chance to run."

He nuzzled her cheek, his warmth seeping into her skin. "Handling you will be my pleasure." Then a shadow of doubt crossed his face. "What about your brothers? Can they tolerate an ex-outlaw in their midst?"

She grinned wickedly. "That's the beauty of family. They have to. We're all stuck together no matter how much trouble we cause."

"I'll try to behave myself," Qaade said with a chuckle, but she could see him beam with the contentment of a family to call his own.

"Is that a promise?"

A slow, sexy smile touched his lips. "Depends. Do you trust a pirate?"

His eyes were full of love and courage, and every adventure she could ever want. "With all my heart."

UNLEASHED
C. J. BARRY

Lacey Garrett was about to be free. Her fiancé had run off with her business, her savings, and stuck her with his cat. What had she done to stop him? Nothing.

But she'd just been beamed to another planet. Here, she wasn't an ordinary Earthwoman; she was part of a team. Here she could help a man like the roguish starship captain Zain Masters. Here, she could face *krudo,* interplanetary defense systems, and galaxy-wide conspiracies. She could even defeat the monstrous Bobzillas that looked like her ex-fiancé! For Zain, Lacey could do anything—because his kisses, his touch, everything about him felt like destiny. And that destiny was the true Lacey Garrett . . . *UNLEASHED*.

Dorchester Publishing Co., Inc.
P.O. Box 6640
Wayne, PA 19087-8640

___52573-9
$6.99 US/$8.99 CAN

Please add $2.50 for shipping and handling for the first book and $.75 for each additional book. NY and PA residents, add appropriate sales tax. No cash, stamps, or CODs. Canadian orders require an extra $2.00 for shipping and handling and must be paid in U.S. dollars. Prices and availability subject to change. **Payment must accompany all orders.**

Name: _____

Address: _____

City: _____ State: _____ Zip: _____

E-mail: _____

I have enclosed $_____ in payment for the checked book(s).

For more information on these books, check out our website at www.dorchesterpub.com.
_____ *Please send me a free catalog.*

UNRAVELED

C.J. BARRY

To continue her father's life's quest, Tru Van Dye has to leave the insular colony of Majj scientists where she was raised and find Rayce Coburne. Yet the virtual-reality program she acquires to gird herself against the man's touch is for naught—his presence overwhelms her. Tru's clever plans, her control, everything is coming unraveled.

Rayce Coburne tried to give up treasure acquisition. He despises dealing with icy customers. And Tru Van Dye is worse than usual—a prissy woman who will blackmail him with all his hopes and dreams. Still, there is a way he can fight back: A kiss a day is the perfect strategy. Unless the spinning he feels inside is Tru unwrapping his heart.
